Never Going Back

KWEEN PEN

Never Going Back
Kween Pen

For Danielle

Contents

Acknowledgments

As is customary and very necessary, I first give honor to **God** from whom all my blessings flow. Thank you for yet another opportunity to be the voice of those who have remained silent for so long. I offer you my unending gratitude for the amazing favor You have had over my life and the gift You bestowed upon me.

Thank you to my darling children, **Aniya and Antoine, Jr**. Being your mother has been such a blessing from the very beginning and continues to grow me as a person to this day. Continue to strive for excellence. I'm here to cheer you on the entire way.

To My Love: I can't thank you enough for everything you've done to help me elevate in every aspect of life over the past few years. Your keen eye for the bigger picture has opened my eyes to things I never thought of. Thank you for doing nothing more and nothing less than being an all-around amazing man.

To my best friend, **Danielle Holley**: the words "thank you" are never enough. From your suggestions and constructive criticisms to your amazing sense of humor to the manifold of ways you've helped me grow my talent, you've been amazing. Thank you for test reading everything I've ever written and always providing honest feedback when I need it most. You are a light in my world when my tunnel can seem so dark. Thank you, Bestie Boo!

To my unwavering group of amazing cousins: Cort, T, Sirion, Sinora, and Sabrina: once again, thank you! You guys don't know how much your encouragement has meant to me over the years. I can't express my gratitude enough to you.

To my wonderful former mother-in-law turned best friend, Paris Pittman: thank you for everything, from lending a listening ear and a shoulder to lean on to test reading and providing suggestions. Thank you for always being there.

To my team: the outstanding group of people who made this book what it is. First and foremost, a colossal thank you goes to my editor and typesetter, **Cyn Alexander.** Thank you for always pushing me to be a better writer and sharing my vision of always publishing quality work. You are an absolute jewel and an amazing asset to this industry. To **Iesha Bree:** the best cover/graphic designer to ever do it. You've been an absolute doll to work with on these last couple of projects, and I can't thank you enough. You are incredibly talented, and you always understand the assignment! Thank you, sis! A million thank you's to my promoter, **Authoress Crystal Alexis.** I can't thank you enough for everything you've done on every single project we've worked together on. Your consistent quality has been impeccable and much appreciated.

To all my readers near and far: thank you for giving a girl like me a chance. A special thank you to those who have stuck around and continue to invest in and enjoy my work. It's the loyal, long-time readers who keep us grounded and the new readers who give us hope as authors. Each and every one of you are appreciated.

Love and light!
Kween Pen

Prologue

IYANA STRUGGLED to catch her breath as she collapsed onto the pillows piled on the floor, doubled over in laughter. Bryan was on her back, still frantically fingering her most ticklish places.

"Okay! Okay!" Her pearly whites gleamed in the empty room's bright lighting reflecting off the eggshell painted walls as she surrendered.

Bryan finally showed her some mercy and rolled over to lie next to her on the plush carpet, smiling just as widely as Iyana released a relieved sigh, but when he gazed into her face, Iyana wasn't there. She appeared to be spaced out, her mind transporting her to another place and time, one they both ran from long ago. It was evident in her expression the pain of that era of their lives, pain caused mostly by himself, was still prevalent.

Her eyes. Those big, alluring round eyes that had always gazed at him with so much adoration and understanding, even when he wasn't deserving of their grace. He didn't deserve her, and he knew it. Neither did he deserve the second chance she gifted him, and that made him appreciate it even more. He knew he wouldn't lose her again. This him, the new him, couldn't lose her again, so he was determined he wouldn't.

Her smile became his trophy, his only goal, and his sole focus. He had just extracted from her a joyous round of laughter after a long night of cute smirks, warm glances, intertwined fingers, and locked elbows. He was in a heaven he had never known with a woman he had almost always known, and he didn't want the night to end. Desiring to pull her back into the present and rid her of the thoughts of things that no longer existed, he thinned out the air, thickened by the absence of her consciousness by inserting a simple question into the silence.

"What's wrong, babe?"

The wide smile on his face couldn't have contradicted his question more if it tried. Iyana shook her head as if to both shake the memories out of her head and deny there was anything bothering her.

"I'm just..." she hesitated, not wanting to kill the evening's vibe with her hidden truth. Peering into Bryan's eyes as they awaited her answer, encouraging her to be honest, assuring her she could, Iyana took a deep breath and finished her confession. "I'm scared."

"Scared? Scared of what?" He frowned as he sat up on one elbow, palm pressed against the side of his own head. He moved closer to her and placed his free hand on her folded legs.

Iyana stared at her manicured fingers folded in her lap as she perched on the throne of pillows. When her eyes returned to meet his, there were pools in the wells that may as well have been as deep as the Pacific and as blue as the waves off the coast of Tahiti because they made Bryan's heart drop just the same.

"This. Us. What we've become. Who we used to be." She shrugged.

"What'd I tell you? Huh?" he quizzed her as he grabbed her hand and held it tight. "What did I tell you? I'm never going back to who I used to be. I ain't that nigga no more, Yana."

She gazed back up at him as tears streamed down her cheeks. His expression was reassuring, and his eyes were sincere. He himself was a breath of fresh air. She exhaled deeply and nodded at him in understanding, assuring him she believed him. He gave her another questioning glance, to which she responded with another nod of confirmation and a teary smile.

"Come here," he whispered as he pulled her to himself and wrapped his arms around her. "I love you, babe. I love you. Right now, that means more to me than it ever has. You mean more to me than you could ever know, Iyana." He rocked her gently as she cried softly into his chest, releasing one last cry. When she pulled away to wipe her face, he inquired, "Are you okay?"

She simply nodded, and Bryan grabbed his shirt off the floor behind him to dab her eyes. Locking eyes with him as he gently dabbed the tears on her cheeks, Iyana searched for remnants of the man he once was. His gentleness and sensuality were new. His compassion and understanding were refreshing. Her fingers graced his hand, and she pressed her cheek into his palm, finding a level of comfort with him she never had. The silence between them was deafening and stated everything they didn't. Their lips greeted each other as old friends, and she welcomed the embrace of a man she never believed to be capable of that type of love.

A THREE-STORY BUILDING resembling a warehouse just outside Midtown in Memphis, Club Emotions was once the hottest club in the city, attracting all the ballers and bad bitches with its weekly Monday Night Boxing event, daily drink specials, frequent celebrity appearances, and exclusive VIP sections with tempered glass floors raised high above the rest of the partygoers.

Bryan's Air Jordan 12 Retro tennis shoes were stomping up the steps to the VIP behind Yo Gotti's entourage, and his mind was preoccupied with plans to win back his ex-girlfriend, Zaria, who broke up with him two months before, when he happened to glance over his shoulder and notice Iyana and a group of her friends entering the dancefloor, drinks in their hands and smiles on their faces. All five of her friends were dolled up, faces caked with layers of make-up, hair done up with weave, but Iyana was the one who caught his eye. The exact opposite of everyone else in her crew, she wore minimum make-up, and her natural hair was in a cute, neat style that accented her doe eyes.

Iyana noticed the lingering eyes on the stairs and smirked at him before gazing away and returning to her friends. Bryan had always been one of Yo Gotti's hangers-on, hoping to be ushered into the booth to record a track or two, though he had no real rap skills and couldn't carry a tune if it came with a shoulder strap and handle. He always portrayed himself as a bodyguard, assistant, or even his best friend when he introduced himself to women, using Gotti's name to pique the interest of the gold diggers he chased, though it was obvious he wasn't built to be guarding anybody, and he hadn't been eating well enough to be a millionaire rapper's best friend. Entering the VIP section long enough to claim a spot at a table and pour himself a drink, Bryan returned to the stairs and scanned the room for the dark-skinned cutie he spotted on his way in.

He finally caught sight of Iyana and her friends near the bar as a group of men approached them, trying to shoot their shot. Iyana appeared to be more amused by the drunken man leaning on the bar in front of her than interested in or attracted to him, which was evident by the bout of laughter Bryan could see she fought back.

"Excuse me, my man," Bryan interrupted from behind the leaning suitor. "Can I holler at my lady real quick?"

The guy peered over his shoulder at Bryan with a raised eyebrow. "Dis sho' lady?" he echoed with slurred words, motioning toward Iyana with his cup and spilling his drink on his own shoes.

"Umm hmm." Bryan nodded.

"Well, shiiiiiit! Why you ain't said dat shit den?" he countered at Iyana before retreating down the bar, gripping the ledge for balance. Iyana giggled as she watched him trudge away, and then she returned her attention to Bryan.

"Thank you for rescuing me," she shouted over the music while nursing her Tanqueray and pineapple juice. She examined Bryan, taking note of his chain, watch, and Gucci shoes but not realizing in the dimly lit club neither the diamonds nor the shoes were authentic.

"We're celebrating my best friend's birthday. I'd hate to ruin the party," she mentioned as she nodded over her shoulder at her best friend, Celeste, who was draped with a pink satin sash that read *I'm a Cancer and I'm a dancer.*

"It's no problem. I know a damsel in distress when I see one." He licked his lips as he grinned at her. "I'm Bryan, by the way," he introduced himself and offered his hand to shake.

"Iyana," she replied, gently placing her own hand into his.

"Iyana. That's an elegant name," he complimented seductively, allowing his gaze to linger on her curves. Standing five inches taller than Iyana, Bryan leaned his chestnut-colored cheek in closer to her ear and offered, "I know you're here with your girls. Would y'all like to come up to the VIP with me? Gotti's up there."

"Gotti? *Yo Gotti?*" Iyana's friend, Bria, interrupted their conversation as she stepped around Iyana with her large breasts and wide hips that were accentuated by her long, bone-straight black weave and skin-tight black bodysuit with a rhinestone-studded silver belt. A full six inches shorter than Iyana's five-foot-seven frame, Bria's espresso-toned skin shimmered in the flashing blue lights inside the club as she squealed, "Oooooo, Yana, we should go, girl!"

"Girl, shut your ghetto ass up!" Iyana rolled her eyes at Bria. "Ignore her," she insisted, turning back to Bryan. "She still hasn't learned *free* isn't always *best.* She's had a couple of allergic reactions that should've taught her that," she scolded jokingly, referring to the swelling Bria experienced in her lips six months prior after accepting a free sample of lipstick from a new beau and the hives she broke out in a year before as she sipped drinks sent to her table by a stranger who was unaware she was allergic to mango.

"Nah, it's cool," Bryan chuckled, amused. "You should come, though. Bring your girls. It's safe."

"I don't know..." Iyana hesitated, glancing back and forth between Bryan and Bria, uncertain of his intentions.

"Oh, come on, Iyana!" Celeste, who stood four inches taller than Bria, urged her from over Bria's shoulder. "Let's have some fun!"

"Alright," Iyana reluctantly agreed with a nervous grin at Bryan.

"Don't worry. I'll take good care of y'all." He winked at them and led the way to the VIP section, where bottles and money were flowing like the Mississippi River.

IYANA TRIED to go about her normal life after that night at Club Emotions, but Bryan always wiggled his way into her day. The news that he recently broke up with a long-term girlfriend sent signals to Iyana's antennas, and she soon picked up on the fact that he was essentially homeless. Bryan's ex-girlfriend was evicted from her apartment, leaving them both with nowhere to go. He slept on his friends' couches and when all else failed, in his car, which was the only thing he possessed of mentionable value.

Bryan was an only child, the offspring of a crackhead and her pimp, who had been long ago sent on to Glory by one of his other hoes. He bounced from home to home all his life and stored clothes in his grandmother's storage shed because she couldn't afford to treat her house again for the bedbugs he dropped off hidden in the folds and seams of his bagged, soiled clothing. Neither could she continue to deal with the disrespect of coming home from a twelve-hour shift at work to find some random hoochie bouncing on her grandson's lap on her leather living room sectional while rap music blared so loudly neither Bryan, nor his companion, heard her car door close or her key turn in the lock. It happened too many times before she was finally fed up, and she returned him to the same streets she tried to rescue him from.

Iyana spent weeks making quick runs for Bryan, that always ended up taking hours. Falling victim to his sob stories composed to create sympathy for him in her heart. She gave him money to rent a room at a rooming house, but he always spent the money on other things to survive. Oblivious to Bryan's constant ploys to insert himself into her life and make her feel obligated to him, Iyana eventually allowed him to move into her one-bedroom apartment two months after they met to keep him out the streets and the abandoned apartments he lived in.

From the beginning, Iyana had problems getting Bryan to commit despite the establishment of their relationship being his idea. Though he lived with her, there was still a roster of females calling his phone and requesting his time and attention. Every time Iyana mentioned it, his only excuse was he was trying to cut everyone off gradually to avoid confrontation and it took time. Meanwhile, Zaria never stopped calling, and from what Iyana could tell, Bryan never stopped answering.

"I'm playing nice with her," Bryan tried to explain to Iyana on numerous occasions. "I've still got a bunch of shit at her house, so when she calls, I try to go ahead and pick up what I can while she'll let me. Don't trip. I got this. The last thing I need is for you to over-react and try to make something out of nothing."

A shirt, a pair of shoes, a brand-new pair of pajamas and slippers was all Bryan ever returned with. Iyana kept reminding herself she wasn't stupid. Those things didn't appear to be belongings he went to retrieve, but gifts he visited Zaria to receive, and Iyana could guess what questions he answered correctly to win those prizes.

Occasionally, for a couple weeks at a time, Bryan's phone rang more than usual, and he spent more time in the streets, claiming to be out job searching. Again, Iyana knew better. *What job is accepting applications and conducting interviews at ten and eleven at night?* she questioned herself. *I don't care if it is for a night shift position. All that kind of business is usually conducted during the daytime.*

However, Bryan always had an excuse to appease her and make her question her own intuition. His response was always, "My interview was at night because that's the shift I applied for," or his favorite, "You're overthinking the whole situation." No job ever resulted from the late-night meetings and interviews, and eventually, the phone calls died down to only Zaria's weekly calls for Bryan to pick up more belongings.

"Just leave the rest of that shit over there," Iyana demanded one evening as Bryan jumped up to run to Zaria's house for the second time in three days, interrupting what was supposed to be a night of quality time for the two of them. They had been living together for six months, and Iyana had grown tired of Bryan's lingering past. "Whatever is left over there can't be that important. You seem to be getting along fine without it. You must not need it."

Of course, he left anyway after mentioning the name brand clothing he refused to let Zaria keep and promising to return shortly. Iyana knew better than to believe the blatant lie and simply showered and went to bed.

Around two in the morning, Iyana groggily stumbled to the bathroom to empty her whining bladder. When she opened the door, there was Bryan, standing there like a deer in headlights, pants and underwear at his ankles, water running in the sink. He was scrubbing nothing but his dick and balls with soap and a washcloth. Still not fully conscious and clearly not in her right mind, Iyana closed the door and went back to bed without giving what she saw a second thought and falling back asleep without using the bathroom.

The next evening when Iyana arrived home from work, Bryan was in an especially lovey-dovey mood. Iyana, however, was not.

"If you want attention, go on back over your hoe's house. I'm sure she'll be calling to summon you soon anyway," she shot at him after shaking him off her and heading toward the bedroom.

"What the fuck is that shit supposed to mean?"

"Exactly what I said. What? You actually have time for me today?" she questioned as she paused in the hallway with a scowl and her hands on her hips. "You don't have a midnight job interview tonight? Zaria doesn't have a pair of drawers for you to pick up?"

"Ain't nobody called me back on my applications," he replied, intentionally avoiding her last question.

"That's because you have to actually submit an application to get a call back, and even if you did, there ain't a company in America conducting job interviews at fucking midnight. A damn job interview," she scoffed. "Yeah, interviewing some *ass*!" she barked over her shoulder as she turned and continued down the hall.

"Exactly what the fuck is that supposed to mean?" he repeated.

"Oh please, Bryan! How stupid do you think I am? You ain't spending six hours or more at no bitch's house just to pick up a damn shirt. You're picking something up, alright, but it's damn-sure more than a pair of basketball shorts," she snapped and rolled her eyes at him as she stepped out the heels she wore to work and returned them to their shelf in her bedroom closet. "A mother fucker better not bring me back nothing Latin from that hoe's house. That's all I know."

"Latin?" he pondered, confused. "Fuck is you tumbout?"

"Treponema pallidum... chlamydia trachomatis... trichomonas vaginalis... herpesviridae," she rambled.

"I don't know what all that shit is, but I recognized Chlamydia and Herpes, and if you're insinuating I'm fucking off, you're wrong. I don't even know where you got that idea from."

"Syphilis, chlamydia, trich, and herpes," she retorted, "and I got that idea from the vision of you sneaking into the house in the middle of the night and washing your dirty-ass dick off in the bathroom sink."

"That don't mean shit! You're reading too much into that shit!

You need to gone on with that foo-foo-ass shit, mane! Ain't nobody got time for that shit."

"That don't mean shit? Why would you only need to wash your dick and nothing else?"

"I was out all fucking night. What do I look like lying next to you with sweaty balls? If you roll over and want some dick, you could catch an infection from that shit."

"Get your whole nasty, sweaty-ass body in the shower, then! Don't wash only your dick and nothing else!"

"I was tired and didn't feel like standing in the shower. I was going to shower in the morning. I just didn't want to jump in the bed with a sweaty dick. That was a courtesy to you," he declared.

"A courtesy to me?" Iyana repeated, turning the thought over in her head that maybe Bryan was being considerate. Bryan could tell he had her retreating and moved in to seal the deal.

"Iyana, we live together. What the fuck can I do without you knowing?" he tried to reassure her.

"That doesn't mean a damned thing! I got you out a bando, sleeping in the dark on old couch cushions. You needed somewhere to stay. That's probably all I am to you, a roof over your head and a convenient piece of pussy. That shit ain't stopping you from doing shit you want to do."

"A roof over my head? Is that what you think? Is that the lie you've been telling yourself?" Bryan questioned quietly as he approached her with puppy-dog eyes, ready to lay the same fake-sincere sentiments on her that always worked like a charm. "I love you, Yana, whether I live with you or not. I'd never betray you like that. You've sacrificed too much and given me too much for me to ever disrespect you like that. I'm sorry if I've made you feel that way, but that's not what's going on. I swear you're over-thinking things and reading too much into nothing. C'mere, baby," he explained and engulfed her in his arms. "Don't you know I love you? Huh?"

"I love you, too." She sighed as she gave in to him yet again.

Unaware Bryan was only saying what he knew she wanted to hear and being the man he knew she desired, Iyana, an only child with an absentee father, believed she found the man who was meant to come into her life and stay forever.

"You must've had a long day. That job got you stressed. I understand. Let me run you a bath and rub your feet. Will that make you feel better?"

"Yeah." Iyana smirked. "It would."

Chapter 3

"WHERE HAVE YOU BEEN? Why haven't you been answering your phone?" Iyana questioned late the next evening as Bryan breezed down the hallway and into the bedroom, passing right by the bathroom where Iyana was in the mirror, pinning up her hair.

"I've been ripping and running, babe. My phone has been in the car all day."

"You could've at least called me back," she mentioned as she turned into the bedroom door, coming face-to-face with Bryan as he was leaving back out.

"My bad. I've been busy. I'll be back in a minute, though," Bryan shouted hastily as he rushed back out the door.

"I'll ride with you. I'm not doing anything, and I'm off tomorrow," Iyana offered while grabbing her tennis shoes.

"No, babe. Stay here. I'll be right back," he urged as he tried to pull the door closed, but Iyana snatched it back open and stood in the doorway as he returned to his car.

"Bryan, who is that in the car?"

"I don't have time for this right now," he shouted over his shoulder as the caramel complexioned female with a long weave ponytail draped over the shoulder of her blue jean jacket eyed Iyana from the passenger seat of Bryan's car. "Go back in the house," he ordered as he opened the car door.

Iyana did as she was instructed and immediately frowned at herself, wondering why she had obeyed the order. *Things are never as they seem,* she reminded herself as she returned to the bathroom mirror. *Stop being so paranoid and trust him before you fuck up your relationship,* she fussed.

As hard as she tried to shake it off, the uneasy feeling in Iyana's gut would not leave her as she laid across the bed watching TV alone that night until she fell asleep, and it was only amplified the next day when she ran to the local deli on her lunch break and discovered all her cash was missing from her purse. She knew Bryan was the culprit, but her heart wouldn't let her believe he would steal from her.

"Babe, I need to use your car. I need a hose replaced in the Maxima," Bryan announced the next Friday night while coming out of the bedroom to the living room where Iyana was sprawled across the sofa watching TV and scrolling down the menu of the restaurant where she booked reservations for the next day's Valentine's Day dinner.

"The keys are on the bar," Iyana stated dryly.

"Cool. I'll be right back."

Three hours later, Iyana called Bryan's phone while sitting on the couch, but it went straight to his voicemail. Unable to reach him, she decided to order delivery from Uber Eats since she couldn't pick up food, but when she entered her card information, it was declined.

"Huh?" she wondered aloud. Hurrying to the bedroom, she

plopped down on the bed with her purse after snatching it from the corner of the dresser, preparing to check the card information saved on the app, certain there was plenty of money in her account, and certainly more than enough to cover dinner.

"Where is my damned card?" she questioned aloud as she thumbed through her billfold and found an empty slot where her card should've been.

Quick thinking led her to call the card's automated system, and she discovered all her money was withdrawn from her account at a series of ATMs within the past three hours.

"What the fuck?" she screeched as she chose the option to speak to a live representative. She froze her account and changed her PIN number, but it was already too late. There was nothing left for anyone to withdraw.

Iyana returned to the couch and cried herself to sleep in devastation, worried about Bryan's whereabouts but aware he was the only person who could've possibly taken her debit card and withdrawn all her money.

The sun peeked through her living room curtains as she awoke, still alone in the house. There were no missed calls on her cell phone and no unopened text messages. Noon came and went with no sign of Bryan. When she hadn't heard from him by five, she called the restaurant and cancelled the Valentine's Day reservations she made for six. By eight, she was crying again, and by midnight, she was in a rage.

At seven the next morning, Iyana was fully dressed as she called her best friend, Celeste.

"I need you to pick me up and run me somewhere." She was as vague as possible.

"Where's your—"

"We're going to go get it. Can you please just come get me?" she rushed her best friend.

"Yeah, yeah. Sure. Here I come," Celeste assured her, her curiosity and concern evident in her voice.

Iyana thought she would pace a hole through the floor as she impatiently awaited Celeste's arrival. Her mind racing a mile a minute, she knew there was only one place her boyfriend and her car were guaranteed to be. She hated bringing her friends into her personal business, but Iyana and Celeste had been best friends since the first day of second grade when they both walked into their classrooms wearing the same red, white, and blue flower-printed outfit with ponytails and barrettes. Now, both adults, Iyana and Celeste were nearly inseparable. They would ride or die for each other at all costs.

When Celeste's text came through alerting Iyana she was outside, Iyana snatched her purse and coat from the sofa and rushed out the door to hop into the passenger seat of Celeste's dark blue Honda Accord. She noted her best friend's new wig, a long chestnut brown installment with a side part and perfect barrel curls, and how it complimented her smooth almond complexion. *I like this style on her. I'll compliment her on it later,* she assured herself.

"Don't be side-eying me," Celeste blurted as she pulled up to a red light.

"I'm not side-eying you," Iyana denied with a light chuckle. "That wig looks nice on you."

"Are you trying to butter me up?" Celeste accused as she turned to glare at Iyana. "Don't be trying to act all nice while I'm taking you wherever we're going and getting into God knows what. I ain't no fool, Yana, and I know better than to fall for your antics. You can be nice to the whole dinner plate, but a buttered roll still gets bit," she stated, and turned back to the road as the light turned green.

During the rest of the ride across town, Iyana remained quiet and evasive as she fed Celeste a story about Bryan having to run somewhere and telling her to come pick up her car. When they pulled onto Zaria's street, Iyana felt her skin glow red from its own heat at the sight of her white Mercedes A-class parked in the driveway of the house where Zaria lived with Bryan's younger cousin, Renisha, and her seven kids. Celeste pulled into the driveway, parked behind Iyana's car, and watched closely as Iyana hopped out of her car and stormed up to the front door of the house.

BOOM! BOOM! BOOM! BOOM! BOOM! BOOM! BOOM! Iyana beat on the door as hard as she could, hoping her banging sounded like the police or even gunshots.

"Can I help you?" a young chocolate-skinned woman who resembled Bryan answered the door, rubbing her eyes, trying to adjust to the morning sun.

"Where is Bryan?" Iyana demanded.

"Bryan? I don't know. He ain't here."

"He's not here? But my car is here. Where are my car keys?"

"Your car?" the woman repeated with a frown. "Car keys. Okay, hold on. Let me check," Ms. Groggy-Sleepy yawned as she turned and closed the door. Iyana waited on the porch with her arms folded and foot tapping against the painted concrete. When the woman finally returned, she handed Iyana the keys. "Hey. I'm sorry. I don't know anything about whatever is going on, but here are your keys."

"Thanks," Iyana mumbled as she took the keys, rolled her eyes, and sucked her teeth at the woman before turning on her heels and heading to her car. *Stupid bitch,* she thought, *acting like she don't know who I am after I brought this nigga over here to pick up his shit the day he moved in with me. She knows who the fuck I am, and she knows what the fuck is going on, too. She can keep covering for that nigga and the bitch. I ain't dumb by a long shot. The nigga is probably laid up in there with the bitch right now.* She gave Celeste a thumbs up so she could leave as she unlocked her car door and hopped in.

"Ugh!" she growled as she glanced around the interior. Throwing the door back open, she dropped a cheap dollar store Valentine's Day card and an empty box of chocolates on the ground in the driveway. Furious at the signs Bryan spent the entire holiday with his ex, she grabbed the single red rose left perched between the seats, broke the stem in half, plucked all the petals, and tossed all the pieces onto the lawn.

Noticing the photo keychain that usually hung from her rearview mirror was missing, Iyana opened the glovebox, assuming Bryan had tossed it inside, but found the glovebox completely empty when she attempted to check its contents.

"My registration, insurance card, all the shit I had in here. Where is my shit?" she rambled.

There was nothing in the back seat, so Iyana got out and popped the trunk. Inside, she found a grocery bag containing the missing contents of her glovebox as well as the missing photos of her and Celeste, the pieces of the broken keychain scattered among the other contents. Disgusted, she snatched the bag out of the trunk, was careful not to slam the trunk and abuse her Mercedes on Bryan's behalf, got into her car, and pulled off.

"If that was where you wanted to be, you should've been there with her all this time instead of over here interrupting my fucking life!" Iyana bellowed into the phone while she changed clothes after work the next evening, livid she had not heard from Bryan in three days.

"Over here with you is where I want to be," came Bryan's voice behind her. She whipped around and glared at him in shock as he stood in the bedroom doorway with a smug smirk on his face. If looks could kill, Bryan would've been buried and decomposing already.

"How dare you?" Iyana seethed with an eerie quietness as she hung up the phone. "How dare you? You left me in the house all day and spent two nights with that bitch! I had to search for my own damned car after you stole all the money out of my bank account to spend on that hoe. You have the balls to bring your ass here after all that?"

"Iyana, baby—"

"Don't you fucking *baby* me! I want you the fuck out my house and the fuck away from me! Get your shit, Bryan Kimbrough, give me my key, and get *the fuck out my house!*" she screeched and lunged at him, but he caught her and wrapped her tightly in his arms, leaving her unable to move, no matter how much she squirmed.

"Damn, you smell good," he noted as he inhaled.

"Fuck you! Let me go so I can fuck you up!"

"Now you know you don't want to do that. What you really want to do is fuck me, and we both know that. That's what the real problem is. You need your dick, and you wanted some last night and the night before," he remarked.

"You have to be a stupid motherfucker to think I want you anywhere near me, especially on top of me, after the shit you pulled."

"What are you mad about? The money?" he questioned, minimizing his own actions as he released her and pushed her away. "I got my hose and radiator fixed and bought some new tires. My old tires were bald as a baby's ass. You don't want me riding around with bald tires in the rain and snow, do you?"

"The money? This shit ain't only about no money," she barked. "Fuck you, your tires, your radiator, your whole damn car. Get the fuck away from me, you piece of shit!"

"Baby, I'm sorry. Okay? I know you wanted to go out the other night. I just," he heaved a heavy sigh, "I went to see her because she said she would kill herself if I didn't. She's not used to spending Valentine's Day alone. What was I supposed to do?"

"Call the police! Let them handle her crazy ass! Call her damn mammy! You have a girlfriend and a whole different life now! You're not obligated to her! She's not your responsibility! You think I don't know what's going on? You put all my shit in the trunk and rode around telling that bitch it's your car. I found the receipt from Ruby Tuesday wedged between my seats when I made it home. Y'all had a whole date night, didn't you? Cheap-ass date for a cheap-ass hoe! Fuck you! Go be with that bitch!" Iyana spat.

"She knew that wasn't my car. I put your stuff in the trunk so her nosey ass wouldn't get your address from it. The receipt from Ruby Tuesday was for the drinks and wings I had at the bar while I was waiting for my cousin, Kevin, to get off work. I picked him up and took him home," he explained. "Think about it. You didn't see more than one meal on that receipt, did you?" His eyes pleading his innocence, Bryan stared into Iyana's eyes as the simple date he and Zaria enjoyed at Iyana's expense on Valentine's Day replayed in his head. The order of fifteen hot wings and fries and his tongue licking buffalo sauce from Zaria's fingers was enough to get him right back where he wanted to be: in her bed.

Iyana digested his words, believing she over-thought the situation and jumped to conclusions, as he always claimed she did. Bryan's eyes begged her to believe him, but the whole time he was sure she would.

"But you spent the night with her," she mumbled. "You spent two nights with her, and you wouldn't even answer the phone for me."

"I spent the evening, yes, but I was up all night at Kevin's house working on the Max, changing the radiator and hose out. When the tire shop opened the next morning, I got tires put on the car. I wasn't laid up with her," he denied.

The silence that followed was confirmation Iyana believed him, and Bryan closed in for the kill. Stepping closer to her, he grabbed her by the waist and peered down at her.

"See, baby," he whispered as he lifted her chin. "All you have to do is let me explain. I wasn't doing anything wrong. I'm just guilty of caring too much. That's all. You still got me. I'm here with you all day, every day. You're not going to lose me," he assured her.

Ashamed and feeling guilty for accusing Bryan of such betrayal, Iyana nodded. She sealed her own fate with a kiss, and she wrapped her legs around Bryan's waist as he lifted her by her hips and laid her on the bed.

Chapter 4

"BABE! I'M HOME!" Iyana chimed cheerily as she entered the apartment after a long day at the office four months later. She found her passion working with underprivileged children as a caseworker and child advocate at a local non-profit. At twenty-six years old, Iyana had been working for the same company for four years and enjoyed her job and its perks and benefits so much she had no plans to leave.

"Sssshhhh! Babe! Go left! Left! Left! Fuck! What are you doing? Shit!" Bryan barked as his soldier was gunned down beside two of his teammates on the TV mounted on the living room wall. "Damn it!" he growled as he took off his headset and launched it into the seat of the recliner across from him.

"Any luck with a job today?" Iyana inquired, ignoring his frustration on her way to the kitchen.

"Don't start, Yana," he warned with his face in his hands.

"What? I was just asking. It'd be nice to have some help with the bills, especially with the bigger TV, the lights being on all day, the air conditioner constantly running, and the stereo blaring. Yeah, it'd be nice," she rambled sarcastically as she glanced at the TV Bryan had convinced her to purchase the week before as if she was deep in thought, throwing hints like daggers at Bryan and not missing even once.

"Really? You come in here and break my concentration, cost me a mission I've been working on for three hours, and then insult me?"

"Three hours? Imagine three hours on a paycheck!" she snickered, ignoring his swelling anger.

"You're just going to insult me to my face, and I'm not supposed to say shit?" he bellowed as he rose from the couch.

"You're just going to sit on the couch and play video games all day like we don't have bills?" she challenged.

"You're the one who insisted you didn't want me hustlin'!"

"No, I don't want you hustling. I want you to get a real job, a legal job! Is that too much to ask?"

"The streets are all I know. That's the only clock I've ever punched. I hustle! I get it out the mud! I finesse, I slang, I push! Period!"

"Just because that's all you know doesn't mean you can't learn something new. When you know better, you do better. I would think I've shown you better by now," Iyana reminded him as she came around the kitchen bar to face him.

"It ain't about what you've shown me. I'm a man. I have to get it on my own. I can't be taking pointers from no bitch!"

"Oh, so I'm a bitch now?" Iyana gasped, taken aback and offended by his disrespect. "A whole year we've been together. I've done nothing but encourage and support you, and this is how you treat me? This is how you treat the person who accepted you wouldn't have the money for a present or to treat me to dinner and cooked a homemade meal to celebrate our anniversary instead, so you wouldn't feel bad? This is how you talk to the woman who carried you on her own back and took care of you like a child when you couldn't do shit for yourself?"

"Ughhh!" Bryan roared as he lunged at her and wrapped his hand around her throat, lifting her into the air and pinning her against the wall. "Say it again! I dare you! Say that shit again, and I'll drop kick your ass right here!" When Iyana merely whimpered in fear, unable to breathe, he warned her, "I suggest you remember who the fuck you're talking to. I'm still the man in this motherfucker, not your damn child."

He opened his palm and allowed her body to drop to the floor. Iyana grabbed her neck, coughing, with tears streaming down her face.

"You want some fucking help?" Bryan growled as he snatched his car keys off the seat of the couch. "I'm about to give you what the fuck you're asking for."

With that, he stormed out the house, slamming the door so hard behind him, it sounded like a gunshot. Iyana was left on the floor, racking with sobs and in disbelief at what had just occurred.

"Umm," Iyana moaned in her sleep that night as a hand tenderly slid up her thigh, interrupting her slumber.

"Hey," Bryan whispered in her ear.

"Hmm?" She stirred. "Huh? Ugh! Move!" she moaned groggily.

"Wake up."

"I'm awake. Watch out," she insisted as she removed his hand from her thigh.

"Turn over," he instructed as he moved closer to her, pressing his body against hers.

"What? Are you crazy? I'm not about to do anything with you! Get the fuck away from me," she croaked sleepily as she rolled away from their intense combined body heat.

"You still tripping on that shit? What the fuck do you need? Some money? Here, you wanted help with the bills, right?" he countered while pulling a stack of bills from his pants pocket, tossing the money onto the pillow next to Iyana's face. "There's your bill money. Now, turn over and give daddy his prize."

Iyana sat up in the bed in disbelief.

"*Prize*? You want to be rewarded for committing crimes and bringing me drug money? What did you have to do to get this money? Huh?" She picked up the stack of money and shook it at him. "You take your damned drug money and get the fuck out my bed!" she ranted and threw the money back at him. The knot struck him in the chest and bounced to the floor.

"You've been nagging at me about needing help for forever. You don't get to choose how I make my money. I made it. That's all you need to know. You want me to pay my way, right? How much do I have to pay for some ass? Huh?" Bryan swiped the stack of cash from the carpet and peeled off bills. "One hundred? Two hundred? Three?" he rambled as he tossed the money at her.

"I ain't no hoe, and you're not about to treat me like one," she seethed, beyond offended by both his words and the pungent stench of liquor on his breath as she stood on the opposite side of the bed disgusted with him.

"Every bitch has a price. I have yet to meet a hoe that won't go."

"Get the fuck—"

"I'm not going anywhere," he interrupted her with his hand around her throat for the second time that night.

"Ugh! Ugh!" she squirmed and fought, but to no avail. Bryan had her pinned against the wall with a grip she couldn't break.

He used his left hand to play in the juices coating her naturally wet pussy. No matter how she flailed, it was useless. Familiar with all Iyana's spots, Bryan knew exactly what to do to force her body to submit to him.

"Please," she choked, her eyes begging him to stop as he slipped a finger inside her.

"You don't have to beg, baby. Daddy got you," he taunted her. He moved his finger in and out to relax her tense and constantly moving body. Recognizing the little effect it had, he slipped a second finger inside her.

"Bryan, please, stop," she whimpered desperately, but he recognized the pleasure mixed with the pain in her voice, and it urged him on.

Using his thumb to rub her clit, he forced her body into submission, released his grip on her neck, and laid Iyana down on the bed, positioning himself between her legs.

"Give daddy his prize," he repeated before taking her clit between his lips and gently suckling on it.

"No, Bryan," she moaned. "Stopppp! Pleeeease!" She was no longer fighting him, no matter what her lips were saying. He sloppily licked and sucked until she could no longer fight the orgasm bubbling in her gut and screamed out in ecstasy.

"Bryan, please, please, please, stop," she huffed and puffed, trying to recover. "Stop this. Please, stop this."

Instead of honoring her request, Bryan removed his pants and underwear, tossing them in a corner on his side of the bed. Iyana leaped from the bed to attempt an escape, but he caught her by the wrist and snatched her back onto the bed.

"Where you going? Huh? You ain't going nowhere," he grunted as he wrestled with her flailing arms.

"No! No! Bryan! Get off me!" she screamed as she swung at him.

"Stop fighting me!" he roared once again and squeezed her neck so tight she was sure he would kill her. Iyana clawed at the hand wrapped tightly around her throat, gasping for air while still trying to force him off her.

Prying her legs open, he shoved himself inside her and moaned as he stroked. Tears spilled down the sides of her face into her ears, and Iyana rendered herself helpless. Defeated, she decided to stop fighting and allow him to finish, praying it would be over more quickly if she made the ordeal easier for him, certain it would be less painful for her to endure.

"You're sitting up here tripping and shit. You should feel blessed I'm fucking with you. I done had plenty of bitches that look better than you. Pretty-ass bitches, supermodels, but I'm here with you, fucking the shit out of you, licking on you until you cum. I'm here 'cause I love you, girl. All these other bitches out here that want me, and I'm here with you. Girl, you better give me this pussy!"

Staring blankly at the ceiling, she ignored his remarks and willed her mind to wander far away from what was happening in her little one-bedroom apartment. Bryan continued thrusting deep inside her, his grip around her throat just loose enough for her to pull slivers of air into her lungs.

"You like that? Huh? Huh? Tell me you like it."

Iyana remained silent. She tuned him out and psyched herself into believing it wasn't happening and Bryan didn't even exist at the moment. His thrusts quickened, and his grunts became deeper, but Iyana felt nothing as she lay silently, absent from her own body.

"Fuck!" he issued a guttural squelch, and four pumps later, he became a fish out of water, jerking and shaking in orgasmic convulsions.

Iyana breathed deeply as Bryan released his grip. A sudden over-whelming feeling that she was filthy rushed over her, and she turned over and balled up into a fetal position.

Bryan was snoring loudly and nearly comatose when she went into the bathroom to clean up. She grabbed a blanket and spent the night on the couch.

Chapter 5

PEONIES. Iyana's favorite flowers were peonies, and Bryan knew it. Every time he messed up in any way, he would buy as many peonies as he could find at the local grocery stores and flower shops and fill their apartment with the dazzling blossoming flowers. Every month after the first time she spent the night balled up on the couch feeling violent and disgusted with herself, Iyana would fill huge trash bags with the dead pink and yellow flowers. The occurrence became bi-weekly, and eventually, it became a weekly routine.

Thanks to Bryan, Iyana now hated peonies. He turned such a breathtaking part of nature into a reminder of the pain and embarrassment she endured the night before they were gifted to her. The flowers came to symbolize disrespect and abuse and her tolerance of both instead of the work of art they had always been in her eyes. In time, Iyana stopped even waiting for them to die. She tossed them into bags as she came in the door before she even kicked off her heels.

For months after that incident, between the peonies, Bryan and Iyana enjoyed good times in each other's company. They spent peaceful evenings at home, lying across the couch and watching TV, dancing or pranking each other. They even had the occasional date night.

However, there were always nights Bryan didn't come home at all. There were days he borrowed her car and brought it back with no gas or littered with trash. There were the hundreds of dollars she loaned him to flip and never saw a profit from. It became a never-ending cycle of drama and trauma that threatened to become a massive train wreck.

"You don't love me like that," Bryan accused Iyana one night seven months after the first incident as they snuggled on the couch watching *Fatal Attraction.*

"You want a woman to be so obsessed with you she stalks you? You want a woman to kill for you?" Iyana puzzled.

"I want a woman who loves me so much she'd kill for me, yes. I need a ride or die chick, in it to win it, Bonnie and Clyde. Fuck how it turns out."

"I do love you, Bryan," she whispered, "but if everything I've already done for you hasn't convinced you of that fact, taking a life for you certainly isn't going to help the cause. Everybody wants a ride or die, but I ain't Bonnie, and you definitely ain't no Clyde."

"You're just weak as hell, that's all," he scoffed in disgust.

"Call it what you want. I'm not one of these chicks who's going to take a charge and do a bid for a nigga. If you do your dirt, you're going to do your own time. I'm not taking anyone's life for you or anyone else, either. You call it weak and disloyal. I call it having common sense and decency."

"I don't have common sense?" he challenged her. "Because I want a loyal, down-ass bitch I don't have common sense?"

"There are plenty of things you don't have. Common sense is one thing on a long list."

"Bitch!" Bryan bellowed and pushed her off the couch onto the floor.

"Here we go with this shit." She sighed, completely exasperated, as she picked herself up from the carpet and dusted herself off. "You can keep all the dramatics tonight, B. I'm not in the mood."

"I don't give a fuck what you're in the mood for. You ain't gone sit here and insult me."

"You initiated this whole conversation. You're the one sitting here stating facts as if I'm supposed to try to convince you otherwise. Now you're mad because I agreed with you. Your reverse psychology backfired. Suck it up."

"You think this shit is funny?" he challenged as he rose from the couch.

"Go on somewhere with that shit, Bryan. I told you I'm not in the mood for the bullshit today."

"Oh, you're not in the mood?" he repeated as he shoved her. "Just today, all of a sudden, you're not in the mood?" he boomed and pushed her again as she tried to block his hand.

"No, I'm not. Now move," Iyana fussed as her back pressed against the wall as a result of a third push.

"Make me move, Yana. Move me," he dared her.

"Bryan, get the fuck out my face," she demanded.

"And if I don't?"

"Bryan, get—" She tried to shoulder her way past him, but her cheek was met with the palm of his hand. Iyana gasped in shock and immediately felt the impact of his open palm twice again. Holding her left cheek in her hand, she cocked back with her right fist and landed a punch to his nose, sending several drops of blood flying.

"Ughhh!" he growled as he stumbled backward while holding his nose.

Iyana seized the moment to scramble out the corner and run to the bedroom. Her wine glass crashed on the door frame next to her head as she slammed the bedroom door closed and locked it just in time to hear a shot glass burst against it.

"Open this door, Yana!" Bryan bellowed as he furiously yanked on the doorknob.

"Get the fuck out, Bryan!" she roared behind the closed door.

"Open this mother fucking door before I tear it off the hinges!"

"No! Get the fuck out!"

"Bitch, open this door!"

"Get out!"

"If I leave, I'm not coming back!"

"That's fine! Leave the key on the table!"

"Arggghhh!" he growled again and threw himself against the bedroom door, forcing it open.

Iyana hit the carpeted floor with a thud and shrieked as Bryan's fist made contact with her eye. Absorbing blow after blow, Iyana prayed he would stop while clawing at his face and neck, breaking skin on his arms.

"Get off her!" Celeste's voice boomed as Iyana considered kicking him in his nuts.

Bryan's fist paused in mid-air as he glanced over his shoulder just in time to see Celeste's entire body lunge onto his back. She pummeled him with punches to the head with all her strength, hoping to knock him out.

"Celeste!" Iyana shouted, shocked to see her best friend.

"You get off her, you piece of shit!" Celeste shrieked as she continued punching Bryan in the back of the head.

"Bitch, get off me!" Bryan bellowed.

"Get your ass out her house, you fucking asshole!" Celeste demanded and jabbed him in his right eye.

"Aaahhh! Fuck! Fucking bitch!" he groaned and slammed her back into the wall. Celeste slid down off his back as he stumbled out the bedroom. "Fuck this shit! Fucking bitches! Iyana, this ain't over, bitch!" he declared as he grabbed his keys.

"Fuck you!" she bellowed behind him as the front door slammed.

"Yana, you need to change your locks," Celeste quietly advised three days later as she made Iyana a plate of the blackened salmon, Italian spinach, and rice pilaf she cooked. Celeste had made sure to call during her lunch breaks at work to check on Iyana over the past two days since she couldn't miss work to babysit Iyana and nurse the black eye and split lip that forced Iyana to take off work, no matter how badly she wanted to. Finally, making it to her off days and able to spend the day with her best friend, Celeste was not biting her tongue or sparing Iyana's feelings about the fight she had to rescue her from. "He took his key with him. He could come back anytime."

"It is what it is," Iyana grumbled, and waved her off.

"Girl, that man is dangerous! He could kill you! Hell, if I hadn't showed up when I did, he would have!"

"What were you doing here, anyway?" Iyana frowned at her as she accepted the plate. After multiple five-minute rushed conversations, Iyana was finally able to ask Celeste the question that had been puzzling her since Celeste busted into her apartment like Superwoman to save the day.

"You pocket dialed me. I heard what was going on and jumped in my car. I didn't even waste time grabbing shoes. You know I ain't having none of that shit. A mother fucker ain't gone put his hands on you and I know about it and not do shit about it," Celeste informed her.

"The perks of your best friend living around the corner from you." Iyana shrugged. "I was fine, though," she mumbled.

"You were not fine. Girl, your neighbors were outside huddled up. The poor old lady that lives beneath you was out there in her housecoat and slippers. She didn't know what to do. I'm honestly surprised nobody called the police because the whole complex heard y'all fighting."

"I'll be okay, Celeste. Really."

"Oh, I know you're going to be okay. I'm going to make sure of it. I'm going to help you bag up all his shit, and we can drop it off wherever it needs to go. Then we're going to change these locks and—"

"Celeste! Celeste!" Iyana interrupted her. "I can take care of this myself. Okay? I can handle it."

"Just like you were handling it the other night?" Celeste paused in case Iyana decided to answer her rhetorical question. "Look, I know I'm not exactly a role model. I know I'm ghetto. My nails and lashes are long, my tongue is slick, my temper is quick. Yes, I'd rather smoke a blunt than read a book, and I'd rather drive the boat than ride one. I don't care how low you believe my standards are. They're exponentially higher than yours when it comes to men. You're a damned good woman, Yana. That nigga ain't had shit the whole time y'all have been together. Everything he has is because of you, including his clothes and his car. He's probably living out that raggedy-ass Maxima since you put him out, sleeping on his partner's couch, bumming loose cigarettes off everybody. He's a bum, sis. You need to let that nothing-ass nigga go and move on."

"Yeah. Yeah, I do," Iyana agreed. "You're right. He really ain't shit without me. I made him who he is."

"You deserve better. I've never been one to get in your business or try to tell you what to do. I just know this nigga ain't worth your time. You can do so much better than him."

Celeste allowed her words to sink in for a few minutes before continuing. "Look at you. You've been laying on this couch for three days. You need to get up and bathe, put on some clothes. I'll do your make-up to cover the last of this black eye. You can't keep missing work because of him. Don't let that nigga interrupt your grinding. Get dressed. Let's go shopping. That'll get your mind off things."

With an armful of bags and a wide smile, Iyana returned home that evening to find a single red rose on the bar in the kitchen with a card beneath it.

I fucked up. I'm sorry. Please forgive me, the note read. **P.S. The peonies didn't cost enough to make up for this mistake.**

Iyana balled up the card and tossed it in the trash with the rose. *You thought the rose would make more of a statement than the black eye I'm having to cover up? Tuh!* she thought as she walked through the apartment, checking for any missing or disturbed items, but there was no other sign Bryan had been there. Nothing else had been touched.

Chapter 6

THE NEXT DAY, Iyana returned to work, her bruises covered with concealer. She had dinner with Celeste and Bria that evening, but she never mentioned the rose. She went about her daily routine with no sign of Bryan until five days later when she arrived home from work, and there was a dozen red roses perched on the bar in a glass vase.

Part of Iyana hoped Bryan would come back. The other part hoped she never saw him again. *I've got so much extra money without him here,* she thought. *I have peace of mind. I feel so free right now. I never needed him, and I don't need him now. He needed me. He was using me. I'm changing these locks tomorrow.*

She spent her weekend changing the locks, repositioning the furniture in the living room, and bagging up clothes she no longer wanted. Then she accompanied Celeste on a trip to the nail shop and stayed up late watching movies, eating ice cream, and drinking wine.

When she arrived at work Tuesday morning, there were two dozen yellow roses on her desk. She sat her purse down, scanning around to see who was watching, before plucking the card from the arrangement.

I Miss You.

It was Bryan's handwriting. *You miss me, huh?* She scoffed. *I just bet you do.* Iyana dropped the card in the trashcan, and on her way home, she stopped behind a grocery store and tossed the whole bouquet in their freshly emptied dumpster and thoroughly enjoyed the loud crash of the glass vase.

"Home sweet home," she sighed as she dropped her purse on her couch and kicked off her heels, exhausted from a day of glancing over her shoulder, expecting to see Bryan pop from behind dumpsters and doors to try to get an opportunity to speak to her. Now in her own home, she felt as if she could breathe again. "Safe at last."

She poured herself a glass of wine and let the shower run while she undressed in the bedroom. Scrolling on her phone, she found a 90s playlist and hopped in the shower after double-checking the locks on the doors.

"Real love... I'm searching for a real love..." she sang as she twirled out of the bathroom, toweling her hair dry. She unexpectedly found her face pressed firmly against the wall in the hallway with a hand tightly gripping the back of her neck.

"Yeah," a voice all-too-familiar murmured with lips and nose pressed to her neck. "Look at that fat ass jiggling and glistening, fresh out the shower. I missed you, baby."

"How did you get in here?" Iyana whimpered.

"Come on, baby." Bryan smirked. "You didn't honestly believe you could lock me out my own house, did you?"

"This is not your house. It's mine. You're not on the lease, and you don't pay any bills here. You have no business here, and you're not welcome. There's nothing here for you."

"Oh, there's something here for me. It's all for me," he hissed in her ear as he pressed his hard dick against her back, alerting her to his

40

nakedness. She squirmed, desperately trying to get loose, but to no avail. "Are you done fighting me? Are you done?"

"Get off me, Bryan. Let me go."

"Nah nah. I'm not about to get off you. I'm about to get up in you," he informed her, the smirk on his lips evident in his voice.

"Let me go, Bryan!" she shouted.

"Don't try to make a scene and get your ass slapped," he warned. "You had the neighbors all in my business last time for no damned reason. Don't fucking play with me."

"Bryan, let me... aahhh!" she yelped as he slid all six inches of his hard manhood inside her from behind.

"Yeah. You miss this dick, don't you? Tell me this dick feels good to you," he grunted as he thrusted.

"Bryan, stop, please," she begged, fighting tears.

"Tell me this dick is good to you, Yana. Tell me you missed it, baby."

"Please stop," she cried, with her tears streaming down the wall.

"Don't fight it, baby. Take this dick."

"Bryan—"

"That's it. Say my name. Say my name. You say it so sexy. I love hearing it coming from between those sexy-ass lips," he moaned as he continued to pump deep into her.

"Ugh! Ugh!" Iyana groaned, disgusted by her own inability to fight her body's natural reaction.

"Yeah, that's it. Poke that ass out for me. Let me get up in that spot so you can cream on daddy's dick."

When Iyana did just that, Bryan pulled her from against the wall by her hair, forced her to the bedroom with his dick still inside her, bent her over the bed, and drilled his dick deep into her spot until she was both crying and crying out.

"Didn't I tell you not to play with me?" he challenged as he pumped, his hand still gripping her hair so tightly he pulled out plugs. "Didn't I?"

Iyana didn't respond. She lay there taking it, feeling guilty about having an orgasm, hoping he finished soon, and wondering what she did to deserve what was happening to her. *This is so sick,* she kept thinking. *He's so sick!*

"Damn, this pussy is so good," he grunted as he threw his head back and hungrily grabbed a handful of Iyana's ass. *I'm so glad I didn't stop taking my birth control,* Iyana thought as she recognized the signs Bryan was about to bust.

"Fuck yeah! Shit! Ummm... aaahhh!"

As the familiar warmth filled Iyana's womb, tragic defeat filled her heart. Incredibly disappointed in her own body's betrayal and disobedience to her will, Iyana waited until Bryan was snoring before she rose from the bed and sulked to the bathroom.

This wasn't supposed to feel good, she scolded herself in the mirror as she waited for the water to warm to clean herself up. *It'll be okay,* she promised her reflection. *It'll be okay.*

Chapter 7

"BRUH, WHERE YOU BEEN?" Bryan's cousin, Kevin, jeered a week later as Bryan exited his car and walked up Kevin's driveway. "I ain't been seeing you around lately. You ain't been coming through, nigga. What's good?"

"Mane, me and my bitch got back together. You know how that shit go. A nigga gotta play nice for a little while 'til shit die down."

"I figured that's what was up. What about Serita? Shawty been coming through here looking for you," Kevin informed him.

"I've been seeing her calls and texts. Next time she comes through, tell her I'm away on business, and I'll get up with her when I can. I gotta take care of this shit first. A nigga gotta have somewhere stable to lay his head. Plus, them new J's finna come out. If I run that pipe deep enough, I'll be able to get the shoes and the fit to match. Know what I'm saying?" Bryan cackled and slapped fives with the group of guys shooting dice on Kevin's front porch.

"Damn, mane. Shawty taking care of a nigga like that?" Marcus, one of Kevin's friends, smirked while Kevin threw the dice.

"Hell yeah. I got her right where I want her. You know how these bitches work. You fuck 'em good, hit that spot, fuck they heads up, they'll buy a nigga a whole new wardrobe round this bitch," Bryan bragged.

"Damn right! Fuck you mean!" Kevin whooped. "You gone get her to fix your car, too?"

"Nah, I'mma just take her credit card when she ain't paying attention and go handle that shit. The Max don't need much no way. A couple sensors and a new thermostat 'cause that muhfucka been sticking and shit. I'll slip the card back in her purse when I'm finished, and she won't know shit 'til the bill come. I'll handle the aftermath. I'll just fuck her real good, and she'll forgive a nigga. I ain't worried about it."

Kevin glanced over at Marcus, recognizing the envy in Marcus' eyes as Bryan continued to brag. Marcus considered making a pass at Iyana and taking her from Bryan so he could get in on some of the good fortune. *This nigga is running his mouth too fucking much,* Kevin thought while Marcus jealously contemplated, *I've been looking everywhere for a bitch like that. This nigga has it made.*

"Aye, Kev. I'mma holla at y'all, mane. I got shit to do. I just stopped by to kick shit for a second and let a nigga know I'm alive out here," Bryan announced as he and Kevin shook hands.

"'Preciate that shit, nigga. Holla at ya boy, mane!" Kevin yelled at Bryan's back as Bryan walked back to his car.

"I got you, nigga," Bryan assured him. "I'll get up with y'all later."

"My nigga! Boy, where you been at?" Bryan's mother jeered as Bryan exited his car after parking in front of the house on a street lined with trash and run-down duplexes where she had been living off and on with her boyfriend.

"I've, umm... I've been around. You been okay?" he inquired as he walked up the driveway and met her in the middle of the front yard where she had been scrubbing a white couch cushion with a toilet bowl brush she was dipping in a bucket of rainwater to the amusement of her neighbors.

"Hell naw! How the hell I'm supposed to be okay? Huh? You ain't been by here to check on me in forever."

"I've been busy, that's all. Had to handle some business."

"What you got for me? What you got?" she questioned while her hands rubbed together, creating a sound like sandpaper.

"I, umm, I... look..." Bryan hesitated. *She looks horrible, nothing but skin and bones. She's going to smoke herself to death. She ain't even been eating. I can't keep helping her do this to herself. This shit ain't right.*

"Quit ya stalling. Whatchu got? I know you got something." She frowned at him as she fussed, waiting for him to go into his pockets.

"Yeah," Bryan mumbled, digging deep into the front right pocket of his jeans. When he came out with a small bag of crack rocks, he watched the smile spread across his mother's dry, cracked lips as her ashy, fidgeting hands grabbed at the bag. "You need anything else, Momma? Food or something?" he inquired as he sized up her emaciated body. If she were a dog, the Humane Society would've been called long ago.

"Naw, I don't need no goddamn food," she growled, picking up on his insinuation. "Got plenty of shit in the house. I'm straight. This all I need. Come get ya money," she instructed as she headed toward the broken front door of the duplex.

Following her inside, he stood at the door, waiting for her to return from the bedroom. His eyes scanned the bedbug-ridden furniture in the living room and the sink in the roach-infested kitchen. The stench of mold, mildew, rot, decay, and crack and marijuana smoke hung in the air and threatened to suffocate him. *One day, I'll have enough of some bitch's money to get her up out of here and put her in rehab*, Bryan promised. *One day.*

"Here you go," his mother's voice snatched him back to reality. She handed him three fives and a taped-together ten.

"What's this? Ma, you know you're short, right? You know this ain't enough."

"Make it enough. Shit."

"Ma, this ain't even half—"

"Boy, what you gone do? Huh? Beat my ass like I'm yo' bitch? I said make it enough. Now, go on somewhere. Get ya ass outta here."

"See, that's the problem. I'm doing right by you, but you shorting me my money because you know I can't do shit about it because you my momma."

"Shorting you yo' money? After all the money I spent raising you? It ain't yo' money no way! That's that girl money. She'll be okay. She ain't gone miss the shit. She prolly don't even know you got the shit, knowing your slick, sticky-fingered ass. Go on bout yo' business so I can smoke. Bye, nigga!"

Bryan left the house seething and pissed only because he couldn't react, respond, or retaliate. He was mad because it was the norm for them. She cared nothing about his well-being, and if he was honest with himself, he knew she never did. Every time she ever called him, she was never concerned about him, only his whereabouts with her fix. As bad as that was, she wasn't paying him for the fifty and one-hundred dollars-worth of crack he dropped off at a time.

"You don't have to sleep on the couch tonight," Bryan quietly told Iyana as he stood in the doorway between the hallway and living room in her apartment later that evening. Iyana was balled up on the sofa with the same blanket she slept with every night for the past week.

"I'm straight," Iyana responded dryly, completely uninterested in being in his presence.

"I don't want you to sleep on the couch tonight," he clarified. "Come get in the bed so we can cuddle and watch a movie, talk things out and make it right."

"I'm straight," she repeated.

"Well, I'm not."

"Look, I'm doing all I can do by allowing you in my house right now—"

"*Allowing? Your house?* This is *our* house. We both live here."

"No, this is *my* house. I'm on the lease by myself, just like I pay the bills here by myself. I'm doing *all* I can do by *allowing* you to be here," she emphasized. "I suggest you get accustomed to sleeping alone and be grateful you have somewhere to sleep at all," Iyana repeated sternly as she sat up on the couch after pausing the show she was watching. "Because at this point, you're testing the shit out my patience, and I'm not going to take much more of this shit."

"I suggest you move past what happened so we can move forward. You're holding up progress by sleeping in the living room instead of in the bed with me," Bryan scolded her.

"Don't try to talk to me like I'm a child! This is my house! You're holding up my progress by being here at all!"

"I'm here because you want me here!"

"You're here because you broke in, you fucking burglar!" she yelled. "I didn't invite you here. I didn't call or text you. You kept coming over here while I was at work and leaving flowers, so I changed the locks. When you couldn't get in, you sent the flowers to my job instead and broke into my fucking house. Let's not forget the facts."

"Are you sure that's how that happened? You have a bad memory.

I think you're remembering that wrong. Plus, I'm still here. You never asked me to leave."

"Would you have left if I did?"

Silence ensued as the two glared at each other while Iyana waited for a response she knew she would not receive. Iyana felt as if steam was seeping from the collar of her t-shirt. She was baking, boiling on the inside, furious that he felt so entitled to everything she owned simply because she allowed him to move in.

I have to get her back here in the bedroom so I can get her back in check, he thought.

"Look, I'm sorry. Okay? I got upset and let my temper get the best of me. I've been stressed out lately about not having a job and having to watch over my shoulder out here in the streets. I took that shit out on you, and that shit wasn't right. Things got out of hand, and I apologize for that. Can you forgive me, please, so we can move past this?"

"I've already forgiven you. I'm a Christian, and I refuse to allow you to have that kind of power over me, but I won't forget," she assured him with a finger pointed at his nose. "You can take your ass back there and get comfortable because I'm fine right here where I am."

"Well, I'mma just come—"

"If you lay your ass on this couch, I'm going in the bedroom, barricading myself inside, and locking you the fuck out," she threatened as he approached the sofa. "I'm not sleeping next to you, Bryan. I'm not ready. I'm not comfortable."

"With me? You're not comfortable with me? C'mon, baby—"

"No, Bryan." Iyana sat up and shooed him off as he approached her with open arms.

"Baby, stop acting like this. You know I love you—"

"Stop, Bryan," she shot back and shoved him away as he stood in front of her. "No."

"Aight. Aight." He threw his hands up in surrender. "I'll let you have this one. I'll respect your space. It's cool." He retreated to the bedroom alone, defeated.

Lord, please, don't let him come back in here bothering me tonight, she prayed.

I'll let you have this one today, Bryan thought, *but tomorrow... tomorrow I'm going to have you spread eagle across this bed.*

Chapter 8

DAYS PASSED with Iyana still refusing to sleep in the bed with Bryan. She wouldn't even go into the bedroom when he was home, and she stored her purse in the trunk of her car to prevent him from swiping anything out of it. The amount of time it took for Iyana to come around had Bryan frustrated. He grew impatient with her and resolved he needed to be more aggressive in his approach.

"Hey, hey, hey... come here. C'mere," he cooed while grabbing her arm and pulling her to him as she exited the bedroom closet one evening, four days after his first attempt to get her back into the bedroom.

"Let go of me, Bryan. I'm not doing this with you today." Iyana rolled her eyes.

"I miss you, baby. I just want to smell your scent," he wooed her as he pressed his nose against her chest and inhaled. "It's lonely at night back here by myself. I miss sleeping with you wrapped in my arms. Don't you want me to hold you, Yana?"

Iyana didn't respond as she stood between Bryan's legs with his arms wrapped around her waist, his cheek pressed against her breasts, while he remained seated on the edge of the bed. *He's like a child*, she noted. *A twenty-eight-year-old child. He got in trouble, and now he's pouting and throwing a fit because he doesn't like the length of the punishment.*

"C'mon, Yana Baby. I'm so sorry for how I was acting. Forgive me, baby. Please," he begged with his face in her chest. He inched his fingers up her back and beneath her blouse, enjoying the feel of her soft flesh. *She likes this shit,* he assured himself. *She loves that special attention and that touchy-feely shit. I bet that pussy is dripping already.*

Bryan peered upward into her eyes as he unbuttoned her blouse. She refused to lock eyes with him and accept defeat, yet defeat felt so good. She missed his touch, the loving caress of gentle fingers roaming her body, the familiar scent of the man she loved, the feeling of being needed and wanted. It had been weeks, but it felt like a life-time ago since the last time he actually made love to her at a time when she actually wanted him to do so.

Sliding her silk blouse off her shoulders, his fingers glided down her back until they met the clasp of her bra and unhooked it, allowing her succulent Hershey Kisses to fall free of their restraints.

"Look at you," he whispered, "so gorgeous." His palms massaged her breasts before his tongue circled her right nipple and pulled it between his lips. Iyana inhaled and closed her eyes, enjoying the plea-sure. When a light moan escaped her lips, Bryan thought, *got her.*

Running her hand over his high-top fade and down the back of his head, Iyana lost her control over the situation. She reminded herself it was only a moment of surrender to get what she needed from him. *Men do it all the time,* she thought, unaware it was exactly what Bryan was currently doing.

She relaxed in his arms, and Bryan reveled in victory. He switched his focus to her left nipple and gently laid her on the bed while posi-tioning himself over her.

"Where you going in this little pencil skirt? Hmmm?" he teased as he unbuttoned the skirt she wore to work. "Walking around here in those sexy-ass heels with that switch you do when you know I'm watching. You're a walking advertisement. What are you selling? Sexiness? Look at these," he complimented her, running his fingertip over the edge of the red lace thong that matched the bra he removed. "You make these muhfuckas look good."

He slid the thong over her hips and dropped it on the floor next to her bra and blouse, licked his lips, and bit his bottom lip while running his eyes over her silken chocolate skin.

"You so muhfuckin sexy, Yana. I can't get enough of you. I love the shit outta you. You know that?"

Iyana watched in silence as Bryan moved downward as she braced herself for what she knew was coming. From the moment he ran his tongue over her wetness, she screamed on the inside. Determined to make him work, she only allowed light, barely audible moans to escape her lips, and it worked like a charm. Bryan went into overdrive to extract those high-pitched screams and full body tremors his head game always caused.

For over an hour, she allowed him to lick and suck as she cried out in gut-wrenching orgasm after orgasm, repayment for his abuse and mistreatment. When she finally couldn't take anymore, she pushed him away with her palm to his forehead and fought to catch her breath. Clutching at her chest, she watched Bryan step out of his gray sweatpants and pull his white tank top over his head, intentionally flexing his muscles. His hardened pole pointed straight at her juicy opening, Bryan slowly stepped toward her, preparing to put it down like never before.

Iyana spread her legs and allowed him inside, releasing the sweetest moan Bryan ever heard as he entered her. He stroked her slowly, aware she liked to make sweet, slow, passionate love in the beginning. Bryan bent down, pressed his chest against hers, and wound his hips as he ran the tip of his tongue over her lips before slipping it between them, allowing her to taste her own juices. He slid his arms beneath her, engulfing her and holding her tight as he stroked her slowly, taking his time and patiently giving her the intimate pleasure he knew her body craved. Once she had her fill of the slow grinding, she put her own legs over his shoulders, repositioned her lower back more comfortably, and gave Bryan that *fuck me* expression he had been anticipating.

"No," he refused and shook his head.

"No?" Iyana repeated, confused.

"Bend over for me, baby," he instructed her, and she obeyed.

Two strokes in, Iyana sensed something wasn't right. Four strokes in, she knew she wasn't imagining things. A weird burning sensation inched up her walls, creating an incredible discomfort she tried to ignore. As Bryan drilled into her spot, the discomfort drifted from her mind, and she rode the waves of pleasure surging through her body.

"Oh God, Bryan! Right there!" she finally cried out.

"I know, baby," he cooed.

"Fuck me, Bryan! Fuck me harder! Beat this pussy up!"

"You want me to beat it up, baby?"

"Yes! Fuck! Yes! Tear it up, baby!"

"I'mma tear it up for you, baby. I'mma give you this dick you've been missing."

"Oh, Bryan! Fuck yeah! Fuck this pussy good, baby!"

"I'm fucking the shit out this pussy for you, baby. I'mma make up for all that time," he declared as he hit it harder and dug deeper.

"Oh shit," she grunted. "Oh shit."

"That's it, baby. Cream for daddy. Put that icing on this big-ass beef cake."

"Oh fuck. Oh fuck, yes. Yessssss. Fuuuuuuuck."

"That's it, baby. Say my name. What's my name?"

"Bryan, oh my God. I'm about to... oh, Bryan... oh! Oh! Oh, fuck! Yes! Aaaahhhh!"

Iyana's body went into a series of convulsions, and she squirted juices all over Bryan's thick rod as he managed three more strokes before he released deep inside her, and they both collapsed onto the bed.

Bryan slid behind Iyana and wrapped his arms around her, placing tender kisses up and down her neck and shoulders. As disgusted by his touch as she found herself, the familiar softness and comfort of her bed caused her desire to slip back into the isolation of the living room couch to be forgotten.

"Baby, you should distance yourself from that Celeste girl. She's not the friend you think she is," he whispered to her.

"What do you mean? Celeste and I have been best friends for years."

"She's not your real friend, Yana. Real friends don't text your boyfriend after y'all have a fight. How did she get my number, anyway?"

"I didn't know she had your number. She texted you?"

"Yeah, she did. You've been telling her too much of your personal business, bragging about the shit I do to you. She offered to do things, begged me to do to her what I do to you. She doesn't care about you or your feelings at all, Yana. She's only trying to see what she can get out of you, including your man. I held it down, though. You know I'm all yours. You can always depend on me to be loyal to you, baby." Bryan gave Iyana a few minutes for the information to soak in before he pulled her closer and sighed into her neck. "Forgive me, Yana. I'm so sorry, baby," he whispered into her hair as she lay silent in an attempt to ignore him.

"Watch out, B," she huffed as she pushed his arm off her and sat up in the bed.

"Yana—" He grabbed her arm and peered at her with pleading eyes as she snatched away.

"Damn, nigga! Can I pee? Can I clean up? Is it against the rules to wash my ass?" she snapped, annoyed by her own defeat.

"My bad, my bad," he apologized as he threw his hands up in

surrender, and Iyana turned and continued down the hallway to the bathroom.

Closing the bathroom door, Iyana plopped down on the toilet top with her face in her hands, desperately trying not to burst into tears. *What have I done? Why did I allow any of this to happen? I shouldn't have let him back into my space. And Celeste? How could she? After everything I've been through with him, why would she want anything to do with him?*

Bryan, on the other hand, laid in bed with a smug grin on his face, satisfied with knowing Iyana was currently in the bathroom questioning her entire friendship with her best friend and preparing to cut ties strictly because of him. He successfully sowed the seeds of distrust he knew were necessary to get Iyana right where he needed her to be.

Chapter 9

"WE SHOULD TAKE A TRIP," Bryan suggested a week later while they sat at the dining room table in her apartment eating dinner.

"A trip?" Iyana frowned. "With what money?"

"I've got a bit of extra money saved up. It can be something simple, just the two of us. We could use a getaway."

"I don't know," she hesitated, the skepticism evident in her voice.

"C'mon, babe. We've never been on a trip together. It'd be fun. Let's go somewhere close. How about Nashville Shores? They open in a couple weeks. We could drive out there and spend the day at the water park, get a hotel room for the night, and drive back the next morning. You know, something simple."

"It sounds like it could be fun," she admitted as she turned the thought over in her mind. "Maybe on a weekend?"

"Yeah, that way you'd only have to take off that Friday."

"I... I can't," Iyana mumbled after turning the thought over.

"Why not? It's a few weeks from now. We've got plenty time to plan it out."

"I know, but I just... I just can't. Okay?" she repeated and quickly rose from the table, rushed to the bathroom, and locked herself inside.

"I'm so stupid," she whispered aloud while sitting on the toilet top with her face in her palms. "Why do I keep going through these motions? Why do I keep letting him do this to me?"

Bryan remained at the table confused, repeatedly glancing toward the bathroom door, waiting for Iyana to return. He finally decided to check on her, but when he approached the door, he could hear her talking. He frowned as he pressed his ear against the wooden door.

"I can't keep doing this. I can't keep living like this. It's a lie. It's all a lie. I'm not happy here. Why am I pretending?"

Assuming Iyana was on the phone talking to another man, Bryan, in a jealous rage, beat on the door.

"Open this door, Iyana! Open this door right fucking now!"

"Go away, Bryan," she replied calmly.

"You're in there on the phone with the next nigga feeding him lies, talking about you ain't happy here! Open this fucking door!" he roared.

"I'm not on the phone. My phone is still sitting on the dining room table," she stated equally as calm and opened the bathroom door. "I was talking to myself, Bryan, myself and nobody else. I was reminding myself I'm not happy here, which is not a lie, and I'm not feeding anything to anyone, unlike you," she challenged as she stepped closer to him. "Is that the lie you feed to your hoes when they find out about me? That you're not happy here? Is that what you're upset about? Did it sound too familiar? Have you been telling them I don't do for you what they do for you, that I don't love you like they love you?" she taunted.

"You don't know what you're talking about. I don't have—"

"You don't have any hoes? Right? That's what you were going to say, isn't it? You don't have any hoes. You're not fucking off. I'm crazy. I don't know what I'm talking about. I'm overreacting, right?"

"Right," he answered, sounding as stupid as the expression on his face looked.

"If that's the case, why am I itching, Bryan? Why am I having all this nasty-ass discharge? You haven't noticed an awfully bad smell? If I'm overreacting, why is my doctor prescribing me medication for chlamydia? If I don't know what I'm talking about, how did I get chlamydia when I haven't fucked anybody but *you*? Answer that shit! Since you have the answer to every fucking thing, since you know so damn much, riddle me that, motherfucker!" Iyana was livid. Her eyes were red, and her fingers were trembling with the itch to slap slob out of Bryan who stood there at a loss for words. "Get the fuck out my way," she scoffed and pushed him to the side.

"I don't know what you're talking about, Yana." Bryan followed her up the hallway toward the dining room.

"Oh, you don't know what I'm talking about? That's real funny because the expression on your face seemed to be a whole lot wiser to what the fuck is going on than you're claiming to be right now," she chuckled, "but that's cool because you never know what I'm talking about. I guess I'm speaking Spanish or fucking French or some shit. You never know shit, honestly. So, why don't you grab the twelve pieces of shit you brought in here, including your chlamydia, and take them with you as the door DDT's you on the way out?" she hissed with an exaggerated smile.

"Are you putting me out?" Bryan was genuinely surprised and appalled.

"Call it what you want. Putting you out, relocating you, giving you the boot, all I know is you need to find yourself on the other side of that door."

"I ain't going no-damn-where. You're sitting here acting crazy with your made-up-ass ailment, throwing out accusations and hoping one sticks. I ain't no fucking dart board, Yana. You can kiss my ass. I ain't leaving," he declared stubbornly and returned to the table to finish his food.

"I'm asking you nicely. I even gave you a big pretty smile to go with it, but I won't keep being nice about it. You need to leave, Bryan, before I call the police and have you removed. I sincerely don't want to put these white folks in our business, but it ain't like you don't have anywhere to go. You can take your STD and go lay with the hoe you got it from. I don't want it. Return to sender, nigga. All I know is you need to make a move toward the door within the next thirty seconds, or you'll be on the way to jail within the next thirty minutes. It's your choice, and it makes me no difference at all because at this point, I genuinely don't give a fuck. Now play."

Iyana planted her feet with her arms crossed, unwavering in her decision. Bryan attempted to read her but was unable to do so. He opted to be smart about the situation and leave like she requested, reminding himself he'd be back in no time, as he always was.

Chapter 10

NO TIME WAS ABSOLUTELY CORRECT. Before Iyana's round of antibiotics was up, Bryan was back at her house as if nothing had ever happened. As much as she tried to play it off, Iyana was tired of putting him out and letting him come back. She was tired of feeling played and accepting so much less than what was owed to her. Deep down inside, she knew she deserved and could do so much better. She was so blinded by what she thought was love for Bryan, and by his continuous manipulation, she couldn't gather enough strength to leave him for good.

Bryan knew that as well, and he made a point not to allow Iyana too much time without him. He didn't allow her time to think or evaluate what was going on around her. To keep her under his spell, he kept her mind in a foggy haze, consumed by the extreme pleasure he bestowed upon her body when their flesh collided.

In the meantime, Bryan had a whole roster of women he visited during the day while Iyana was at work, including Serita, the woman he spent most of his time with when Iyana put him out, and Zaria. Unbeknownst to Iyana, Bryan gifted her belongings to his side chicks, with Zaria being the main recipient. Body sprays, purses, shoes, DVDs, a camera, even some of Iyana's clothing were all taken one by one to his side chicks' houses. Bryan had never stopped seeing Serita after he and Iyana got back together all those months ago, and she was more than content with the occasional visits he bestowed upon her while Iyana was at work.

"I'll be back in an hour or so," he announced one night a month after sewing the seeds of distrust between Iyana and her best friend, while lacing up his Jordans, the same ones he vowed to convince Iyana to buy for him. "I've got to make a couple serves."

"An hour?" Iyana questioned.

"Or so," he repeated.

"Yeah, okay," she replied, the skepticism evident in her tone.

"I'm going to take your car, baby. Mine is acting up," he announced while heading toward the door.

"Maybe you don't need to go then," she remarked as she stepped out of the kitchen.

"I gotta make this money, baby. I won't be long," he promised as he grabbed her keys on the way out the door.

Iyana went about her normal evening, unwinding and preparing for bed. Two hours after Bryan left, she remembered her phone bill was due and picked up her purse to retrieve her credit card, only to find her entire billfold missing.

"What the—" she growled. "Now I just know the fuck he didn't!"

Impulsively, Iyana called her debit card's automated system to check her balance. While entering her card information, she reminded herself it was nearly impossible for Bryan to withdraw money from her card, as she hadn't given him the new PIN number after she last changed it. Her funds remained untouched. However, her card was locked due to the five failed transactions at different ATMs due to the culprit entering an incorrect PIN each time. That was all Iyana needed to hear. She sprang into action, aware she had to recover her card to pay her bill before two in the morning to prevent her phone service from being deactivated.

One thing Bryan was never made privy to was Iyana's ability to track her car's location at any time through the Mercedes Me Connect app. When she opened the app on her phone, she realized it was exactly where she suspected it to be... parked outside the apartment Zaria moved into only a couple months before. Reluctantly, she picked closed the app and called the only person she knew she could count on, without a doubt other than Celeste.

"Bria, you up, girl?" she inquired when Bria answered after the second ring.

"Yeah, I'm just chillin', watching TV. What's up?"

"I need a favor."

"Cool. What's up wit' it?"

"Can you run me somewhere to pick up my car?"

"Of course, but why you ain't call Celeste? She lives closer to you," she questioned.

"Celeste and I aren't speaking right now, and where I'm going, I need somebody with me who's strictly with the shit," Iyana explained as she wondered how Celeste had been and what she was doing.

It had been over a month since Iyana had spoken to her best friend, and though it was by her own choice, Iyana could not deny the fact she missed Celeste. Celeste had called her multiple times over the course of that month, but Iyana refused to answer her calls or respond to her texts. She was simply too hurt by the betrayal and still in disbelief that her best friend would go behind her back and try to hook up with her boyfriend. *I'm going to call her,* she kept promising herself, but she just hadn't gotten around to it. She wasn't sure if she would be able to maintain her composure when she finally confronted Celeste about the accusations, so she concluded their first contact shouldn't be over the phone.

"You called the right person because you know I'm with all the fuck shit," Bria proudly assured her. "Let me throw on some shoes and grab my pistol. You know I don't leave the house without it on me. I'll be on my way in just a second."

"You know that's some bullshit, right?" Bria scolded Iyana after Iyana explained why she and Celeste weren't speaking while in the car on the way to Zaria's house.

"How so?"

"You seriously believe this no-good, lying-ass nigga over your homegirl who's been rocking with you since second grade?"

"What did he have to lie about, Bria? He had nothing to gain from lying. I honestly don't think he made that shit up."

"*No purpose? Nothing to gain?* Oh, he achieved his goal with that shit. You're living out his goal right now. The nigga has a history of being on some fuck shit, and this situation ain't no different, Yana. He tried to pin you against Celeste to isolate you. He wants you to feel alone, like nobody gives a fuck about you and nobody's loyal to you except him. He doesn't want Celeste around because she'll protect you, and she's your voice of reason. He knows she's a real friend, and she'll ride this motherfucker until the wheels fall off. She's in the way of his plan," Bria explained. "You need to call Celeste and talk to her about it. I guarantee she'll have a completely different story than the bullshit he's feeding you. Hell, as long as y'all have been friends, you at least owe her that much."

Iyana thought about Bria's advice as they pulled into Zaria's apartment complex. Iyana used the app to sound the horn and flash the lights on her car, not caring it was after midnight and hoping she was disturbing Zaria's neighbors, so they'd file a complaint.

"Hold on for a second. I've got to get my car keys back."

"You know I got you, girl. Me and Blue Bell will be in the cut watching," Bria assured her with a pat to the gun laying on the passenger seat. "How the hell do you know where this girl lives, anyway?" she questioned before Iyana turned to walk off.

"Bryan's stupid ass showed me texts from her begging for money for her light bill. She sent a picture of the bill, address, and all, and I made a mental note of it. He thought he was being funny and shit, but I'm way too observant for that type of shit," she explained.

"Niggas never learn, mane." Bria shook her head in disgust.

Iyana first examined the outside of her car before peering through the windows to check the interior. Beer cans, liquor bottles, and empty cigar and candy wrappers littered the front seats. She took a deep breath to calm her growing anger before marching up to Zaria's door and beating on it like she was Mike-Will-Made-It.

Two knocks later, she stood face to face with the one person who was a constant interruption in her relationship: Zaria. Medium-complexioned, too fat to be skinny and too skinny to be fat, built like a box, and as plain-faced and beady-eyed as a woman could be without being flat-out ugly, Zaria opened the door with crust in her eyes, wearing nothing but a silk robe her fingers were holding closed between two breasts that lost any pertness they ever possessed long ago.

"Is Bryan here?" Iyana skipped the formalities, her attitude obvious. Zaria stood there without saying a word, looking like she was seeing a ghost.

"Ummm... yeah... but he's sleep. You want me to—" she offered, pointing over her shoulder, but Iyana interrupted her.

"Naw, let him sleep. Let me get my car keys, though."

"Yeah, yeah. Sure. Hold on a second," Zaria agreed, and closed the security door. The wooden door was left cracked, and Iyana could see the lights and hear the music of a stereo system playing R&B in the background. Squinting a bit to see better into the dark apartment, Iyana scoffed.

"This bitch's bed is in the living room?" She almost laughed out loud.

"Here you go," Zaria quietly offered Iyana her keys when she returned.

"I need my shit out his pockets, too." Iyana scowled at her, daring her to pretend to be ignorant of what she meant.

"Ummm... okay," was Zaria's response before she went back into the house and quietly rummaged through Bryan's pockets, being extra careful not to wake him for fear of being caught. When she returned, she stated, "I found your debit card. I think the rest of your stuff is still in the car, though."

Iyana leered at the woman as she took her card from her, turned, and marched off. Zaria watched her until Iyana unlocked her car doors, and then Zaria quickly closed and locked her doors.

"Look at this shit," Iyana mumbled in disgust. "This is a Mercedes, not a goddamned Infiniti."

She gathered all the trash in her car, stalked back to Zaria's door, and piled it all in a heap against the door. Pulling out the parking space, Iyana signaled to Bria and pulled off.

"No gas in the motherfucker," she growled as she exited the apartment complex and pulled over at a gas station a block down the street.

"You good, sis?" Bria inquired as she pulled up next to Iyana who had just inserted the nozzle into her car.

"Yeah. About to get some gas and head home," she assured her while pressing buttons on the gas pump. "Thank you, sis."

"Girl, you know I got you anytime, and Celeste does, too," she reminded her with a wink.

"Duly noted, sis. I'll handle that."

"Alright, hit me up if you need me."

"Bet," Iyana nodded. When the gas finished pumping, she hung up the nozzle and got back into the car in time to hear her cell phone ringing. "Who the hell..." she mumbled as the screen glowed with a number she didn't recognize. "Hello?"

"Ummm... is this... is this Yana?"

"Who is this?"

"Zaria."

"Oh."

"Ummm... I got your number from Bryan's phone. He sleeps with his eyes open, so it's pretty easy to unlock."

"Okay."

"I just... I just wanted to apologize. We didn't want you to find out like this."

"Find out? I've known about the two of you for quite a while. This only confirmed what I already knew."

"Oh, okay. Well, I just thought I'd apologize. I'll... ummm... let you get back to whatever you were doing."

"You don't owe me an apology. He does, but he can keep that shit. I don't want it. You can keep him, his apologies, and everything else that belongs to and comes with him over there with you. I've got a whole drawer of his *I'm sorry's*. I don't need anymore, and I don't need him or his community dick," Iyana hissed at her.

"I honestly didn't want you to find out we were getting back together like this," Zaria repeated, "or that we were still having sex."

"Seems to me like y'all never broke up, honey. You have a good night, though," Iyana spat sarcastically and hung up.

Bryan repeatedly called Iyana's phone the next day. He left voicemails until her mailbox was full and sent texts that she deleted without opening. He finally stopped calling at about six that evening after being ignored all day. At eight, she returned his calls, instructed him to meet her at the laundry mat across the street from Zaria's apartment, and hung up before he could respond.

When she pulled into the parking lot, Bryan exited the business, uncertain what to expect. Iyana popped the trunk and dropped two large plastic shopping bags of his belongings on his feet.

"Here's all your shit from my house. I'm done with you. You're a piece of shit, a liar, and a cheater, and I don't want shit else to do with you," she spat with a venom in her voice he had never heard. "I told you from the beginning to be with her, if that's where you wanted to be. You insisted you were done with her and wanted only me, and yet, here we are. I brought you all your shit so you can stay here with her, where you want to be, and you won't have to come back to my house for any reason."

"I don't want to be with her. I want to go home with you," he corrected her.

"That's quite difficult to believe since she's under the impression you two have made plans to get back together." She smirked as she revealed she knew much more about what was going on than he believed.

"I'm not getting back with her." He frowned, trying to maintain his lie.

"Honestly now? That's the impression you have her under, and believe me, I'm more than glad to roll with it. Like I told her, y'all never broke up, anyway."

"I don't care what impression she's under. I don't want her. I want you!"

"You want me?" She cackled exaggeratedly, purposely making Bryan angrier. "You want me so bad you were dick deep in your ex last night? Oh, that's a good one!"

"I'm not cheating on you, Iyana!" he declared.

"Oh, now you're not cheating? This keeps getting better! Nigga, please spare me the bullshit! The bitch answered the door in a kimono with her titties hanging to her knees. Clearly y'all had been fucking, and she had no problem admitting that much."

"Of course, she told you some shit like that. She wants you to leave me so she can have her nigga back because in her head, I'll always belong to her. She's used to us breaking up and me always coming back, and the last time, I didn't do that because I've been with you. She's playing mind games with you, and you're falling for the shit."

"You're telling me y'all didn't fuck?"

"I ain't touched that girl. I went over there because she said she wanted to talk, and I must've dozed off while I was there," Bryan explained.

"But she answered the door naked in a robe."

"I don't know what the hell she was wearing when she answered the door. She probably had just got out the shower. I don't know. I was sleep," he urged.

"Why did she lie then?"

"I told you she wants me back. The quicker she gets you out the picture, the quicker she thinks I'll be back."

Iyana was quiet for a second as she mulled over his words.

"Look, if you're going to believe her and let her run you off and win, I understand. If you want me gone, I'll grab my shit and go," Bryan huffed impatiently as he reached for the bags, but Iyana quickly snatched them back.

"I shouldn't give you shit," she seethed, "but since you barely have anything and what you do have is trash, you can have this shit."

"Thanks, I guess."

"I'm not going to keep dealing with this shit, Bryan. I'm tired of the bullshit," Iyana warned.

"Look, it's cold out here. I'm not about to stand here and listen to you fussing and shit like I'm a child. Can I have my house key back or naw? Damn!"

"Here!" she shouted and handed him the key to her house back, but he took both his key and her car keys from her hand.

"Give me my fucking car keys, Bryan!" she demanded.

"Shut the fuck up with all that rah-rah shit! Got all these people out here staring at us."

"I don't give a fuck about these folks watching! Give me my keys!" she shouted again.

"Get yo' ass in the car and let's go! Shit! Save all the damn dramatics!"

Just like that, he was once again back in the house.

Chapter 11

WITH EACH PASSING DAY, Iyana grew increasingly resentful, and Bryan grew increasingly comfortable. With his comfort came even more disrespect. He was secure in his position and doubted Iyana would ever actually get rid of him, no matter what he did.

Iyana pulled up at Kevin's house one day after work a month later to pick up Bryan as he asked her to do. Bryan requested to use her phone, explaining his battery was low, and Iyana nonchalantly obliged and waited in the car while he went back inside. When he finally hopped in the car, he was eerily quiet, and they rode in silence the entire way home.

"Think before you answer this question," Bryan advised her once they were in the house. "Who is the nigga?"

"What nigga?" Iyana frowned, genuinely confused.

"Aht. Aht. I told you to think about what I'm asking you before you answer. I'mma let you think about what you did for a second."

Iyana stood in the middle of the living room floor staring at Bryan, completely lost. She didn't even try to think about it. There was nothing to think about, and yet, Bryan stared at her, waiting for an answer.

"Now," he began as he approached her, tossing the phone at her and hitting her in the chest, "who... is... the—"

SLAP!

Bryan backhanded Iyana so hard she fell with a thud against the wall and dropped to the floor. Taking the opportunity to pounce on her, he squeezed her throat as tight as he could with his left hand while punching her in the face with his right. She clawed at his arm, trying to release his grip on her neck. With him on top of her, she was unable to breathe and left feeling helpless. She was certain he would kill her.

"Bry... Bry... I..." she whimpered, unable to speak but desperately trying to tell him she couldn't breathe.

"Weak-ass bitch!" he growled as he continued punching her in her face and head with his knee in her chest, trying to get full control of her.

Iyana's head pounded from the swelling of the knots. She could hear her own heartbeat in her ears as her left eye closed with the swelling. Her tongue crossed pieces of a broken back tooth, her own blood's metallic taste infuriating her. With a sudden burst of anger-driven strength, Iyana kneed Bryan between his legs, forcing him to release his grip on her neck.

Gulping air, Iyana jumped up and tried to make a run for the hallway, but Bryan caught her by the leg of her slacks, and she fell face-first onto the carpet. He pulled her toward himself, but when she was close enough, she kicked him in the face with her heel. Though he roared in pain, Bryan still didn't let go. Instead, he snatched her and grabbed a handful of her hair.

"C'mere, slut," he growled and resumed punching her, this time in the back of the head. "You want to hoe around, huh? You want to be a hoe?"

Iyana felt herself slip out of consciousness for two seconds, and her bladder released. Instinct kicked in, and she kicked and flailed wildly to get him off her, releasing no more than a quiet grunt.

"Get off me, Bryan," she growled through gritted teeth as she swung, punching him squarely in the nose. "Stop!"

Bryan fell off her to grab his bleeding nose, allowing Iyana too much time to recover. She kicked him in the leg with her heel and took off running, locking herself in the bedroom.

"Open this fucking door, bitch!" he roared while beating on the door.

"I'm calling the police!" she threatened.

"You gone call the police? On me? Fuck you, bitch!" he barked.

Iyana listened as he grabbed his keys and slammed the front door, but she didn't move until there was no movement in the house for fifteen minutes.

Her breathing sporadic and reduced to sobs and shudders, Iyana picked herself up out the corner of the bedroom and rested on the edge of the bed, trying to collect herself. When she finally found the strength to stand up to head to the bathroom, pain shot through her entire body, from her toenails to her hair follicles. Breathing her way through each step, she clicked on the bathroom light and stared at herself in the mirror in both shock and shame. She was unrecognizable. Her face was bloody, bruised, knotted, and swollen. Her eyes were both black, and her lips and nose were busted.

She called her job and left a voicemail for her supervisor, informing them she wouldn't be in for the rest of the week without providing a reason, drove herself to the hospital, and checked into the emergency room.

Iyana spent two days in the hospital being treated for three bruised ribs, a sprained wrist and ankle, and symptoms of a panic attack. Afraid Bryan would be at her house, she prepaid for three days at a hotel and called Bria once she was locked safely inside her hotel room. When Bria called Celeste, she filled her in on the little knowledge she had of what had been going on with Iyana, making her promise not to chastise Iyana before they went together to visit her.

"You don't have to explain anything to me," Celeste reassured her as they ate in an awkward silence during a visit on Iyana's third day at the hotel. She and Bria brought brunch with them to prevent Iyana from ordering room service for the third day in a row.

"Celeste, I—"

"You don't have to explain. I understand," she firmly interrupted her. "I know you want to apologize," she assured her more softly, "but it's totally unnecessary. I was hurt in the beginning, of course, but I could tell what was going on all along, even before Bria explained it to me. I saw it coming way before that night I pulled him off you. That's what these types of guys do. He created a distrust so he could isolate you. The only reason he didn't plant the same type of seed in your head about Bria is because he wasn't aware enough of her. He didn't know how close y'all are because of the picture we painted when you met him. You're never really on the phone with her or out to eat or shopping with her, so he didn't view her as a threat. In reality, even though she's not your best friend, she's still a tremendous friend."

"Yes," Iyana nodded as she sliced a corner of her omelet off and dipped it in Hollandaise sauce as she smiled at Bria, "she truly is."

"She told me the lies he fed you. I'm sure I don't have to tell you it's not true, but I want you to see the actual truth for yourself," Celeste stated, and slid her cell phone across the table to Iyana.

Celeste and Bria ate their omelets and hash browns and drank their mimosas in silence as they watched Iyana read the entire thread of text messages between Bryan and Celeste.

Hey there
Who is this?
Bryan
How did you get my number?

From Iyana's phone

Where's Yana?

She sleep

So you snuck & went thru her phone & got my number?

Yep. What's up witchu

What's up? Don't come texting me like we're cool. We're not friends. We don't have anything to talk about.

You don't have to be so mean. I know we're not friends, but I want to be. I want to be so much more than friends.

More than friends? Nah bruh. I'm straight on that.

I saw how you were looking at me the other night when you stopped by.

Excuse me?

And I have to admit that dress was sitting right on that ass.

Okay, idk if you're high or what, but you're way out of line.

Come on Leste. You and I both know it was you I was after that night at the club.

No you got who you were after. It was pretty clear who you wanted. You ran all the guys away from her at the bar.

I was trying to get her to hook me up with you.

Even if that were the case, that's not how it turned out.

So how about we correct that mistake

The only mistake is me allowing my best friend to get involved with the likes of you.

Why? Because you wanted me for yourself? I knew it

Ha! No! Because you're a piece of shit!

No, I'm the shit

That's debatable.

So I'm tryna see what's up? What's good?

Ain't shit up. Why are you still texting me?

I'm trying to get a trio going with you and one of your homegirls. I heard you into women. Shit, I am too!

I don't know who told you that but you've got me mistaken. I'm not into women and I'm not into you. Now get the fuck off my phone.

Well I'm an excellent teacher. You can try it out with me.

I ain't trying shit but to get you to leave me the fuck alone.

Come on girl. You know you want to hit a threesome with me. Every woman has a homegirl they think is sexy as shit.

I'm done talking to you. You have a real problem. I really wanted better than this for my best friend. If you're not happy, you should leave her alone but texting me is not an option.

So you're going to act like you don't want me? I'm a grown man. I'm real about mine. I think you're sexy as hell and I'd love to bend you over and long stroke that pussy from the back.

Stop texting me.

I'm serious, Leste. Come through. Yana's gone right now.

First she was asleep. Now she's gone. Please get off my phone..

You can quit playing hard to get. I know Yana done told you how I be having her climbing the walls. Come let me taste that pussy. You look like you taste like cherries and peaches.

I have herpes and I'm having a really bad outbreak right now.

Girl stop. You play too much. Come see me.

I told you to stop texting me.

Come see me and then I'll leave you alone.

I'm not coming to see you and you're still going to leave me alone. I'm about to block you. Good night.

"Why didn't you tell me?" Iyana demanded as she glared at Celeste while passing her phone back to her. "Why didn't you show me this?"

"Would you have believed me if I told you?"

"What do you mean? You're my best friend!" she yelled.

"You were so in love with him, Iyana," Celeste mumbled quietly as she shook her head. "You were so blinded by all his lies. You wouldn't have been able to wrap your head around him betraying you. It would've been turned around on me, and just like

76

he created a divide between us and had you not speaking to me for a month, he would've concocted some sort of excuse or rationalization to turn you even further away from me. Your best friend? Yes, I am, but I also know manipulation and brainwashing when I see it, and I know eventually everything done in the dark comes to the light.

"You let him do this to me. You let him do this to *us*. Why, Celeste? I don't understand."

"I didn't *let* him do anything. There was nothing I could do to stop it. Anything I could've done would've only made the situation worse and turned you even further away from me."

"As bad as this situation is, Yana, I have to agree with Celeste," Bria intervened. "Staying out of the situation as much as possible was the wisest thing she could do to minimize the damage to y'all's friendship."

"Celeste, I—"

"I already told you, you don't have to apologize. You don't owe me an apology. I love you, and I understand."

"I was so stupid." Iyana hung her head in shame. "We've been friends for decades. I don't know how I ever let some guy make me doubt you. *You* of all people!"

"It's okay, Iyana. I promise. I understand," Celeste assured her.

"I don't. How? How did I allow this guy who has nothing and is nothing to take control of me, of my life, of everything?" She frowned as she questioned.

"It's not that simple. He forced you to allow him. He manipulated you until you turned a blind eye and believed all his lies. There's nothing for you to apologize for. He should be ashamed of himself, but of course, he's not," Bria spoke up. "Don't you dare take responsibility for the mental and emotional abuse he put you through. That's exactly what he wants. He wants you to take all the blame."

"It just is what it is." Iyana sighed heavily. "All that is over now. I'm done with him. I'm about to go home and change my locks again and move on with my life. You two care to join me?" She wiped her mouth and rose from the table.

"Naw, sis. You got it. We've both got to get to work," Bria informed her.

"Oh, okay." Iyana chuckled. "Mention a little work and everybody scatters to the wind."

"Seriously, if you need some help, let me know, and I'll come by when I get off," Celeste offered.

"It's cool. I should be fine. It's only a couple of doorknobs. How hard could it be?"

Repeatedly checking for Bryan's car as she waited in the parking lot, Iyana sighed as she accepted Bryan was nowhere to be found. After ten minutes of praying, hyperventilating, and threatening a panic attack, she grabbed the bag of new doorknobs off the passenger seat of her Mercedes, mustered up the courage to exit her car, and took her time climbing the stairs to her apartment.

Her heart raced as she unlocked the door and stepped inside, but she was relieved to find there was no one in her living room, perched waiting for her on the couch. She dropped her purse onto the table next to the door and stood in the center of the living room floor for ten seconds before she realized something was indeed amidst deeper in her house.

Iyana stepped stealthily down the hallway toward her open bedroom door, but she made it no further than the bathroom before she was sure of what was taking place in her bedroom. The smell of sex was thick in the air, and the sounds were unmistakable.

"Oh my God!" she whispered loudly from the bedroom doorway as her heart dropped to her knees. There was Bryan perched over a caramel-complexioned female with a low fade who had her legs thrown over his shoulders, enjoying him long-stroking her and digging her back out. Iyana's voice alerted the woman of her presence, and she gasped at the sight of Iyana, quickly pushing Bryan off her in a panic.

"Yana!" Bryan gasped.

Iyana hurriedly retreated to the living room with Bryan stumbling, tripping, and falling over the pants around his ankles as he tried to catch her, dick swinging everywhere.

"Oh my God! Oh my God!" she whimpered as she reached for her purse. Bryan's hand landed on her arm to pull her back, and Iyana quickly spun around and punched him as hard as she could before rushing out the door.

"Who was that, Bryan?" the naked woman questioned him from the hallway.

"Serita, don't worry about who the fuck that was," he snapped at her. "Put your clothes on and let's go."

"Yana? Yana, baby?" Bryan called in a sing-songy voice as he slipped his key into the lock two days later with a bouquet of red roses and a bottle of Moscato in hand. The door creaked open with caution as Bryan peeked his head inside, hoping Iyana wasn't still mad.

Squinting in the blinding darkness, he flipped the light switch on the wall to reveal an apartment stripped completely clean. Like The Grinch when he stole Christmas, Iyana even took the hooks off the wall. It was empty, cleaned, and ready to be rented to the next tenant. Iyana moved out and moved on... without him.

Chapter 12

WITH IYANA GONE, her number changed, her friends not answering his calls, Bryan once again had nowhere to go. After sleeping in his car for two days, he decided to call Serita and try to make amends, if for nothing else, to have somewhere to live.

It took quite a bit of convincing, but as conniving as Bryan was, he slithered his way into Serita's home with her four children and became her fifth child to pick up with Serita where he left off with Iyana. The late nights turned into early mornings, but Serita was still satisfied solely to have a man around. He spent days at a time at Zaria's house, hoping she would take him back while she debated whether she even wanted him and wondered why he hadn't suggested he move in with her.

"I needed my car to go to work today," Serita fussed as Bryan undressed in her bedroom after being gone two days three weeks after moving in with her. "I've been calling you and texting you. You're going to get me fired."

"You're not going to get fired. I had some business I had to tend to. You'll be okay," he blew her off.

"I'm not going to be okay. I have to work to be able to pay my bills. You're already taking most of my money. I have to work, Bryan."

"I ain't took shit that wasn't mine," he seethed through gritted teeth.

"You took my rent money last month. My landlord is threatening to evict me if I don't try to catch up. I can't catch up if I can't get to work. I have kids, Bryan! We won't have anywhere to go!"

"Alright, calm down," Bryan cooed as he pulled her onto the bed next to him. "You're not going to get fired. You can go to work tomorrow. I'll even stay here and make sure the kids are okay. Cool?"

"Yeah." Serita nodded and answered quietly.

"Ummm," Bryan moaned as he inhaled. "You smell so good, girl. What is this scent?"

"Soap." Serita jumped up and folded her arms across her chest. "If you think you're going to come in here smelling like day-old pussy with lipstick on the rim of your shorts and think you're going to get some ass, you've got another thing coming. Get your funky ass out my bed," she growled and stormed off to the kitchen before he could say another word.

"Man, where the fuck you been hiding? We ain't seen you in a few weeks. Your girl been on your ass?" Kevin's friend, Marcus, shouted at Bryan as Bryan sauntered up Kevin's driveway the next day.

"Nah, man." Kevin spoke up before Bryan could respond. "Tell him what happened, Cuzzo," he chuckled knowingly as he threw a pair of dice against the wall of his porch and snapped his fingers.

"Fuck you, Cuz. That shit ain't funny." Bryan shook his head in shame as he stood on the steps watching the game with his hands deep in his pockets.

"What happened?" Marcus pried.

"Mane, look. I beat her ass that night the last time I was over here, right? I guess she got scared and didn't come home for a few days. I'm thinking when she does decide to come home, it'll be at night. She'll miss her own bed and come home to get some sleep. I took the Serita hoe to the house to get away from all them damned kids at her house. You know she don't know shit about my gal, and I just wanted to fuck in peace."

"This sounds like it's about to go all the way left," Marcus commented as he dropped a twenty-dollar-bill in the stack of money on the top step.

"Shut up, nigga. Let the nigga talk," Kevin instructed with a frown.

"So, me and Serita up in the house. She already asking questions because my gal got the house laid out and decorated. It's obvious a bitch lives there. So, we in the bedroom, and I'm dick deep in the bitch with the hoe legs over my shoulders and shit, jugging her real good. It's the middle of the fucking day, so I'm thinking we're good. My gal's ass is at work, right?"

"By the way this story is going, I doubt that." Marcus snickered.

"Man, I get at this angle that makes Serita's loose-ass pussy feel a little tighter, like a pants leg instead of an open window, you know? My gal walks in and catches an eyeful of every damn thing. I jump up and try to catch her when she heads for the door, and she hauls off and punches my ass in the damn nose."

"Damn!" Marcus split his sides at Bryan's misfortune.

"She leaves. I make Serita get dressed, and we bounce. I drive past the apartment once or twice a day, but her car was never there. There weren't any lights on, nobody was home. I got tired of acting scared and shit, picked up some roses and wine from the grocery store, and went home a couple of days later. Man, I got in the house, cut the light on, and the bitch was empty as hell. The bitch done moved completely out the damned house, changed her number, and ain't said shit to me at all."

By that time, Marcus was doubled over on the porch, holding his stomach, splitting his sides at Bryan, who stood there embarrassed. Bryan allowed them to find entertainment in his pain, aware it was all his own fault, but he still tried to keep up the façade. He didn't care.

When Marcus finally regained his composure, he inquired, "Where you been staying?"

"With Serita," Bryan admitted.

"Serita and all them damn kids? You were trying to get away from her kids for a quick fuck session, and now you have to deal with them daily. Damn! If that ain't some serious karma for your ass!"

"Did you find out where she moved?" Kevin pressed.

"Man, naw. Her friends all blocked my number. They wouldn't tell me shit, anyway. She ain't been to work. I've been sitting across the street from her job hoping to catch a glimpse of her coming and going, but she ain't been there, and she ain't been at none of her friends' houses, either. I don't know what's up with her. She done fucking disappeared."

"Damn, cuz. That's fucked up, but she ain't Casper. She's somewhere around. You just gotta find her."

"Man, fuck that shit," Bryan huffed in defeat. "I ain't got time, patience, or resources to be hunting this bitch down. I told the bitch to stay down, and she jumped up and took flight. I ain't got time for no hoe who can't follow instructions. It just is what it is."

"Damn, man. That's cold." Marcus shook his head.

"It's a cold world." Bryan shrugged.

Chapter 13

"YOU'RE NOT GOING to keep coming over here fucking on me if you're not going to move in with me." Zaria sighed as she puffed her blunt a month later.

"You know why I won't move in with you?" Bryan quizzed her as he took the blunt she passed him and pulled from it.

"Why?" she questioned, curious to know the answer.

"Because you ain't gone do shit but put me out."

"How about you don't do shit to get put out, and then you wouldn't have to worry about that?"

"I ain't gotta do shit to get put out. The wind blow the wrong way, my shit outside in the parking lot. The Sun set a little early, the locks changed on the door."

"That's not true, and you know it. Every time I have ever put you out, I had a damned good reason. You make me put you out, B. The lying, the cheating, the stealing... you be begging to get thrown back to the streets. If you just act right—"

"Act right? What the fuck is *act right?* What the fuck is that?"

"That's the problem right there. You don't even know what it means to be a good man. You don't know how to treat a woman right, and you expect any woman you deal with to accept your bullshit and keep quiet about it. I'm not putting up with that bullshit. I'll be by myself and live alone before I accept that shit. I'll find myself a couple fuck buddies and be single indefinitely," she stated matter-of-factly as she pulled from the blunt again.

"No, the fuck you ain't!" he growled and snatched the blunt from her. "You better not be fucking nobody but me. That's *my* pussy. You belong to *me*. I better not catch you giving my pussy to no other nigga." *This bitch done been listening to too much Megan and grown herself a pair of off-brand nuts,* he thought as he side-eyed her.

"See, that's your problem! You always think you own some shit. You ain't running shit over here, Bryan," Zaria stated as she sat up in the bed. "I'm a grown-ass woman. I pay all the bills in this motherfucker. You don't contribute to shit, and you ain't dependable. I run this shit over here. You come over here and drop dick off when I call you. I don't do a damn thing on your time, and you don't get shit unless I tell you to come get it. I hate to bust your little bubble, but you actually ain't got no power at all. You don't control shit in your life. You depend on women for everything. I might not like your dumb-ass girlfriend or the smart one you had, either, but one thing I can say is we all let you believe you were in charge but had complete control over your entire existence."

"Bitch!" Bryan roared and jumped up.

"Oh, now I'm a bitch, huh?"

"Shut the fuck up!"

"Shut up? Oh, okay. See, let me explain something to you, B. The wonderful thing about this being my place is when I'm ready for you to leave, you have no choice but to get out. Disrespecting me is the first way to be shown the door. You want me to shut the fuck up? How about this: *get the fuck out.*"

Zaria rose from the bed and stood with arms folded over her bare breasts as she smirked at Bryan, having played a winning hand. Past the point of being done with his shenanigans and disrespect, she knew she'd always win because she had reached the point at which she refused to allow him to control her like he once had.

"Get out? You want me to get out? Fine then! Don't fucking call me no more," he huffed as he got dressed and headed toward the door. Zaria watched him throw on his clothes and appeared unbothered while she silently hoped he didn't try to choke her out as he had done so many times before.

"Oh, sweetie, should I stop paying the phone bill, too?" she taunted him.

"Fuck you, bitch!" he spat as he grabbed his keys.

"You wish! You just make sure when you see another nigga pulling up to get this pussy, you mind your business. Okay, sweetie? Bye!" she crowed and quickly shoved him out the door and closed and locked it just as Bryan attempted to snatch it back open to get to her. She cackled exaggeratedly as she enjoyed his banging on the door, pulling on the knob, and screaming profanities at her. Aware the thought of her being with another man would set him off, she was now sending him back to his *other* other woman after he did to Serita exactly what he was forbidding Zaria from doing to him.

"Stupid-ass nigga," she mumbled as she entered her bedroom after the banging stopped. "You have to be in a relationship to cheat. I'm a free agent, and I'm about to play all the games. He expects me to be faithful to his cheating ass? He ain't even my nigga. He's community penis, for the streets, and that's where I'm sending his garbage ass." Chuckling as she hopped into the shower, she reassured herself with, "Game on, and I'm Player One."

"Where the fuck you been? I've been calling you for hours," Serita drilled Bryan the moment he came through the door.

"Out handling business," was his only reply.

"Yeah, okay. Handling somebody else's business! You smell like pussy!"

"Serita, gone on with that bullshit, mane! Ain't nobody in the mood for this shit today."

"I don't give a fuck what you're in the mood for! Hey! Un-uhn!" she shouted and jumped in front of him. "Don't take your ass in my bedroom! You're not sleeping in my bed smelling like the next bitch. The best you're going to get tonight is the couch."

"The couch? I ain't no fucking guest!"

"Says who?" she challenged with an attitude.

"Bitch, have you lost your fucking mind? I live here!"

"Again, says who? You sure don't act like you live here. I could've sworn I've been living here alone the past few days."

"I'm out here trying to make money to bring home, and when I come through the door, you're tripping. I bet you won't trip when the money comes in, though."

"The money never comes in, Bryan. It only goes out! Miss me with your bullshit! You can hit the sofa. I've been sleeping alone the last few nights. I don't see why tonight should be any different," she hissed and slammed her bedroom door before locking it.

WHAM!

When Serita came out of her bedroom the next day dressed for work and preparing to take her kids to school, Bryan was waiting at the bedroom door. The moment she stepped into the hallway, he slapped her head into the wall with a loud thud, and she collapsed in a heap on the floor.

Stunned and trying to gather herself, Serita glanced at Bryan, towering over her with pure evil in his eyes. A sudden streak of crushing pain shot through her chest, and Serita found it difficult to breathe.

"Play with me again, bitch," Bryan sneered as he bent down, his nose an inch from hers.

Serita heard the threat, but she was in too much pain for it to register. She hyperventilated while clutching at her chest, tears rolling down her cheeks as her left eye swelled.

Bryan stormed straight out of the house without even glancing back. Serita's twelve-year-old son came out his room to find his mother unconscious on the hallway floor and called 9-1-1.

Bryan had never hit Serita before, and his physical violence took her completely by surprise. Though it was the first time, it would not be the last.

Serita spent a week in the hospital after doctors discovered an underlying heart condition. Bryan's violence and the newly discovered ailment scared Serita so badly she vowed Bryan would never hit her again without consequences, and any attempt to assault her would be taken as an attempt on her life.

No matter what she promised herself in the hospital, when she returned home, it was a different story. The first week, Bryan was barely home, and he tried to have as little interaction with her as possible, spending most of his time flipping money he stole from Serita and sliding between the thighs of several women in his flock. When he didn't feel like going home, he spent the night with whatever woman was the most eager to have him around a little longer than usual.

During the following two weeks, he went home every other night, mostly to make sure the locks hadn't been changed. When Serita returned to work the following week, she was advised by her doctor to only perform light duty. Instead, Serita took extra shifts and worked overtime to make up the money she missed while Bryan kept her car and from being in the hospital. With Bryan barely around, her kids spent twice as much time with her mom, and her house was empty twice as often.

"I'm proud of you," her mom admitted one night two weeks later while Serita picked up her kids. "You're overcoming this disease. You're taking care of your kids. You even got rid of that no-good nigga."

"Oh, he still lives there," she revealed. "He's just hardly ever around."

"Why don't you put him out? Get rid of him. He's not serving you any purpose. Baby, you've got enough kids. You don't need somebody else's grown child to take care of, too," her mother advised her.

"He's no bother to me. He takes a shower and sleeps while I'm at work. By the time I get off and make it home, he's gone again. At most, we see each other in passing," she explained.

"How does he know your schedule? It changes so much, and you take so many last-minute shifts. How could he possibly know when you'll be home?" her mother questioned. Her question sparked a curiosity in Serita, who wanted an answer as well.

"Listen to me," she warned Serita as she handed over her sleeping two-year-old son. "You're settling for having somebody in your house. Just having some man around is not enough if he does nothing to contribute to the household or to you as a person. You can't allow yourself to become so desperate to have someone around that you're willing to lay all your standards down by the riverside. Now, I know we've never had much, but that doesn't mean you can't aim higher and strive for more. This man is doing nothing but bringing you down, and just because he's not active about it right now doesn't mean he won't jump back into full gear. These types of guys have a knack for doing just that at the most inconvenient moment. You hear me good when I tell you to get rid of him, baby. Let him go before he does more damage than he's already done."

"I hear you, Momma. I'm tired, though. I need to get home so I can get some sleep."

"Get you some rest, baby. You've been working so hard lately. Don't let me hold you up."

Her mother's words went in one ear and out the other. Serita was so busy working she wasn't paying any attention to Bryan, who was sure to stay out her way as much as possible.

Serita took Friday off to take her two oldest children to the dentist. While they were getting set up in the back, Serita went to the front counter to handle their co-pays.

"They both have thirty-five-dollar co-pays," the receptionist informed her.

"Can you run it as one transaction?" she inquired.

"Yes, ma'am. We sure can," the receptionist smiled sweetly and agreed as Serita handed over her debit card. Her smile faded when she returned with the card in hand and informed Serita, "Ma'am, your card has been declined."

"That's impossible." Serita frowned. "Run it again."

"I tried to run it three times," she stated.

"What? There's money on there. I got paid today." She shook her head in confusion.

"I'm sorry, ma'am. We can't run it again, but we can take cash."

"I don't have seventy dollars on me, though. It's on my card. I don't understand why it isn't going through. Can you bill me for it? That way, they can get their work done, and I can pay it when I figure out what's going on."

"I'll have to get approval from Dr. Moore," she stated before she stepped away. When she returned, she explained they usually only billed amounts over one hundred dollars, but Dr. Moore made a one time exception for her. Serita thanked them profusely and stepped into the back with her oldest son, who was fifteen.

"Mom, what's wrong?" he inquired, seeing her upset and confused expression.

"Nothing, baby," she denied.

"The lady came in here and said something to Dr. Moore about the payment. Is everything okay? Didn't you get paid today?"

"Yeah, but I'll figure it out." She smiled weakly at him. "I don't know what's going on, but my card has been in my purse, and nobody has been at the house but us. There's nothing that could've happened with the card."

"Bryan was there for a few minutes last night."

"Bryan?"

"Yeah, he came by while you were asleep. I got up to use the bathroom, he asked where you were, and when I told him you were asleep in your room, he said he was going to peek in to check on you and head back out," he explained.

"Oh my God," she gasped and immediately called the number on the back of the card. The automated system informed her Bryan withdrew all of her paycheck and also over-drafted another four hundred-eighty dollars. With the overdraft fee, Serita's account was in the negative over five hundred dollars. She was livid.

My rent, she thought. *My light bill. My kids. This motherfucker!* She listened to the list of transactions from Bryan using ATMs all over the city to withdraw four to six hundred dollars at a time until he was unable to withdraw anything else.

When they were finished at the dentist, Serita dropped the kids off at school and immediately drove to Kevin's house, where she knew Bryan would be.

"You just missed him. He left here about half an hour ago. I thought he was going to your house," Kevin informed her.

"Did he spend any money over here?" she queried.

"He shot around some, but he won about eight hunnid off Big Pooh before he left," he mentioned. She thanked him before snatching off headed to her house to catch Bryan. She pulled up in time to whip her Toyota Camry into the driveway behind his car and block him in.

"Move your car, Serita," he demanded from his driver's seat.

"I ain't moving shit! Get out the car!"

"Serita, I ain't got time for your bullshit. Move your fucking car!"

"No! I said get the fuck out the car now!" she ordered.

"If you don't move your fucking car, I'm going to move that bitch for you!" he threatened.

Serita grabbed a brick from the corner of the flowerbed and held it in the air.

"What? You're going to hit my car with this raggedy-ass Maxima? If you want your windshield, you'd better get your bitch ass out the car right motherfucking now!"

Bryan cut the car off and threw the door open.

"Who you calling a bitch? You gone bust my windshield? Huh?

Bring your ass in the house," he growled and snatched her by the arm with a grip so tight she couldn't pull away. He unlocked the door and forced Serita into the house before slamming the door behind them.

"Where the fuck is my money, Bryan?" she seethed.

"Who the fuck do you think you're talking to? You need to lower—"

"Fuck all that!" she cut him off. "Where the fuck is my money?"

"You need to chill out. It's all—"

"Don't you tell me to fucking chill when you snuck your ass in my purse and stole my whole paycheck off my bank card before I even had a chance to spend a single penny of the money I worked hard for. Don't you tell me to chill. Don't say shit to me at all. Give me my fucking money!"

Bryan stepped toward her but quickly retreated when Serita held up a can of mace, with her finger poised to let it rip.

"Here," Bryan growled as he pulled money from his pockets. Serita snatched it, counting it as he pulled it out. "That's it. That's all I have left of it," he stated after he had given her twenty-eight hundred dollars.

"What's that?" she questioned, pointing at something sticking out his jacket pocket.

"These?" he replied, pulling the paper out. "Lottery tickets. Scratch offs."

"You bought those with my money?"

"Well, yeah, but—"

"Then they're mine. Give them to me," she demanded as she snatched them out his hand before he could respond. "Where's the rest of it? Where's my money?" she pressed after counting thirty dollars in scratch off tickets.

"I spent it."

"Where? On what?"

"Different shit," was his only answer.

Serita folded the bills in her hand and shoved them in the back of her underwear, allowing Bryan to think the money was in her back pocket. She patted Bryan down vigorously, searching for more money.

"What is this?" she quizzed, as she pulled a wad of money from the pocket of the gym shorts beneath his jeans.

"That's mine!"

"Yours?"

"Yeah. I won that. That's mine!"

"No, no, no, no." She shook her head. "You used my money to win it, so this here belongs to me." She counted out eight hundred seventy dollars. "You did pretty good, too. Damn!" she bragged and folded the money.

"Hey! I only owed you six or seven hundred more. The rest is mine," he argued.

"Oh, no, sweetheart! It would've been yours until you stole my money and put me through all this shit to get it back. After everything you've taken from me, I think this little extra hundred dollars should be the least of your worries."

"You're going to give me my money," he growled and tried to grab her with one hand and reach into her back pocket with the other, but he came up empty-handed with a face full of pepper spray. "Arghhhh!" he roared and stumbled around her living room, desperately rubbing at his eyes. Serita quickly unlocked and opened the door and shoved Bryan blindly outside, sending him tumbling down the steps of the porch. She closed and locked the door as he hit his head on the concrete, adding to his pain.

Serita remained locked inside with no intention to let Bryan back inside as he howled and beat on the door, attracting the neighbors' attention. One of the elderly neighbors called the police, who called for an ambulance when they arrived.

Serita spoke with the police and moved her car from behind Bryan's while he was in the back of the ambulance, and once she was locked inside the house again, the officers made Bryan leave after warning him not to return.

Serita didn't leave the house until it was time for her to pick her two younger kids up from school. She paid the two months' rent she owed, her light bill, and the balance at the dentist's office before returning home with her babies and cooking them all a dinner of steak, baked potatoes, and broccoli and cheese.

BRYAN SPENT a month gradually getting back into Serita's good graces. Apologetic texts led to brief phone conversations, which led to longer conversations. After three weeks, Serita finally agreed to meet him in a public place. Another week passed, and they were cordial again. After a month and a half, Serita gave in and let him move back in.

Her mother warned her she was setting herself up for destruction. Her best friend advised her she was making a huge mistake. Despite all their warnings, Bryan knew the one cure for all ailments with women, and he had her dickmatized by the end of their first night of make-up sex.

Though he was back in the house, Bryan treaded lightly. He knew he was already on thin ice with Serita, and he didn't want to get caught up in anything that could jeopardize the one stable home he had again. He dealt with all his side chicks at a distance to keep them off Serita's radar and tried to be at home as little as possible until around Serita's usual bedtime, returning in time to shower, climb into bed, and give Serita her daily dose.

For two months, every time Serita questioned him about his whereabouts, he diverted the conversation. When she complained about him staying out late, he came home early the next two nights. While she spent most of the day at work, Bryan was out selling crack, smoking weed, and fucking bitches. While Serita believed he learned his lesson, he was getting her back comfortable and complacent to give him room to do what he wanted.

"Where you been?" came Serita's voice in the still darkness of the living room one night as Bryan snuck in late.

"I lost track of time hanging with the boys," he instinctively lied.

"You can head right back where you came from," she instructed from her recliner.

"What?"

"You think you're slick," she reported, staring him square in the eyes in the blackness. "You think you can put up this front like you've changed and you're doing right? The whole time, that shit was suspicious as hell. You're a dog, Bryan. You can house-train a dog, but they still have the tendency to catch fleas."

"What the hell are you talking about?"

"Don't play dumb with me. We both know you've been fucking around all over town. I waited to see how long you would keep up this game. I've got pictures of you in damn near every neighborhood in the city, different bitches in your car, you in theirs, your hands on asses and up skirts. I've seen half the shit with my own eyes," she revealed with a chuckle.

"You've been stalking me?"

"Stalking you? Nah. I just followed and observed occasionally. It was quite entertaining. Here I was letting you think you had me fooled, and you fell for that shit just as hard as you thought I fell for your bullshit ass lies." She snickered. "You give a nigga a little pussy and he'll think he has you wrapped around his finger. You ain't noticed I haven't asked you for no dick in weeks?"

"Ain't nobody been lying to you, Serita," he assured her, trying to save himself.

"Please! Please! Save me the damn dramatics! You insist on

putting on a show even though you're clearly caught. I'm done being your audience. I'm not buying the tickets. Miss me with the whole theatrical production."

"You've been fucking following me?" Bryan ignored her and repeated as the situation sunk in.

"Yep. Sure have," she admitted. "I've seen the hoe you've been laying up with over on Seventh Street. I know all about the bitch you've been fucking in the Hillview Village Apartments. I even followed you, at a distance, of course, when you went to see that trick that lives in the Bella Vista, too. But my manager, Bryan? My damn supervisor?" she sneered in disgust as images of his indiscretions flashed through her mind.

"I don't know what you're talking about," he denied. "I ain't did shit with nobody's manager."

"Save the bullshit," she scoffed. "Please don't insult me with the same shit over and over. I may not be the prettiest, the classiest, or even the smartest fish in the pond, but I'm certainly not the dumbest, and I'm certainly not blind."

"Mane, gone on with all that bullshit, mane." He dismissed her. "Ain't nobody got time for all this extra-ass shit."

"I don't give a fuck what you do or don't have time for, B. That's what you're not understanding. I truly don't give a fuck. I wondered how you always knew what time I got off work. I've been working crazy hours, coming home at random times, and you always knew when I would be home. I set up some shit with a couple of coworkers. We swapped shifts, so I'd be off work at times the schedule showed I would be at work. Believe me, I'm a smarter bitch than you think. The FBI ain't got shit on a woman on a mission. I found you every single time. I followed you, took pictures, and let you do you while I sat back and observed. I let you dig yourself into a deep-ass hole you couldn't climb your way out of if you had Super Mario's pipe system."

Serita observed Bryan's reactions as she spoke, anticipating the conversation taking a violent turn. As Bryan's brow furrowed with his growing anger, Serita egged it on, encouraged, and welcomed it.

"Mane, look, I'm tired. I'm finna get in the shower and go to bed. I don't know what type of shit you on," Bryan blurted dismissively and headed toward the hallway.

"Aw naw. See, that's what you're missing." She stood up and stepped in his way.

"Move, Serita," he growled.

"I ain't moving shit. You finna get your ass the fuck up out my house. Now," she stated with an eerie calmness.

"Who the fuck do you think you're talking to? I don't know who you think you are," he barked while stepping into her personal space, "but you don't run shit. You got me fucked up. Get the fuck out the way."

"Oh no, I *do* run shit. I run *this* shit. This is *my* house. My name and no one else's is on the lease. All the bills are in my name and paid by me. *You're* the one who ain't running shit. Now, get the fuck out."

"Serita, get the fuck—"

"I said get *out*!" she bellowed.

"Bitch, who the fuck is you yelling at?" he boomed and grabbed her by the neck. "Get the fuck out the damn way."

"Let me go, Bryan," Serita choked out with tears forming in her eyes from the sudden decrease in air supply.

"Stop fucking playing with me, then! I told you to get your ass out the way, but you want to be hard-headed and shit."

SLAP!

"Stupid-ass bitch!" he spat as his open palm made contact. "Get the... fuck... out the... way!" he barked, slapping her as he spoke while holding her in the air by her throat.

Serita tumbled to the floor when he released his grip, holding her neck where his hand once was, swiping at the involuntary tears rolling down her cheeks, and gasping desperately for air. She collected herself as Bryan towered over her, barking and cursing, threatening to beat her even worse than before.

"Dumb-ass bitch! Your stupid ass don't learn, huh? Fucking spying on me like you're Secret Squirrel or some shit, making assumptions. A nigga out here tryna get this money, and you're in here talking about some bitches. That's all you're worried about is who I'm fucking. You need to get your broke ass up and go to work and stop sitting in here looking busted and disgusted. I should slap your ass to sleep for fucking playing with me."

As he continued ranting, Serita listened to him, silently calming herself and taking deep breaths to increase the oxygen in her blood. When she regained her strength, she jumped up, her right fist closed tight, and upper cut him, relishing in the sight of his head flying back and the shock on his face. When he reached out to grab her, she took off running to the side table next to the recliner and swiped her taser off the top of it.

EHHHHH! EEEHHHH! EEEEEEHHHHHH!

Chapter 16

BOOM BOOM BOOM BOOM BOOM!

"Who the fuck is it?" croaked Zaria's sleepy and agitated voice from inside her apartment.

"It's me!" Bryan announced as she cracked the wooden door open.

"What do you want?"

"I want to come in. I'm ready to move in." He smiled weakly.

"B, you can't be here. I told you I'm done with you," she reminded him as she pulled her black silk robe tighter around her nakedness.

"Come on, baby. I told you I'm ready. I've changed."

"Too little too late." Zaria sighed and shook her head.

"But, baby—"

"Baby, who is that at the door?" came a male's deep baritone from behind her.

"It's nobody, baby. Go back to bed. I got it," she called over her shoulder.

"Yo! You got another nigga up in there?" Bryan boomed furiously.

"Not just another nigga. *My* nigga. Who are you to question me about who I have in my house, anyway?"

"This how you do me?"

"Nigga, who are you supposed to be? You're the nigga outside the door trying to get in, remember? What have you ever done for me? Not a damn thang! So do me this one favor, Bryan. Lose my number, forget my address, and keep it pushing," she growled before rolling her eyes and slamming the door in his face.

"Look who decided to reappear! Nigga, I'mma start calling you Casper, as much as you like to disappear and shit!" Kevin cackled at his own joke. Bryan took a seat on the opposite end of the couch inside Kevin's house and silently stared at the football game showing on the flatscreen mounted on the living room wall.

"What's up, my nigga? How you been, man?"

"Man, cuz, not too good, honestly." Bryan dropped his head.

"Damn, mane. What the fuck is up? Who I need to pull down on? You know I'm always ready for that action."

"Mane, a nigga fucked up out here in these streets. I mean, I still got some work, but Moms been shorting a nigga for a while now, making it hard for a nigga to even break even, let alone see a profit. I don't know how long I can stretch the little bit of money I have. I'mma have to hit a lick or something. I need a come up."

"What happened to Serita? I thought you was breaking shorty's pockets? She ain't giving you enough to re-up?" Kevin inquired.

"Man, me and shorty ain't rocking no more," he revealed.

"Damn, mane. What the fuck?"

"Mane, she was following me and shit, and I ain't know. I thought her ass was at work. I was fucking the store manager, so I thought I had her schedule. Shit, Serita got hip to that shit and swapped shifts with her coworkers and followed me while I kicked it with the other hoes. I came home a little late one night, and shawty was sitting in the dark in the living room waiting for me. We got to arguing and tussling, and the next thing I knew, I was rolling around on the floor being fried to death by a damn taser. I was lucky to get out that motherfucker alive."

"Daaammmnnn!" Kevin jeered and burst into laughter. "Serita tased you? That shit is crazy as hell!"

"Shit ain't funny, yo!"

"I mean, it is, but it ain't. When was this shit?"

"About a week ago."

"Damn. Where you been staying? Over at Zaria's?"

"Nah, man. I went over to Zaria's when I left Serita's. The bitch wouldn't even open the door for a nigga because she had some other nigga laid up in there talking about 'Baby, who that is at the do'?'" Bryan explained while deepening his voice to imitate the unseen man in Zaria's apartment.

Sitting on his cousin's couch, he felt the same as the day he showed up at Kevin's parents' house twenty years before and told them he hadn't eaten or been to school in five days because his mother had left the house with a strange man, forbid him from opening the door or leaving the house, and had yet to return. Kevin had the same sympathetic look on his face as the day Bryan's mother came to her brother's house in search of her son and snatched him out the front door to return home for the beating he knew awaited him for disobeying her instructions. Bryan and Kevin had been close since that week Bryan spent sharing Kevin's bed and his clothes. Over the years, times got hard as his mother's drug addiction spiraled out of control, but Bryan always knew he could count on his Uncle Marlowe, Aunt Georgia, and Cousin Kevin whenever he needed help. That knowledge was what landed Bryan on Kevin's couch, telling him the truth about what was going on in his life after every woman in his life moved on without him.

"Damn, mane! You done lost all your hoes! Man, you're seriously having some bad-ass luck around this bitch! This shit is crazy as hell!"

"Yeah, mane. I don't know what the fuck I'm going to do."

"If you ain't been at Zaria's, where the fuck you been?"

Bryan considered his relationship with Kevin for a minute, contemplating whether he should be honest with him before answering. As the memory of Kevin's compassion during some of the most embarrassing moments in Bryan's life played in Bryan's head, Bryan responded, "I've been sleeping in my car."

"Nigga, in your car?" Kevin repeated in surprise.

"Yeah, mane. I've just been parking in a parking lot or on a quiet side street to get a couple hours of sleep, hoping don't nobody fuck with me or call the police."

"Damn, man! Talking about a fall from grace! God damn!"

"Yeah, mane. I'm almost out of money and ain't got nowhere to stay. Ain't none of my hoes fucking with me. Most of them were already sick of my shit, anyway," he explained. "I'm fucked up out here, for real."

"Damn, mane. I see. What you gone do? What's your next move?"

"Shit, man, I was kinda hoping you'd let a nigga stay here, bum your couch for a while until I can get back on my feet."

"Here?" Kevin frowned.

"Yeah, here with you."

"Nah, man. You can't stay here." Kevin shook his head.

"Damn, cuz. Why not?"

"I got my gal staying here. Shawty already been on my ass about all the niggas hanging out on the porch all day. I know damned well she ain't having that shit. She like to prance around naked and shit. Hell naw, cuz."

"Damn, my nigga. I wasn't gone make a pass at yo' gal or nothing, nigga. I wasn't gone be here long. She can put some clothes on for a month or two. Shit."

"A month or two?" Kevin scoffed with an amused frown. "Mane,

106

she ain't gone let your ass stay a *day* or two, let alone a couple months. Nah, mane. You got to come up with something else 'cause this ain't it over here."

"Damn, cuz! You just gone leave me out on the streets like this? That's fucked up!"

"Aye, mane! I got a whole-ass woman in this motherfucker, mane! You ain't finna bring yo' fucked up ass over here fucking up what I got going on. We both know you got a fucked-up-ass record with bitches. I don't want to have to kill you, cuz. I love you too much for that, my nigga."

"Whatever, man. It just is what it is. Fuck it."

"Look, I can throw you a couple dollars to get a room for a night or two, but you can't stay with me, cuz. That's out the damn question," Kevin offered.

"I appreciate what you can do, cuz. Something is always better than nothing," Bryan thanked him as he accepted the one-hundred-dollar bill Kevin slid him.

"That's definitely true," Kevin agreed as Bryan stood up to leave. "You make sure you come by here if you need anything else. I'll try to do what I can to help you out."

"Thank you, cuz. I'll get up with you later, man," Bryan assured him as he exited the house with his pride under his shoe and disappointed his cousin wouldn't take him in but appreciative of the help he offered.

Two nights at a little hole-in-the-wall motel on Lamar Avenue for thirty dollars a night was all Bryan could afford after he bought gas and food with the money Kevin gave him. Because he slept in his car every night after Serita kicked him out, Bryan was satisfied just being able to shower and sleep in a bed, even if it wasn't the cleanest or most comfortable. When he checked out after the second night, he knew he would have to make a move if he didn't want to return to the discomfort of his car that night.

With a full tank of gas, Bryan drove across town to East Memphis and pulled into an apartment complex on Winchester just off Lamar Avenue. Driving slowly through the complex, Bryan searched for a lit porch light in the daytime, indicating a unit that was possibly empty. The window blinds were closed on all the units he pinpointed.

After driving further east down Winchester to another complex, he did the same thing, still to no avail. He followed the same routine at two more complexes before he arrived at a group of complexes near a police station. Nervous about the precinct in the vicinity, he almost didn't even try, but Bryan was desperate, and as they say, desperate times call for desperate measures.

Bryan pulled into the second complex and drove slowly to the rear, eying the buildings and mentally noting the cars parked in front of them. As he drove along the back gate, he spotted two apartments at adjacent buildings with the porch lights on. When he drove past, he could see both units were empty through the open blinds. He then drove past the front side of the units and circled back around.

There were only four cars parked in front of the two buildings, one of which had two flat tires and obviously hadn't been moved in some time. He parked at the first building, leaving two spaces between his car and the next, and waited five minutes before getting out.

With his head on a swivel, Bryan twisted the doorknob and was immediately relieved to find it unlocked. He quickly darted inside, closed the door, and locked it behind himself before turning off the porch light. He closed the blinds in both bedrooms but was certain to leave the blinds open in the living room so he wouldn't arouse the suspicions of anyone who knew the unit was supposed to be vacant. Heaving a sigh of relief, Bryan resolved, "This is it. Home until I can find another home."

As quickly and quietly as he came, he snuck away, not wanting to be caught inside the vacant apartment in the daytime in case the property manager was planning to show the apartment to a potential tenant. At a nearby mall, he meandered around aimlessly before visiting a neighborhood park and posting up on a bench to watch the children play, only to find himself reminded of Serita's kids.

Serita. That bitch fucking tased me. She actually tased me, he thought. *I should probably be glad she didn't actually shoot me. She ain't no killer. Still. I can't ever go back there. Good thing she didn't change the locks immediately. I was at least able to sneak in while she was at work and get my shit. It ain't much, but it's mine. Oh well. I'll be okay*, he assured himself, and rose to make his rounds to sell his wares.

Bryan sold everything in his sack, plastic and all, before nightfall. He stopped at a Wendy's for a 4 for $4 and ate in the parking lot while he tried to figure out his next move.

"Hey! Hey!" came a voice and several knocks on his window after he unintentionally dozed off while turning his thoughts over. "You can't sit here. We're getting ready to close. My manager said you gotta go,'" a chocolate-skinned woman informed him.

"That's my bad. I didn't mean to scare y'all. I dozed off while I was eating. I'm finna go," he apologized.

"It's okay. There are always some suspicious-looking cars out here around closing time. The police usually run them off, but apparently, the city's busy tonight because I haven't seen the usual officers all day," she informed him.

"I'll wait until you're locked inside, safe and sound before I pull off."

"Okay. Thank you." The young woman beamed at him, turned, and whisked back into the building.

Bryan grinned and nodded at her as he pulled out of the parking lot, headed to his new temporary home.

Chapter 17

FOLLOWING HIS SAME ROUTINE, Bryan circled the building before parking by the dumpster at the back of the complex. He grabbed the backpack he filled with toiletries and a small bag of dirty clothing and casually entered the vacant apartment as if he was leasing it. He immediately closed the living room blinds and exhaled deeply. *Safe for one more night.*

Thankful he located a vacant unit at a complex that kept the utilities on when tenants moved out, Bryan stripped out the clothes he had been wearing for over a week, dumped them along with the dirty clothes from his bag in the unit's washer, and dropped in a Tide pod. While his clothes washed, he soaked in a hot bath and thought about his life.

All the women he met. All the women he fucked over. All the wrong he did. For the first time, he realized Zaria was right. He didn't control anything in his life. His entire existence completely depended upon a woman taking care of him, and now he was alone without a single female companion, and he had nothing.

With a towel wrapped around his waist, Bryan turned up the heat on the thermostat to protect him from the mid-November chill, tossed his clothes in the dryer, and turned off the dryer's alarm. He lay naked on the bare carpet on the master bedroom floor with his arm thrown lazily over his eyes.

The first night a man is reduced to sleeping naked on the floor of an empty apartment with nowhere to go, no hopes, no direction, and a future full of the unknown is a cold, lonely night. Bryan felt as if he betrayed himself. Everything he did led him to that moment. He resolved he deserved that moment of embarrassment and humility, and he finally accepted it as he lay in a fetal position, shivering, crying, and all alone.

"I may be down, but I ain't out," he avowed to the bare white walls. "I may be down, but I ain't out. I may be down..." He repeated to himself until he finally slipped into a light slumber.

"Where ya been at, boy-boy? I ain't seent ya in a minute!" the elderly man with salt and pepper hair and an accent unmistakably from Mississippi called out three days later as he held the front door of his house open for his only nephew.

"Aw, you know me, Unc. I've been around." Bryan smiled as entered the only house he had ever known his mother's only brother to reside in.

"How you been? Let me look at 'cha!" Bryan's Uncle Marlowe smiled as they embraced and then held him at arm's length to examine him. "Boy, it shole is good tuh see ya! I ain't seent ya since ya nuts dropped!"

"Aw, Unc. C'mon nah!" He chuckled at his uncle's joke. "What's going on down the street? They protesting or something?"

"Mrs. Ida's grandson got himself killed. The guy working the register at that lil' ole raggedy store shot at him a few nights ago when he ran out the door without paying for a couple beers."

"Beer? He's like sixteen or seventeen, ain't he?"

"Yep, seventeen. Anyway, one o' the bullets hit one o' his arteries in his leg. He ran down the side o' Corrine's house down yonder, probably 'tending tuh jump the fence tuh his grandmomma's backyard, but he fell an' bled out on the side o' Corrine's house."

"Oh, wow!"

"Yeah, Corrine said she didn't e'en know he was out there. She just happened tuh be comin' home from the sto', seent the blood stains up the side o' the house and thought maybe a raccoon or a dog had done got hurt over there. She got out the car and went 'round the side o' the house tuh check it out, and damnnear had a heart attack when she seent Ida's grandson laid out back there, dead as a doorknob. He had done been back there a whole day."

"That's why they're down there? Is it Black Lives Matter?"

"Yeah, it's them an' a whole bunch o' other folks. They're marchin' 'cause they want that cashier arrested. The sto' owner won't tell where the guy at, but the police already been telling everybody they lookin' fo' the guy an' 'tend tuh arrest him fo' murder."

"I hope they catch him. That don't make no sense. Shooting at a kid over some beer. He didn't have to lose his life like that. He was probably tryna impress his lil' girlfriend or look hard in front of his homies." Bryan sighed and shook his head.

"No sense in Monday mo'ning quarterbackin' now. It's too late. He's gone nah an' Ida gotta figure out how she gone bury him 'cause his momma on that shit an' ain't nowhere tuh be found. Ida done had custody o' him an' his lil sisters fo' going on ten years now. Anyway, what brings ya by? Ya don't usually be round these parts."

"Nothing. I was around the way and thought I'd stop by to check on you. It's been a minute."

"It's nice tuh know an ole man is loved." Marlowe grinned as he tugged on the front of his motor oil-spotted coveralls and took a seat in his living room recliner while Bryan plopped down on the couch. "Ya almost missed me. I was getting ready tuh run o'er tuh Eugene's an' pick me up a lil' something."

"Aw, Unc, you don't need that shit, man," Bryan groaned as he frowned at the thought of his uncle still drinking corn whiskey.

"Boy, who ya talkin' tuh? Ya better watch yo mouf up in my house! You ain't got too ole fo' me tuh tan your hide, nah! Just done got too big fo' ya britches!"

"My bad, Unc. You're right. That's my bad. I just hate for you to be drinking that stuff, man. It ain't good for you."

"The news say a glass or two o' wine a day is beneficial fo' ya heart, ya memory, and ya skin, and it'll help keep ya cholesterol down an' ya sugar in check. I drink tuh my health!" Marlowe cracked up.

"That's red wine, Unc! You're drinking White Lightning! That ain't near-bout the same thing!" Bryan chortled.

"It's all the same!"

"Naw, it ain't, Unc!" Bryan crowed, unable to control his laughter.

"It's the same tuh me. We all have tuh pick our poison. This one is mine. It ain't no worse than that glass dick yo momma been puffing on. How is she, anyway?" Marlowe's tone turned solemn.

"The same I guess you can say," Bryan mumbled. "Just slowly wasting away."

"We're all lookin' fo' love in the bottom of a glass. Hers is jess a different glass. That's all."

"Yeah. I guess."

"What ya hanging yo' head fo'? I been hearin' about ya."

"About me?" Bryan feigned confusion. "What about me?"

"Word on the street is you're who she's getting' that shit from, anyway. 'Stead o' tryna help her get clean, ya out here selling the shit tuh her."

"Aw, Unc, man—"

"Don't you 'aw, Unc' me, boy. It's one thing fo' ya tuh be out here in these streets throwing yo' life away, but that there is yo' momma, boy. Ya only get one o' those, an' once she's gone, it ain't no coming back. Don't ya help her throw her life away, too."

"I just be trying to make sure she's safe, Unc. These folks are out here mixing all kinds of stuff with the drugs, stuff that can kill her. I take her hit to her so she won't be out here buying off the wrong person and it end up being her last hit," Bryan tried to explain.

"Listen to yo'self. Do ya hear yo'self? Ya out here poisoning yo' own momma, helping her die a slow death an' tryna justify it by saying ya just don't want someone else tuh kill her quicker. Ya can't explain away yo' wrongdoin', nephew. When ya get tuh the front o' that line at the gate, St. Peter ain't gone have time fo' yo' excuses. The line longer than the one outside the club, an' everybody tryna get in. Everybody ain't got an address on that street made o' gold. Ya need tuh be tryna get right wit' the Lord an' get into the housing market befo' all the real estate is bought up."

"Is that what you're going over to Eugene's for, Unc? To buy your next piece of real estate?" Bryan questioned sarcastically.

"Naw, I'm goin' tuh buy myself a belt tuh beat yo' ass wit' since ya think ya grown an' got so much damn mouf!" Marlowe wasn't laughing anymore. "You busy tryna charge me fo' yo' sins, but ya got tuh pay yo' own bill. I got my own indiscretions tuh account fo'."

"I hear you, Unc. I feel you."

"Ya stopped by tuh pay me a visit, an' I ain't mean tuh get tuh preachin' at ya, but I tells the truth up in my house. Somebody got tuh wake ya up an' get ya in line. Ya momma ain't in her right mind tuh do it."

"I get it, Unc. I wouldn't expect nothing less from you. I can respect that."

"Ya just make sure ya take heed tuh what I'm saying tuh ya."

"Yes, sir. I am," Bryan assured him with a nod. "How you been holding up?"

"Well," Marlowe began with a deep sigh, "as best as can be expected, I guess."

"I've been meaning to get over here and see 'bout you for a while. I know it's been hard on you since Aunt Georgia been gone."

"Ole Georgia." Marlowe sighed with a smirk and shook his head at the thought of his deceased wife. "That woman was the sweetest thang that ever happened 'cross my plate. My ole Georgia Peach. I do miss her somethin' terrible, especially her cookin'."

"Yeah," Bryan agreed. "I miss coming over here on holidays for a plate. Her baked macaroni with the long noodles... collard greens with the ham hocks in them... sweet potato pie... man, I miss those days."

"I miss 'em, too, but that's what I mean about ya momma, too. One day, ya gone look up an' be missing her, too."

"Yeah, but Momma can't cook, though," Bryan joked.

"Can't cook? Who can't cook?"

"Unc, c'mon, man! You know Momma can't even boil water."

"Can't boil water? Boy, who ya think cooked dinner while Daddy was gone working at the gin an' momma was busy making dresses? Boy, yo' momma done cooked full holiday meals an' Sunday dinners with no help in the kitchen, an' she don't need no measuring spoons tuh do it!"

"For real?" Bryan was shocked. "She almost set the house on fire trying to boil hot dogs when I was a kid. We always ate fast food or over somebody else's house. I thought she couldn't cook."

"That's because she on that shit! Boy, yo' momma can cook anything grown in a field or raised on a farm! Her damn sweet potato pie will put a Patty pie tuh shame!"

"I never knew that. I had no clue."

"Enough about Marva," he said, calling Bryan's mother by her first name. "She's depressing. Ya seent that no-count son o' mine?" he queried, referring to Kevin.

"'No-count'?" Bryan raised an eyebrow at his uncle.

"I done heard 'bout him, too. Out here slangin' dope an' shackin' up with some lil' fast-tail girl, gamblin' an' carryin' on. Both o' y'all throwin' rocks at the penitentiary," Marlowe fussed.

"I don't know about none of that, but I saw him about a week ago," Bryan deflected.

"Umm-hmm. I'm finna use this bathroom 'fo I head over tuh Eugene's." He groaned while struggling to stand and then shuffled to the bathroom. His fingers hadn't come off the lock on the door before Bryan was on his feet, tip-toeing as quickly as possible into his uncle's bedroom.

Having spent so much time at Marlowe's house as a child, Bryan knew Marlowe always kept a small envelope of cash hidden in a mate-less sock in his dresser. He discovered the stash while curiously rambling through his uncle's belongings as a child. Because he was an old-fashioned creature of habit, Bryan was sure Marlowe hadn't moved his *just in case* money.

Hurriedly snatching the drawer open, Bryan dug beneath the two dozen pairs of mated socks to the far-left corner of the drawer and felt around until his fingers bumped into a sock with a wad of cash inside. The toilet flushed in the bathroom, and Bryan quickly pocketed the money, closed the drawer, and slithered back to his spot on the living room couch, the noise of his movements masked by the water running in the bathroom while Marlowe washed his hands.

"You good, Unc?" he inquired when Marlowe returned to the living room.

"Yeah, yeah. 'Bout tuh head on out. It sure was good seein' ya, nephew."

"You too, Unc. I'll swing by and check on you more often," Bryan promised as he rose from the couch and hugged his uncle.

"Yeah, yeah." Marlowe dismissed him doubtfully. "Ya youngin's ain't got no time fo' an ole man like me. I'll believe that shit when I see it."

Chapter 18

"YOU EAT a whole lot of 4 for $4's for somebody who drives a nice car. You know it's other stuff on the menu, right?"

"I ain't paid no attention to it. I stick with what I know."

"We got baked potatoes and full-sized burgers, too. You like salads? We got some fye-ass salads."

Bryan changed bando's weekly for three weeks, but almost every single day, he found himself back at the Wendy's, checking for the little, brown-skinned cutie with the almond-shaped eyes named Raelyn who tapped on his window.

They became friends after that first night. Raelyn was receptive to his flirting, but when she flirted back, he knew he had her. He usually stopped by to see if she was working that day, but after they hung out after her shift one night, Raelyn slid Bryan her number and gave him her schedule for the week. Now, there they were, a week later, parked in a corner of Zodiac Park after dark, passing a blunt back and forth inside his Maxima.

Bryan sized Raelyn up out the corners of his eyes, puzzled by his attraction to her. True, she was gorgeous, but he had dismissed plenty of beautiful women. She had a normal job, nothing special.

Though Bryan couldn't put his finger on what it was about her that captivated him so strongly, he couldn't stay away from her.

"Bryan? Bryan? Helloooo..." she called as she waved a hand in front of his face.

"Huh?"

"You zoned out? I asked you where you stay. What part of town?" she giggled.

"I... umm... I'm between places right now," he admitted with a nervous chuckle. "I'm staying here and there, you know, with my nigga 'nem and a couple of my cousins."

"Damn, my bad. I didn't know. I shouldn't be so nosy," she apologized, assuming he was embarrassed.

"Naw, you good. I ain't gone be down long," he assured her. "Hustling is in my blood."

"Oh, okay." She smirked. "Do you feel like taking me home? My cousin is doing some work on my car, so he has it until tomorrow evening."

"Yeah. Where you stay?" he inquired while turning the key in the ignition.

When they pulled into Raelyn's driveway, Bryan was both impressed and confused about how she could afford such a nice house in a quaint little neighborhood on minimum wage.

"You want to come in?" She smiled as she opened the passenger door.

"Are you sure this is your house?" he questioned with a raised brow as he exited the car. Raelyn hopped out on her side and led the way to the door.

"Yeah, it's all mine. It used to be my parents', but they moved to Texas when they retired and let me keep the house. I pay all the bills, come and go as I please, handle all the maintenance. It's mine," she explained as she beamed widely over her shoulder as Bryan followed her up the driveway.

"Damn, man! That's love! You're blessed as hell," he complimented as he waited patiently behind her while she unlocked the front door.

"Make yourself at home in the living room," Raelyn offered as she flipped on several light switches and disappeared down the hallway. "I'll be right out."

This is nice, he thought as he slid onto the buttery leather of her sofa. *Her shit is decked out.* Bryan made mental notes of the large TV, glass tables, leather sectional, candles, and family photos everywhere. There was a grandfather clock and all kinds of décor. Raelyn's house was a complete home.

"Do you want something to drink?" Raelyn extended as she stood in the doorway wearing a pair of track shorts and a tank top.

"Naw, I'm good. C'mere, girl," Bryan requested as he patted the spot next to him on the sofa.

"What's up?" She giggled as she plopped down next to him.

"A nigga feeling the shit outta you, girl," he wooed as he licked his lips and pushed her bangs out of her eyes. "No cap. You got a nigga's nose wide open."

"I know. I am feel-able." She shrugged innocently and giggled again.

"What's up wit' you? You got a nigga?"

"Naw, I'm single and free to mingle, but even if I did, I don't see nobody here but you and me, so he must not be that important. I wouldn't be worried about the next nigga if I were you. They shole ain't gone be worried about you."

"You right, you right," he agreed with a nod.

"You wanna Netflix and chill or just chill?" she queried.

"Oh, is just chilling an option?"

"If you're up for it. I'm tryna see what that mouf do." Raelyn smirked slyly.

"Naw, Shawty. I don't eat no pussy," Bryan lied after a brief pause, caused by the initial shock of Raelyn's bluntness.

"Aw, well, ain't no sticking without the licking, baby."

"Oh, for real? That's how you get down?"

"That's exactly how I get down," she confirmed matter-of-factly.

"Damn," Bryan mumbled. Hoping she would change her mind, Bryan waited in silence until it became clear she was unwavering. Giving himself a mental pep talk first, he moved in closer to Raelyn. "I got you, shawty," he whispered, but sensed a hesitancy to allow him to kiss her.

"I don't kiss no lips that ain't got my pussy juice smeared across them, sweetheart."

"Damn, a nigga can't even get no kiss? I'm tryna set the mood and shit."

"I don't need no mood set. This pussy wakes right up when you kiss her," she stated. "Look, this ain't my first rodeo, and you ain't the first bull I've lassoed. I know how you niggas work and you ain't gone get me. You're going to eat this pussy and how good your mouth work is will determine if you get your dick wet. That's how this shit works. If you don't like it, I'll see you to the door. Believe me, I ain't hurting for no head or no tail. You got to pay to play around here, and those are the house rules."

"Chill out, Shawty. I said I got you."

"I'm just letting you know ahead of time, so don't get back here in this bedroom acting brand new because I already warned you," Raelyn cautioned him as she rose from the sofa and glanced at him over her shoulder. "C'mon," she ordered with a nod toward the hallway.

Ten minutes later, while still in disbelief Raelyn had even allowed him inside her house after revealing to her he was homeless, Bryan found himself in her bed, completely naked, dick hard as his heart with his face between her open thighs, her manicured fingertips toying in his high top fade, pushing his face deeper and urging his tongue into her center.

Eager to dip into her wetness, Bryan knew he would have to lick her into submission if he expected to get what he craved. Glancing up into her face, he witnessed the pleasure she experienced in her eyes as her impassioned moans turned him on even more. His slurps resounded throughout the bedroom, making a show of how much he enjoyed the taste of her sweet nectar.

He vibrated the tip of his tongue as it pressed against her clit. Raelyn gasped as she peered down at him and called out involuntarily in heightened ecstasy.

"Oh! Oh shit! Oh my God! Fuck!" she screamed. "Yes! Oh, God! Yes! Right there! Just like that! Don't stop! Fuck! Fuck!"

Bryan lifted her waist as he sat up on his knees, keeping his tongue between her juicy lips and vibrating against her clit.

"Oh God, Bryan! Shit! Yes! Yes! Yes! Oh! Ahhhhhh!" she squealed. With her juices still dripping from Bryan's chin and her breathing still labored, she huffed, "Fuck me!"

"Fuck you? You want this dick, girl?" he teased.

"Yes! Fuck me!"

"Tell me you want this dick, then!" he demanded.

"Put it in! I want this dick! Gimme that big-ass dick, Bryan!" she ordered.

Bryan instantly shoved the entire length of his six-inch dick into her wetness as he held her waist level with his midriff. Raelyn cried out again and again as Bryan pulled his dick out to the tip of the head and rammed the entire rod back inside her, slamming against the bottom of her womb each time. Pounding her vigorously and repeatedly, he tried to knock the moans and screams out of her.

"Shit yeah! That's it, baby! Fuck this pussy!"

"You like this shit, baby?"

"Hell yeah!"

"This shit feels good, don't it?"

"Too good, baby! This shit feels so fucking good!"

"You want me to beat this pussy up?"

"Beat this pussy up, nigga! Beat it up!"

"Turn that ass over and toot it up," he instructed. Raelyn obeyed immediately, burying her face in a pillow in anticipation of him knocking it out the park with his Louisville Slugger.

"Oooohhhh fuuuuuuuuck!" She released deep, drawn out, throaty groans as Bryan re-entered her with the apparent intent to demolish her insides like a wrecking ball.

"You gone take this dick for me, baby?" he implored her as he plowed her with deep, strong thrusts.

"I'mma take it!"

"Tell daddy you gone take this dick then, baby," he pressed.

"I'mma take this dick, Daddy! I'mma take it!"

"Yeahhhh, that's what I'm talking about. Take this dick, baby. Take all of it."

"I'mma take all this dick, baby. All this big-ass dick! Give it to me!"

Bryan was sure the slapping of their skin could be heard all the way to the sidewalk outside as he pounded her relentlessly. Seeking better leverage, Bryan gripped Raelyn's ponytail and tugged her head back while continuing to drill her.

"Oh fuuuuuuuuck! Yeeeessss!" she crowed.

"Yeah, you like that shit. Don't you?"

"Yes, daddy. I love that shit. Fuck me, baby. You're tearing this pussy up," she urged him, and he reached back, slapped her right ass cheek, and watched it ripple like ocean waves.

"Oh fuck!"

"Un-huh! That's it. Take this dick wit' yo' bad ass," he urged and slapped her ass cheek a bit harder, causing a bit of a sting.

"Fuck, daddy! Yes! Pop that ass again!"

Bryan landed two quick slaps on the same cheek, the repeated slaps turning her skin red and causing an increased sting that made Raelyn flood even more. Bryan recognized the effect it had on her and knew exactly what to do next to push her over the edge. His left hand still wrapped firmly around her ponytail, he leaned forward and gripped her throat.

"You gone take this dick? Huh? You gone take it?" he growled in her ear as he continually delivered deep, hard pumps into her womb.

"Yes! Yes! I'mma take it!"

"Oohhhh, you're taking it!"

"I'm taking it, daddy! I'm taking this dick!"

"Go ahead and bust this nut on daddy's dick, baby."

"Oh, daddy! Oh, fuck!"

"That's it, baby. Bust this nut on this dick, girl!"

"Daddy! My spot! Oh! Oh shit!" she wailed.

"Right there?"

"Yes! Yes! Right there!"

"Right there?" he repeated, relishing in knowing he was pleasing her.

"Yes! Yes! Yes! Right there! Don't stop!" she shrieked.

"Nut on this dick!" Bryan demanded as he squeezed her throat harder and dug deeper into her spot.

"Fuck! Daddy! Yes! Yes! Yes!"

"Aaaahhhh!" they both croaked. Bryan released a load of baby batter as Raelyn's juices leaked all over his dick. Bryan rolled off Raelyn's back and collapsed on the bed next to her.

"Goddamn, girl! Shit!" he huffed and glanced over at her collecting herself as she lay beside him with her eyes closed, savoring the moment. "Girl, you got some good-ass pussy! You done worked a nigga the fuck out!"

"Shit, you ain't so bad yourself. I don't think I've ever been fucked like that. I can't believe you ain't got a girlfriend, the way you put it down," she complimented him, boosting his ego but knowing it wasn't the truth.

It was quick as a flash but made his heart drop as if he was rounding the summit of a rollercoaster, staring straight downward at certain death but for two seconds, Iyana crossed his mind, and the regret of losing her crept over him. As quickly as she came, Iyana was gone again, driven out by Raelyn's velvety touch on his stomach and her head snuggling comfortably against his chest.

Chapter 19

"**WHAT ARE YOU DOING HERE?** I told you not to bring your ass back over here," Zaria shouted at Bryan through her locked storm door. It had been three days since the first time Bryan entered Raelyn's house, and now he was at Zaria's door, attempting to retrieve the little clothing he left at her house.

"Mane, chill on all that rah-rah shit, Z. Aight? I came to pick up my clothes and shit. All that extra-ass shit ain't even necessary." Bryan replied.

"You need to go over on Winchester to the Goodwill and talk to them about your clothes because that's where I dropped that shit off," Zaria sassed with her hand on her hip and her lip turned up at Bryan.

"Mane, open this door and give me my shit. I ain't come over here to play with you."

"You seriously ain't got no fucking manners, do you? First, you pop up without calling. Then, you stand at my door yelling, disturbing my neighbors, and making demands. You do realize I don't owe you no favors, right? This is my house. I don't have to open the door for you."

Bryan examined Zaria. She wore long, curly weave, make-up, and lashes. Her brows were arched, and her dress was short, hugged her hips, and displayed her cleavage. He eyed her caramel thighs, recalling the last time they were thrown over his shoulders. The gold anklet resting gently on a decade-old butterfly tattoo accented the icy white of the Air Max's she had just pulled out the box. He never denied he still wanted her. He couldn't resist her, even on the few occasions he tried. When he locked eyes with Zaria, she recognized the lust that had found its way into his pupils.

"Look, bruh, I'm sorry," Bryan apologized quietly, with a softer demeanor. "Can I come in for a second to get my clothes and maybe talk?"

"What's the magic word?" Zaria teased.

"Please?" he charmed.

"C'mon."

She heaved as she unlocked the door against her better judgment and held it open for him, examining him as he slipped past her, hoping to find passion marks on his neck to use as ammunition to rush him back out the door. As he stepped inside, Bryan took notice to the fact Zaria's entire house had been rearranged. A sectional, recliner, and coffee table replaced the bed Iyana noted in the living room the night she stood at Zaria's door waiting to retrieve her car keys. The bed itself had been moved to its proper place in the bedroom. The stereo system had been moved onto an entertainment center, and there was even a decorative rug covering the stained carpet. *She changed niggas and changed her whole life around*, he thought with disdain. *That's alright. I'll show her ain't shit changed.*

"Are my clothes still in your bedroom?" he inquired as he pointed down her hallway.

"Naw, everything is in a box in the spare bedroom," she stated as she pointed down the hall in the opposite direction.

"Aw okay," he mumbled, the disappointment evident in his voice as he opened the door to the bedroom Zaria had been using for storage space.

"I seriously ain't in the mood for talking, so whatever you need to say, say it quick," Zaria advised with her arms folded across her chest when he returned to the living room carrying the cardboard box labeled with his name. Her attitude made it clear her patience was growing thin with him.

"Can we sit down?"

"I wasn't anticipating you being here long enough to get comfortable," she sassed, while tapping her foot impatiently.

"Damn! I can't even sit down for a second?" Bryan frowned.

"First of all, don't come up in my house raising your voice at me! I don't know if you done forgot, but this is *my* shit! In case you didn't pick up on it, that's why you're standing here with your shit in a box, asking for permission to do shit. Second, if I say you can't sit down, that's exactly what I mean. I don't know and don't care where the fuck you've been. You could have bed bugs and all kinds of other shit in your clothes, and you ain't about to let that shit loose in here. You're a dirty-ass dog, Bryan, and I ain't trying to catch your fleas."

"You know, you're sincerely trying my patience, Z," Bryan warned as he placed his box on a side table. "I'm coming to you as your man, and you're seriously getting the fuck out of line."

"*My man?*" She smirked with an amused chuckled. "Nigga, you ain't my damn man! You ain't been my man in years. When you were my man, you didn't appreciate me and didn't know what to do with it. I *been* moved on! *You* refuse to let the shit go! I peeped game a long time ago, B. You get these little girlfriends, and when they get tired of you slapping them around and put you out, you come over here trying to run game to ease your way back in. I'm done with your bullshit. Ain't shit you can do for me except leave me the fuck alone."

"Ain't shit I can do for you?" Bryan seethed through gritted teeth as he took one large step up to Zaria and wrapped his hand so tightly around her neck she immediately clawed at it. "Ain't shit I can do for you, Z? Huh?" he reiterated as his grip tightened.

"Le- le..." She tried to speak but was unable to get the words out.

"Let you go? That's what you want? I bet you do! Bitch, I'mma show you to stop fucking playing with me!"

Tears were streaming from Zaria's bulged eyes as she desperately scratched skin off Bryan's hand, fighting his vice-like grip. Relentless, unmoved by her tears, and in a furious haze, he craved the sight of her unconscious body.

Zaria's body exerted feeble efforts to cough, but to no avail. Her scratching weakened until her eyes rolled back in her head, and her body went limp. Bryan caught her and immediately turned her around, shoved her dress over her hips, and laid her over the arm of her own sofa. In one motion, he ripped off her thong.

"Ain't shit I can do for you? Ain't shit I can do for you? Huh?" he challenged as he unbuckled his pants and whipped out his hardened rod. Forcing her legs open, he shoved his entire six inches deep inside her.

Standing in the pool of urine Zaria's body had released when she lost consciousness, Bryan furiously drilled her, his thrusts creating ripples in her thighs that only made his dick harder. The groggy moan Zaria released as she regained consciousness was mistaken for a moan of pleasure, and Bryan pulled her head back by her ponytail and pumped even harder and faster.

"Ugh! Ugh!" Zaria croaked as she realized what was happening. "No! No! Get off me!" she pleaded.

"Ain't shit I can do for you, right? Is that what you said?" he taunted her. Releasing her hair, he wrapped both hands around her neck from behind and dug even deeper inside her. "Ain't shit I can do for you, but you moaning, and this pussy is talking to me. Your pussy is wet and swallowing this dick up, but ain't shit I can do for you."

"Bryan, stop! Please! Uugghh! Get off me!"

"Shut up, bitch! We both know you want this dick, so shut up and take it!"

"Ugh! No! No! Bryan, please! Stop! Let me go! Stop!" she begged even louder.

"Shut up before I choke your ass out again!" he threatened as he tightened both hands around her neck. "You gone take this dick today!"

"Ugh, ugh, ugh," she sobbed, tears streaming down her chubby, caramel cheeks. "Pleeeease! Stooooop!"

"I ain't stopping shit! You know this shit feels good to you! Nut on daddy's dick!"

"No! Bryan, get off me!"

"Nut on this dick, bitch!"

"No! Bryan, get off *me*!" Zaria screeched and kicked her foot up so hard and so high when it caught Bryan's balls he yelped like a wounded dog. Quickly turning around while Bryan was doubled over in pain, Zaria kicked him squarely in the chest, sending him tumbling onto the floor several feet away.

"Bitch, I'm gone kill you!" Bryan huffed.

"Get yo' ass up," Zaria coughed out, still catching her breath, "and get the fuck out my house."

"I ain't going no motherfucking where!" he gritted.

"Oh! Oh, you ain't gone..." Zaria scoffed, astonished at how brazen Bryan had become, injured gonads and all. After storming off down the hallway, she returned wielding a Louisville Slugger and a scowl that assured Bryan she was prepared to take his head off. "I said get yo' ass out my motherfucking house," she barked, "before I knock your noodles out your fucking head! *Get out* before I call the fucking police, bitch-ass nigga!" As she spoke, Bryan scrambled frantically to stand up, pull up his pants, and dash out her front door.

"You're a bitch, and you're a motherfucking bum! Don't you bring your weak ass around here ever again!" she bellowed and threw the box of Bryan's belongings out the door behind him. The cardboard burst when it plopped against the concrete sidewalk, sending clothes flying all over the lawn. "If I catch you anywhere near here again, the police will be the absolute least of your worries!"

The slam and lock of Zaria's doors echoed throughout the courtyard as Bryan collected his dirty shirts and underwear in the yard, his pants still wide open, while her neighbors observed in disgust.

Chapter 20

EIGHT HOURS after being tossed out of Zaria's apartment, Bryan was right back at Raelyn's house as if nothing happened.

"What is all this shit?" Raelyn gasped as she entered the living room to find Bryan bagging up crack rocks with a mound of cocaine sitting in the middle of her coffee table and marijuana crumbs littering the edge of the table, evidence of the two blunts he had just rolled. "I gave you a key so you could lie down while I was still at work, not so you could trap out my house!"

"Cool out, lil' momma! It's all good," Bryan nonchalantly continued portioning out the drugs.

"It's all good?" she echoed. "Ain't none of this all good! Get this shit off my damn table, Bryan! What the fuck is wrong with you?"

"I'm bagging it up. It'll all be off the table in a few minutes."

"I want this shit off my table *right now*! Like yesterday! Get it off my table before I knock all this shit over! What the fuck is wrong with you, bringing this shit up in my house, dumping it on my table?" she ranted.

"I had to bag it up somewhere. What do you want me to do? Ride around with a scale in the car, too? It's bad enough I got this shit on me. I don't need a paraphernalia charge, too! So don't come in here fucking tripping! This is my house, too! I live here, too!"

"Your house? You don't pay a single goddamn bill in this mother-fucker, nigga! Hell, you don't even pay attention in this bitch! Don't get it twisted. I let you sleep here and shit, but don't nothing in this motherfucker belong to you. I had all this shit before I met you, and all this shit will still be here when you leave. Don't come up in here laying claim to nothing that don't belong to you. Now, get all this shit off my table, wipe it down with a Clorox wipe, and get it the fuck out my house!"

Before Bryan could respond, Raelyn stormed off to her bedroom and slammed and locked the door.

"Fuck you too then!" he bellowed down the hall in her direction. "I ain't gotta be here! I'll take my shit and roll!"

"Oh, yeah?" Raelyn retorted as she snatched the bedroom door open and charged back to the living room. "You've got so many places you can stay that you were sleeping in your car, right? I'mma throw your ass back to the streets where I should've left you. You don't come up in my house acting like you run shit and disrespect me when I correct you. I ain't hard up for no dick, nigga. You can run me my keys and kick rocks."

Bryan pocketed the bags of drugs he had just tied and rose from the sofa.

"A nigga ain't finna argue with you, Rae. I'm gone. I'll be back later," he dismissed her while heading for the door.

"I'm straight on that shit. Drop my keys, though, my guy," she countered with her palm outstretched.

"I ain't giving you shit. I said I'll be back. Now, go on in the house somewhere," he warned as she followed him out the door.

"I don't know what type of bitches you've been dealing with, but you ain't my damn daddy, and I ain't no kind of submissive. I run this shit over here, nigga..."

Bryan didn't hear another word. Zoning out as he got into his car, he shut the door and snatched off. Raelyn sounded like Serita. Serita sounded like Zaria. Zaria sounded like Iyana. Every woman in his life was sure to remind him he had nothing of his own. Everything he had, he had because of a woman. Whether they gifted it to him or he stole it from them, it all came at a woman's expense.

His mother's voice echoed in his head as a memory from when he was nine years old came to mind. *"You ain't shit,"* she spat as soon as the police officer was on the other side of the door. Bryan got caught stealing from the grocery store, and the officer opted to bring him home instead of taking him to juvenile. *"You got caught and still ain't get shit. You ain't worth a shit."*

He shook his head as he headed to his mom's house to drop off her package.

"Ummm... hmm? Huh? Un-uhn!" Raelyn croaked groggily as she rolled over to Bryan, nudging her awake in the middle of the night with his hard dick in her back.

"Hey. Hey, girl. Hey!" Bryan whispered in her ear.

"No, B. Where's my key? You need to leave."

"C'mon, Rae. You're lying in the bed in this damn thong. You got a nigga's dick harder than the corner of the wall when you barefoot and ain't looking where you're going. You knew what the fuck you were doing laying up in here like that."

"Who are you supposed to be, Lenny Williams? Ol' begging-ass nigga! Get the fuck outta here. I'm trying to sleep, and you ain't talking about shit," she hissed, turned back over, and put her back to him. Bryan removed his hoodie while kicking off his shoes, snuggled behind Raelyn, and palmed her ass cheeks.

"Why are you laying here like this with this soft-ass booty out?

Titties just free," he cooed, his hands roaming up her sides to her breasts.

"I said no, now go on somewhere, preferably to hell," she seethed. "I don't give a fuck where you go. Just get away from me."

"C'mon, baby. Let me get a little taste. You know you want this footlong," he whispered while rubbing his hardness against her back again.

"See, that's the problem with those cheap-ass five-dollar foot-longs. Everybody wants them, so they don't understand when someone finally doesn't, and they always claim to be a certain length but never live up to the hype. You're right, though. I can let you get a taste." Raelyn flipped over onto her back and spread her legs. "Come put your head right here and say ahh, nigga."

"I wasn't—"

"Un-uhn!" she cut him off. "You said a taste, right? Come taste this rainbow then." She laid back with her eyes closed and waited.

"Girl, my dick is hard enough to cut through these sheets! You better—"

"Hey! I'm compromising already. My house, my rules. You don't like it, there's the door. The rules are still the same, and they still apply. You can either get down or get up out my bed like I asked you to do. Period. Now, put your face right here and come eat this pussy, or you can excuse yourself right back out my damn door. Your choice."

"So, if I don't eat you out, I gotta leave? Where the fuck am I going to go, Rae? You—"

"Hey! Hey!" she interrupted him again. "You started this whole conversation. I couldn't give a fuck about whether or not you like the direction it's going. You either put your face in my lap or pick which park you're going to sleep in tonight. Take your pick," she stated sternly.

"Mane, damn, mane! Shit!" he complained as he moved into position. "C'mon, pull this thong off, mane."

"I know one motherfucking thing for sure... wasting my time will get you put out even quicker. You do all this complaining, but I don't ever hear a mumbling word against me slobbing on your knob. Now, you better shape up, eat this pussy correctly, and act like you're enjoying it, or you'll be back out the door. I mean, I'd better be about to lose my mind, gripping the sheets, moaning and screaming, back arched, with a mind-blowing, wet-the-bed, big-ass nut busted behind it. Think it's a game and see what happens."

"Mane, is you gone come out them damn drawers or what? A nigga trying to lay down and get some sleep while you coming with all this bullshit."

"You know what? Nah, I'm good, bruh."

"What?" He frowned.

"You heard me. I said I'm straight. You talk so much shit, I don't even want the head no more. I just want you out my damn house. I ain't never seen a nigga that fucks up and then gets mad about the consequences and never apologizes for shit. I ain't got time, bruh. I'll holler at you later," Raelyn dismissed him. She got out the bed and threw on a robe while Bryan stared at her in disbelief.

"What the fuck is your problem?"

"Ain't no problem, baby. It's all good, like you told me," she replied with the same nonchalant attitude Bryan had while sacking up crack at her living room coffee table. "Run me my keys. I'll walk you to the door."

"Like I told you earlier, I ain't giving you shit!" he fumed and took a step toward her.

"Oh okay. That's cool, too. No big deal. C'mon. I'll walk you out."

"You're seriously going to put me out?" His whole demeanor changed once he realized she wasn't bluffing. The reality she was actually throwing him back to the streets set in. The memory of the cold carpeted floor of the bando flashed in his mind and quickly deflated his ego.

"Oh, I'm so sincere. You got to roll, bruh. I've been living on my own too long to let a nigga come up in my house, disrespect me, and try to run my shit. I made it clear the first night you came over I ain't hard up for no dick or no mouth action, baby. I don't chase niggas, either. If you can't respect the dealer and the house rules, don't sit at my table. Plain and simple. Now, if you don't mind, I've got work tomorrow, and I'd like to get some rest." She smiled sweetly as she ushered him toward the door.

"Damn, baby, I said I'll eat the pussy. Why are you acting like this?"

"My actions are a direct reaction to your actions," she stated simply. "You asked to stay. I gave you the stipulations and even broke down the terms. You contested, which I didn't have an issue with. Now, if you would be so kind as to return my keys and vacate my premises, I'd sincerely like to return to my Serta Perfect Sleeper. I was quite cozy."

"C'mon, baby. I'mma lick it for you."

"Aht aht! I gave you that opportunity, and you passed on it. Don't stand here begging and pleading. I'd rather you leave here with your dignity intact because the begging won't get you anywhere with me, and it's a huge turn off, so spare me the melodramatic bullshit for tonight. I'm straight on the head. It's too late for that. I don't even want it no more."

Bryan stared at Raelyn for a minute from the door and decided to leave. Raelyn watched him slink down the driveway to his car. When he pulled off, she closed, locked, and dead bolted the door. *At least I know he can't get back in,* she thought, *because I didn't give him a key to the deadbolts.*

"Mane, look at what the pit bull drug in! I know that ain't Lil B! Hell naw! Where you been, nigga?" Kevin jeered as his cousin trudged up his driveway for the first time in several weeks.

"Mane, you know. I've been around." Bryan shrugged. Thirty minutes after leaving Raelyn's house, he was at his cousin's house to plead his case once again.

"Nigga, yo' girl must be tripping or something? A nigga don't ever see you until you fall out with one of your bitches."

"Let me holler at you for a second, cuz." Bryan nodded toward the house, ignoring Kevin's jokes.

"Fa sho." Kevin held the front door open for Bryan and followed him inside. "What's up, my nigga?" he inquired as he opened the refrigerator in search of a beer. Bryan stood in the living room with his hands deep in his pockets.

"Mane, cuz, I need you, nigga."

"What's up? You got beef with some niggas or some shit? I need to grab the blick?" Kevin frowned, eager to grab his heat and ride for his family.

"Nah, man, I got into it with my new chick, and she put me out. I just need to crash here for a night or two."

"Mane, I told you last time ain't none of that shit over here, cuz. I got a whole gal in there. It's a wrap on that shit."

"I only need somewhere to sleep, cuz. I'll be gone before y'all wake up. She won't even have to know I'm here."

"Nigga, ain't no way in hell I'mma have you up in here, and she don't know. If she fucks around and goes to the kitchen in the middle of the night and sees a whole nigga on the couch, she's likely to blow your ass off. Shawty don't ask no questions before she let that llama loose. You gone be a dead-ass nigga 'round here trying to play that game."

"Damn, cuz. I'm saying, mane! I'm in the streets for a couple days. Help a nigga out."

"No can do, cuz," Kevin declined, shaking his head. "I let you stay here, and we both gone be on the streets first thing the next morning. I'm telling you, shawty ain't having that shit. I don't know what you gone have to do, but you better go eat some pussy or something to get your ass back in the house."

Bryan shook his head and cut his eyes at Kevin, who caught the message immediately.

"Damn, Shawty ain't want no head? Oh damn, my nigga! You must've fucked up big time! What the fuck kind of problems you done caused that head can't solve?"

"It ain't even like that. She different. That shit don't sway her. She damn near thinks like a nigga. She got mad and said she ain't even want the head. She just wanted me to roll, so I dipped."

"That's on you, cuz. All I know is your ass can't stay here."

"Damn, mane. I don't know what the fuck I'mma do," Bryan mumbled and shook his head again.

"What you need to do is learn how to stand on your own two feet and quit depending on these hoes out here. You can't even act right long enough to keep a bitch in check. You need your own shit."

"Mane, I ain't tryna hear that shit right now. I need somewhere to stay *now*. That shit you talking ain't got shit to do with my current situation."

"Aight, I hear you. I said what I had to say and gave you my answer," Kevin stated with a shrug, the finality clear in his voice as he leaned an elbow against the doorframe leading to his kitchen.

"Damn, cuz! I'm saying, though! You for real gone choose yo' hoe over me, cuz? Real talk?" Bryan pressed.

"Aye, my nigga. You ain't gone disrespect my motherfucking gal, mane. Watch your mouth when you're speaking on shawty 'cause she ain't did shit to you, and I don't play about her ass. We cool and all, cuz. We family and shit, but you damned right I'mma respect my gal's wishes *and* her motherfucking gangsta. I'mma hold her down the same way she holds me down. I told you the last time you asked shawty was with the shit. She hot-headed as fuck. She don't even try to play it cool. The last thing I need is for her to up the draco on your ass 'cause I ain't tryna explain shit to Auntie Marva's crazy ass," Kevin snapped.

"I'm saying though—"

"Naw, my nigga! I know what the fuck you saying, and you're dead fucking wrong if you think I'm supposed to disregard everything I got going to help you out after you fucked your own shit up. Real shit, cuz! You're in the situation you're in because *you* fucked it up, not me. *You're* out here doing this crash dummy-ass shit, so don't come treating me like I'm supposed to be your tow truck for your twelve-car pile-up. *You* fucked that up, nigga! *You!* Not me. *You!* I wasn't fucking none of them bitches or beating none of their asses. That was all you. You're royalty in the fuck up monarchy, B. That shit ain't no secret! Now you gotta figure out what to do about that shit, but if you think I'm about to fuck *my* shit up at home to help you with *your* shit, you must be hitting your momma's pipe 'cause ain't no way in hell I'mma risk it all for you when I know for a fact your ass wouldn't do none of that shit for me. If you call that choosing a bitch over you, so be it 'cause one thing for certain and two things fa sho'. Shawty feeding, fucking, and financing a nigga, she gone Alpha Phi Alpha step show in the Delta step about ya boy, and you *ain't*. All these promises you're making are big cap, and there ain't a soul alive who don't know it. I'mma protect my home and my peace at all costs, my nigga, and I don't give a fuck how you feel about it. Now, watch out. I gotta get back to my game," Kevin popped off and meant every word. He nodded toward the door, arms folded across his chest, and Bryan caught the hint. Taking another glance at Kevin, Bryan nodded, turned, and left back out the door.

Chapter 21

"WHO THE FUCK ARE YOU?" Bryan barked and stepped toward a dark-complected male with dreadlocks who was comfortably watching TV on Raelyn's sofa. It had been three days since Raelyn dismissed him, three days since the day from hell. Bryan had spent three days sleeping in yet another bando, but tonight, he had decided, he was sleeping in a bed.

"What, my nigga?" the man questioned.

"I said, who the fuck are you, nigga? Did I stutter?"

"I don't know who the fuck you think you are, but you'd better get the fuck out my face. I promise you this ain't what you want," the man warned as he continued flipping through the channels.

"Nigga, this is *my* house. Get your ass the fuck up out of here."

"Your house?" The man chortled. "You shole ain't got shit in this bitch that says it belongs to you."

"What, nigga?"

"Did I stutter this time?" the man mocked Bryan.

"Nigga, you need to get your ass up off my couch and roll."

"Who's going to make me?" he challenged. Bryan stepped closer to him and cracked his knuckles. "What? Am I supposed to be scared, my nigga? You better get the fuck out of here with that bullshit."

"What? Jack then, nigga!"

"Jack?" the man scoffed. "Nigga, I'll fold your bitch ass up like laundry, hang you out to dry, and still put some lead in your ass!" he bellowed as he rose from the sofa to tower almost a foot over Bryan. "Rae, you better tell this weak-ass, simp-ass nigga, mane!!" he threatened as Raelyn entered the living room to see what was going on.

"Bryan, what the fuck are you doing here?" she barked when she saw him standing in her living room.

"Who the fuck is this nigga you got chillin' in my motherfuckin' house?"

"You've got a whole lot of fucking nerves! You break your ass up in *my* house and got the nerve to interrogate me about who the fuck I have over here! Like I told you the other night. This is *my* shit! You're a guest when you're here. Don't get that shit twisted, nigga!"

"How the fuck I break into a house I live at?" Bryan demanded.

"With a key I requested to be returned that you refuse to give back! The fuck?"

"So what? We get into it, and you think it's cool for you to be fucking other niggas?"

"Fucking other niggas? What did Tyrone Davis say? You ain't find my drawers beside nobody's bed? You ain't seen me laid up with nobody, and even if you did, nigga, we ain't together. I can do whatever and who-the-fuck-ever I want."

"Oh, so, we ain't together now?" Bryan demanded, taken aback.

"What do you mean *now?* We never were together, nigga. We were just fucking. You were cute and had good dick. We ain't in a relationship and never were. I mean, let's be honest. I just met you. I hardly even know you. You gave it up easy, so, hey. I knocked you off real quick, you know?" Raelyn shrugged.

"Mane, this shit is fucking crazy. Now *I'm* the hoe? You're the one fucking other niggas. You're a real hoe. You know that?"

"Aye, mane! You ain't gone disrespect the lady in front of me, bruh," the man, who still stood there, spoke up. "You're in her house. Watch your mouth."

"Mane, Rae, if you don't get this Jolly-Green Giant-ass nigga the fuck out my face!"

"Why don't you get me out your face yourself?" The man stepped closer to Bryan and challenged him.

"You're the one who brought your ass over here uninvited. He's my company. He has every right to be here. You're the intruder," she clarified as she glared at Bryan with her arms folded over her chest.

"Oh, so, it's like that?" Bryan dared her.

"It's exactly like that," she stated matter-of-factly, unmoved by Bryan's nonverbal threats.

"Bet, bitch!"

"Aye, my nigga. Let me see you to the door 'cause it ain't gone be none of this disrespectful ass shit you're trying to be on, bruh. Real talk, my nigga."

"Thank you, Jamel." Raelyn smirked and turned to retire back to her bedroom.

"So, you're going to put me out so you can fuck this nigga?" Bryan barked behind her.

"Would you rather stay and watch?" She cackled. "Correction... I put you out a couple days ago. I happen to be fucking this nigga because it ain't like you're hitting shit, anyway. You can't even act right long enough for me to even be interested in the dick," she shrugged and continued her departure, "or the head!" she shouted over her shoulder.

"Man, fuck this shit." Bryan stomped toward the door. "I got something for you and that bitch, nigga."

"Don't worry, my guy. They call me All-State; all that ass she got is in good hands," he assured him. "But, hey, just find comfort in knowing you won't ever be able to fill that hole behind me, anyway." Jamel howled and slammed and locked the door in Bryan's face.

Bryan returned to the bando he had been sleeping in a few blocks away, but the entire time he settled on the floor of the empty apartment, visions of Raelyn and the possibilities of what she was doing with Jamel at the moment played over in his mind. Finally, an hour later, unable to take his mind off it, his thoughts got the best of him, and he drove back to Raelyn's house.

Although she was quite blunt about what was about to go down between her and Jamel when Bryan left, Bryan still wouldn't allow himself to believe Raelyn was indeed going to sleep with Jamel. At half-past eleven, Bryan parked four houses down the street from Raelyn's house and observed her house for fifteen minutes from his car. There was no sign of movement, no lights turning on and off, no cars pulling in and out the driveway.

Bryan shook his head as he got out his car, unable to believe any female had him acting that way. Hands in his pockets, hoodie pulled over his head, he gave burglar or late-night stalker vibes as he slinked down the street to Raelyn's house, jumped the fence, and crept around the back of the house to her bedroom window.

Bryan immediately recognized the moaning and groaning of two people in the throes of passion. His heart tried to pass the lie that it was the TV turned up too loudly, but when Jamel's voice growled, "Shit, Rae! Damn!" he was forced to face and accept reality.

Standing with his back against the brick next to the window, he listened to the pleasure-filled moans of a woman he wished he were pleasing himself at the moment. His heart hurt... until he turned to peek through the window and realized the curtains were wide open.

There they were, completely naked in his full, unobstructed view. Raelyn lay flat on her back with her head off the side of the bed, mouth wide open, while Jamel towered over her, gripping her throat, force-feeding her ten inches of long, thick, hard dick. The TV was on, but it was obviously muted. In its light, Raelyn's throat rose and fell as Jamel ran his dick in and out her esophagus.

"Fuck, girl!" Jamel moaned. "Suck this dick!"

Jamel's strokes in her throat became faster and harder until he shot nut all over Raelyn's face and lips and into her mouth. Raelyn smiled widely as she watched Jamel's tremors calm to a stop. She grabbed the wet towel from her nightstand, cleaned her face, and laid back across the bed.

"Aw hell naw! I'm not finished with your ass yet. Don't get comfortable," Jamel warned her. He eagerly forced her legs open and dove in face first, instantly sending Raelyn into impassioned screams.

"Oh! Ohh! Ahh! Ahhh! Fuck, Mel! Yes! Fuck!" she hollered, with her fingers entangled in his dreadlocks, her hand pressing the back of his head, encouraging him.

"Is it good to you, baby?" Jamel queried as the tip of his tongue circled Raelyn's clit.

"Oh, baby, yes! Shit! Eat this pussy, baby! Shit!"

Raelyn, who had been up on one elbow with her other hand on Jamel's head, laid down on the bed and spread her legs wide, giving Jamel easy access to lick her any way he desired.

"That's it, baby. Open them legs up and let me up in there. Daddy gone get you right."

"Ooooo, get me right, daddy. Get me right!"

"Don't worry, baby. Daddy got you," he vowed as he flicked his tongue just inside her juicy opening while Raelyn spread her pussy lips with her manicured fingertips.

"Umm-hmm," Jamel groaned in approval and immediately flicked his tongue back and forth over her clit. Bryan's face was nearly pressed against the glass window, watching the festivities so closely he should've had a legal pad in hand to take notes.

"Uh! Mel! Uh! Ahh!" she called out and hyperventilated. "Oh, Mel! I can't take it! Fuck! Uhh!"

"Bust that big-ass nut, baby. Nut in my mouth," he encouraged her.

"Uh! Uh! Right there! Don't stop! Don't stop!"

Jamel closed his eyes, pressing his tongue firmly against her clit as he flicked it back and forth. Raelyn nearly lost her mind.

"Uh! Ahh! Ahhh! Mel! *Mel*! Ahhhhh!"

Raelyn's toes curled as she squirted juices all over Jamel's face while her back arched involuntarily.

"Come here, baby," Jamel cooed as he moved up in the bed and kissed her slowly.

Bryan was paralyzed and unable to peel his eyes away from the spectacle. There was a passion in the kisses they shared that excited Bryan. As he watched from outside her bedroom window with a hard dick, he felt the desire to kiss her like that. He wanted to hear her moan from the meeting of their lips. He was jealous, envious, but more than anything, he was angry with himself for not being the one in her bedroom and inside her at that moment.

As Jamel gazed upon Raelyn's face, entranced by her beauty, he caught a glimpse of Bryan watching from the window in his peripheral. He tried to tell Raelyn, but she grabbed his face with both hands, turned him back to her, and kissed him again. When she winked at him with the eye Bryan couldn't see, Jamel smiled, continued kissing her, and winked back, finding the situation amusing. If it was a show Bryan wanted, Jamel fully intended to put on an entire production.

Wrapping Raelyn's left leg around his waist, he eased back inside her, stroking her slowly as he swiveled in his hips to hit her spots. He planted kisses up and down her neck and then returned to her lips.

"I want you to turn over for me," he whispered.

"Yes, baby. Whatever you want," she answered obediently.

Raelyn moved into position with her ass in the air, back perfectly arched, legs spread wide, and face in a pillow. Jamel rubbed the head of his dick back and forth over her pussy lips, teasing her until she begged for penetration.

"You want this dick, don't you?" he teased her.

"Yes, baby. I want it. Put it in, baby. Put it in."

"Tell me you want this hard-ass dick."

"I do! I want this hard, juicy, thick, long-ass dick! I want it! Give it to me!"

"You want it, Rae?"

"Fuck me, Mel! Please fuck me! Fuck me!"

Jamel shoved his dick deep into Raelyn's sopping wet pussy, causing her to call out.

"What did I tell you? What did I tell you, huh?" Jamel quizzed her while issuing hard, deep, timed thrusts. "What did I tell you about fucking with these lame-ass niggas, Rae? You can get all the dick you want," he reminded her as he swirled his dick around in her wetness, "but you out here fucking with these little scrawny-ass, nothing-ass, leeching-ass, bum-ass niggas."

"Shit, Mel! Shit!" Raelyn panted.

"I'mma show you how a nigga is supposed to be hitting that ass. That little lame-ass motherfucker ain't hitting this pussy right! He ain't hitting it right! Why you moaning like that? Huh? Huh? Why your pussy so wet for me? Huh? Because that bitch-ass nigga ain't been fucking you right! Throw that ass back on this dick!"

The fuck? Bryan seethed as he listened to Jamel insult him without being aware of his presence. *This nigga don't know what the fuck I be doing. I got his bitch-ass nigga. I can't wait to catch this nigga on the street. I'mma let some of that air out of that nigga's chest. Him and that bitch. She ain't defending me or shit. She's just going along with the shit like I don't be tagging her ass.*

Raelyn bit her bottom lip and forced herself to concentrate as she twerked and clapped her ass cheeks with Jamel's dick deep inside her. The thrill of having an audience had Raelyn's juices flowing. Just the thought of Bryan standing at the window, furious and jealous, turned her on even more.

I'mma show out on this dick, she thought as she made her ass cheeks slap against Jamel's thighs so hard the claps resonated throughout the room.

"Yeah... yeah... yeah... yeah! That's it, baby. Throw that ass, girl!" he cheered her on.

I'mma show this nigga how to fuck some pussy, Jamel thought as he watched his dick disappear and reappear repeatedly. *If the little peeping Tom-ass nigga wants to stand at the window and watch, I'mma show him what the fuck he ain't been doing. I'mma make his ass mad as hell how I'm about to tear this pussy up and teach him a lesson about peeping through windows.*

Jamel slapped Raelyn's right ass cheek while Raelyn gazed back at him. Bryan frowned in jealousy. *That's my ass cheek*, he seethed silently as Jamel grabbed her hips, moved up against her, straightened his back so he towered over her, pushed her face down into a pillow, and commenced to digging her back out.

"Oh, Mel! Oh, Mel! I can't take this shit. This shit feels so good. Oh, God!"

"I know it. That nigga ain't been hitting shit. He got you all neglected and shit. This pussy purring for me. He ain't do shit but get you ready for a real nigga. I can feel all the big-ass nuts that nigga done left piled up in there. I'mma dig all that shit out for you, baby. Bust on this dick again for daddy."

"Ohh, daddy. Ohhh. Ohhh," Raelyn growled.

"How that shit feel, baby?" he whispered.

"Ohhh. Ohhh! Ohhh!" was all she could manage to release.

"Yeahhh," he cheered while dropping dick straight down into her welcoming wetness.

They both fell silent as Jamel focused on hitting Raelyn's spot in the bottom of her pussy. Unable to moan, Raelyn could only gasp for breath as Jamel continued to dig deep inside her, hitting a spot that hadn't been touched since the last time they rendezvoused months before.

"Why you ain't moaning, Rae?" Jamel teased. "Yeah, I know what that shit means," he smirked.

Bryan watched from the window, as confused as Jamel knew he would be about why Raelyn was no longer moaning.

"Ugh! Ughh! Ughh!" she finally moaned again.

"That's it. That's it, baby. You're so mesmerizing. Look at how well you're taking this dick. I fucking love you," Jamel encouraged her quietly.

"Ughh! Ugh!"

"Let it out, baby. I know. I know it feels too good. I'm sorry. Let it out. Let that pussy leak on daddy's dick."

"Ughhh! Ughhh! Errr!"

"Here it comes. I'm ready for you, baby. Give it to me."

"Ughhh! Ahh! Errr!"

"Give me all that juicy sweetness, baby. Let it out. Let it out. Pour that cream on this dick."

"Errrrrrrrrr!!!" Raelyn growled. Bryan watched how gingerly Jamel handled Raelyn as she struggled to breathe behind the extreme orgasm and then scowled with jealousy as Jamel's dick slid out her womb with white cream slathered all over it.

"That's my baby," he comforted Raelyn as she collapsed onto the bed, breathing heavily, with her arm thrown across her face. "Ain't nobody been treating this pussy right since I been gone, baby? You're shaking like a leaf, leaking like a faucet, and cumming harder than a Nitti beat. You out here fucking with niggas that can't even make you bust a decent nut. A nigga gone take care of all that shit tonight, though," he promised as he wrapped her in his arms and placed kisses up and down her neck as she recovered.

Once her breathing was no longer labored, his kisses trailed downward until his lips finally wrapped themselves around Raelyn's nipple. Twirling it with his tongue, he pulled back on it, causing her to moan lightly as her sexual senses rushed over her again. A smile crept across his face as he moved from one nipple to the other, licking and sucking gently. His right hand, which was busy massaging her left breast and rubbing up and down her left side, thigh, and ass cheek, roamed downward. His fingers dipped themselves into the pool of juices collected at the opening of her pussy.

"Ooohhh, you taste so sweet," he moaned with closed eyes as he licked his fingers, exaggeratedly sucking her juices off them.

Jamel slid his middle finger in and out of her creamy warmth, gently caressing her walls. When he added his pointer finger, he stared into her eyes, watching her reaction to the slow stroke of his fingers. Her eyes begged him for more, and he obliged with his thumb, gently rubbing her clit as his fingers continued rowing in her river. Added pressure on her clit caused her to moan his name in a stutter.

"Ja- Ja- Jamel," she moaned.

"Does it feel good to you, baby?" His deep voice boomed in the room.

"Un-huh," she whined and nodded.

He kissed her deeply while maintaining the rhythm of his fingers.

"Tell me it feels good to you, baby," he demanded.

"Oh, Jamel. It feels so good," she whimpered. "Ohhh."

Snuggling his face into the nape of her neck, Jamel placed light kisses on her sweat-glossed skin as he lay next to her, pleasuring her. Raelyn's eyes closed as she allowed herself to enjoy his touch, a touch she so desperately missed.

Jamel had always been the only man who could truly please her. He knew all her spots, paid attention to her body, and learned its cues. He could tell by her attitude exactly what kind of loving her body needed. They never argued, rarely ever disagreed, and whenever he called, Raelyn was sure to answer. They knew they belonged together and would make a perfect couple, but Jamel's business in the streets kept him out of town on runs and meetings for periods of time so long he found being faithful almost impossible. Never wanting to disrespect her, Jamel refused to give any woman the ammunition against her to give the impression she was stupid or to treat her as if they had something over her. They agreed to be friends, but they both knew where the other's heart was, and every time Jamel was in town, Raelyn knew she could expect a knock on her door and a bouquet of impressive flowers. Jamel always returned bearing some sort of gift, whether it was expensive jewelry or a piece of home décor, and the gifts were always accompanied by a round or two of passionate lovemaking to curb both their appetites for everything they had been missing while they were apart.

Raelyn's appetite had never been satiated by anyone else. No matter how good sex with any other man ever felt, it was never good enough. Other men were nothing more than appetizers, and Jamel was always the much-anticipated main course.

Unable to see Jamel's fingers inserted into Raelyn's womb, Bryan stood at the window, assuming they were exhausted, spooning, and finished for the night. He resolved to retreat to his empty bando to lick his wounds, his ego completely deflated, and feelings shredded like julienne carrots.

As Bryan turned to leave, Jamel turned over while lifting Raelyn in the air above himself, her legs spread wide as she reached down and held Jamel's dick in position, allowing Jamel to slowly lower her down onto his dick. Bryan was awe-struck. The maneuver was clearly something they had done before, but it was also something Bryan wasn't nearly strong enough to do. Steam rose from the neck of his hoodie with his growing anger, despite the throbbing dick in his pants.

Raelyn tossed her hair behind her as she rolled her hips on Jamel's dick. Bryan was infuriated with jealousy as he watched from the other side of the windowpane. Raelyn never rode him at all. He had always been on top with her barking orders on how she liked it from beneath him. Eager to please her, he never minded the constant direction, but she hadn't made a single request or issued any orders the entire time Jamel dicked her down, and now she was bouncing on his dick and riding him like she was in a rodeo. Bryan was both pissed and turned on at the same time.

"Damn, baby. Look at your sexy ass. You look so fucking good. You ride this dick like a champ," Jamel complimented her.

"I missed this dick, daddy," she moaned. "I get tired of lying to these niggas like they be doing some shit. Don't nobody hit this pussy like you do, baby."

"I know, baby. Every time I leave, I ask you to come with me. I get money, baby. You ain't gotta worry about shit. You know I'll take care of you," Jamel reminded her as he palmed her breasts with both hands.

"You know me better than that. I get my own bag and take care of myself. I don't depend on no nigga for nothing."

"I know, but—"

"Cut this conversation, Mel, and fuck this pussy. I'm tryna bust this nut on this big-ass dick," Raelyn fussed as she rolled all the way down until Jamel's dick pressed into the bottom of her womb. "Fuuuuuuuuuuuck!"

"Yes, ma'am," he obeyed.

Raelyn bounced on his pole, the ecstasy evident in her eyes. Jamel twirled her nipples between his thumbs and pointer fingers, well aware of their sensitivity. She relished in Jamel's moans and groans, knowing she was the only one who could make him feel the way she did. They stared into each other's eyes, unashamed of the obvious pleasure they were bestowing upon each other. As good as it felt, Raelyn remembered she promised herself she would show out when he made his way back to her bedroom again, as they were never sure exactly when their next rendezvous would be.

Rolling to a stop while staring into his eyes, Raelyn turned around on Jamel's lap to face the opposite direction without letting his dick slip out. Glancing back at Jamel before putting her knees down, she laid all the way forward on the bed and gripped the sheets by his feet. Raelyn bounced on his dick with her upper body still flat against the bed, providing Jamel with a clear view of his own dick entering and exiting her womb.

The moans coming from behind her brought her deep satisfaction. Jamel smacked both her ass cheeks with his fingertips, loving the ripples it caused. *I must've died and went to heaven,* he thought, but he knew he would catch hell when his body suffered withdrawals when he left her again. Pushing the thought from his mind, Jamel focused on the pummeling Raelyn was presently giving his joystick.

"Damn, baby! Shit! Fuck, Rae! Damn, this pussy is so good! You're popping that thang tonight, baby. Bounce that ass for me! Damn, you getting that dick up in there!"

"I want you home where you belong," she stated.

"And where is that?" he questioned.

"In the bottom of this pussy," she cooed as she sat up with her hands straight up in the air and bounced on his dick. "How does it look, daddy?" she purred as he watched her titties bounce from behind.

"Damn, baby, you're so motherfucking sexy! I love watching that ass bounce on this dick, and these big juicy-ass titties... damn, I just want to lick and suck all over 'em!"

"Ooooooh, daddy! Say that shit!" she moaned and shook her head from side to side, shaking her long hair against her glistening shoulder blades. Not wanting Jamel to cum yet, Raelyn slowed to a stop and turned back around to face him once again, his thick rod still tucked deep inside her womb. She held her hands up in front of her with her palms facing him, and as if on cue for a stage direction, Jamel intertwined his fingers with hers. She pushed against his hands as she placed both feet flat on the bed and slowly slid up and down, making sure to rise all the way to the tip of his dick just before it could slip out before rolling all the way down until her lips kissed his hairs.

Raelyn's cheeks slapped against Jamel's thighs as they collided. Jamel's mouth hung open involuntarily in amazement as Raelyn gripped his hands and rode his pole.

"Damn, baby! You're riding the shit out this dick!" he huffed. "Do yo' thang! Shit!"

Raelyn admired Jamel's frown caused by his pleasure as she assured him, "I'mma ride this dick for you, daddy. I'mma drop this pussy down on this big-ass, hard-ass dick."

A few strokes later, he pushed back against her hands to signal her to stop, and Raelyn perched on his lap. Jamel lifted her by her hips and fucked her from beneath.

"Hell yeah, daddy! That's it! Fuck this pussy, baby!" she wailed loudly. Raelyn constantly fought against the orgasms Jamel pumped out of her, but to no avail. The harder she fought, the more determined he became, and Raelyn found herself trembling even harder and screaming even louder than before.

"This dick good, baby?" he panted as he pumped.

"Fuck, yes! Shit!"

"Bust a big-ass nut on this dick like a good girl, baby. I want to see that cream running down this dick."

"Ahh! Oh, shit! Yes! Don't stop! Ugh! Don't stop!"

"I ain't gone stop until you cum again for me."

"I'm finna cum, baby!"

"That's what I'm talking about!"

"I'm finna cum hard!"

"Cum hard for me, baby. Squirt all over this dick!"

"Ohhhhhh!"

"Give me all that sweet shit, baby. Give it to me. Make a mess on this dick."

"Ugh! Ugh! Ugh! Yes! Mel! Fuck! Me! Yes! Ahhhhhh!"

Raelyn's body shook in Jamel's grip as juices poured from her center, pooling beneath her in his lap. Encircling her in his arms, he held her as she recovered. When her breathing steadied, he pressed his lips against hers so sensually she nearly cried.

Their kisses grew more passionate until they were breathing heavily once again. Jamel held her tight as he turned her over and laid her on her back. He placed both her legs over his broad shoulders before leaning forward to kiss her again as he slipped all ten inches of his dark chocolate back inside her. A moan slipped from her lips and found its way between his.

As his rhythm quickened, Raelyn was forced to break away from their kisses. Jamel's strokes were so deep, they were forcing moans up from her stomach and out her throat.

"Mel! Ahh! Fuck!" she whined. Jamel was busy pumping away, watching his own dick running in and out of her dripping wetness. "Fuck! Mel! Ugh!"

"Unnnnnn- hunh!" Jamel moaned. "Fuck, this shit is so good!"

He abruptly grabbed both her ankles and put them up over her head with one hand like she was a baby getting her diaper changed. Rapid strokes followed, and the squishing of her juices filled the room as he drilled her.

"That's it, Mel! Fuck! Yes!"

"I know, baby! I know! I'm finna nut all in this pussy!"

"Nut in this pussy, baby! Skeet all in me!"

"I'm finna shoot this shit deep off in that pussy!"

"Shoot it in me! Cum hard, baby! I wanna feel it skeet all over my walls!"

"Fuck, Rae! Shit!"

"Uh! Mel! Uh! Ah! Beat it up, baby. Beat it up!"

"Oh, shit! Fuck! Fuck!"

"Ahhhhhh!" they both moaned as they climaxed together.

Raelyn's legs slid down Jamel's shoulders before he collapsed on top of her, out of breath and completely spent. Raelyn recovered first, and it was her turn to plant kisses all over Jamel's neck and chest.

"Damn, baby, you know you be tearing this pussy up," she whispered with her lips pressed against his neck.

"I'm the man for the job." He smirked at her.

"I mean, you seriously be fucking the shit out this pussy. Nobody does it better than you, baby."

"That's what I like to hear. Are you satisfied? You need some more?" he offered.

"No, no, I'm good. You always get me right," Bryan heard her say.

Both Bryan's head and his dick were throbbing, and he was fuming. The show was over. He witnessed much more than he needed to and some things he shouldn't have.

"Fuck, man!" he grumbled, while pounding his fist into his palm as he trudged back to his car. *I really liked this girl, man*, he thought. *I for real liked her, and she out here fucking other niggas like I don't fucking matter, like I don't even fucking exist. She legit dismissed me and went right in there and fucked that nigga! She got me so fucked up! Fucking bitch!*

Chapter 22

RAELYN HOPPED out her gray Infiniti G35 in her driveway the next evening while on the phone with her best friend, her cell phone wedged between her ear and shoulder, as she grabbed her Brahmin bag off the passenger seat of the car.

"Girl, I don't give no fucks! I'm real-deal pressure out here in these streets, and I applies it! These niggas ain't never had no shit like what the fuck I be putting on 'em," she bragged. "Yes, bitch! The nigga watched damn near the whole time from the window! The nigga stood outside the club like he couldn't even get in! In my Chris Brown voice, bitch!" She fell into a bout of laughter as she fumbled through her ring of keys for the door keys. "Look, let me call you back once I get settled in and shit. I got you. Aight." Dropping her cell phone into her open purse, she stuck the key in the security door.

As she turned the deadbolt on the wooden interior door, Bryan popped around the corner of the house, ran up behind her, and forced her through the door before she could even react.

"What the... get out my house!"

"Bitch!" *WAP!* "Shut the fuck up!" Bryan boomed after punching Raelyn in the face. "I would've been in this motherfucker waiting for your ass to come home so I could choke your weak ass out if you hadn't changed the fucking locks. Trifling-ass hoe!" he seethed as he snatched her by her hair, dragged her across the kitchen floor to the living room, and tossed her on the sofa.

"Get your fucking hands off me, trick!" she snapped as she jumped off the sofa and punched him squarely in the nose. His reflexes kicked in, and he backhanded her, sending her small frame flying back onto the couch.

"I got your motherfucking trick, ole duck-ass bitch!" he growled as he stalked toward her.

"I bet you better not touch me no more," she warned him as she jumped up and stood behind the sofa, using it as a shield to keep distance between them.

"Or what?" he challenged her. "Huh? What the fuck you gone do? You think this shit is a game, bitch? You think you can play with folks' emotions out here? Huh?"

"Nigga, I do who and what the fuck I want," she sassed, "and I couldn't give two fucks who don't like it. I'm a grown-ass woman, baby." She snickered. "If you can't hang, I suggest you stick to the chickens you've been clucking around because I'm the momma hen around this bitch."

"Naw, you're just a trifling-ass hoe, and I'm about to beat your ass like one. C'mere, bitch!" he promised as he grabbed at her and missed when she moved behind the far-left corner of the sofa.

"Get the fuck out my house, Bryan. I ain't gone warn you again!"

"What you gone do, bitch? Huh? Put me out! Make me leave, hoe!" he dared as he swiped at her again. That time, she saw an opening and took off running down the hallway into her bedroom, slamming the door behind her and quickly locking it.

"Open this fucking door, Rae!" he bellowed while pounding on the bedroom door.

"I ain't opening shit! Get out my house or else!"

"Or else what? Huh? What you gone do? Call the police? Call the police, bitch! You gone need 'em by the time they get here!"

"I'm not going to keep repeating myself," she assured him from inside the bedroom. "I done told you to get your ass out my damn house. You'd do best to leave, bruh."

"Bruh? I got your motherfucking bruh, bitch! Bring your ass up out of there!" He repeatedly kicked at the door, desperate to get his hands around her neck.

"Leave, Bryan! Get the fuck out!"

"Bitch, I ain't going nowhere! I'mma be right here! You gone have to come out that room eventually, hoe. You can't live up in there."

"So, you ain't gone leave?"

"Nope."

"You're going to wait outside my bedroom door?"

"Yep."

"After I done told you several times to get the fuck out?"

"I don't give a fuck! I ain't going no-damned-where!"

A long awkward silence followed, and when Raelyn spoke again, it was from directly behind the door.

"So, you ain't gone leave?" she shouted. The cocking of a gun came from inside the bedroom on the other side of the door.

"Oh, shit!" Bryan exclaimed and took off running down the hallway.

Throwing the bedroom door open, Raelyn ran behind him, firing two .9mm shots in his direction. Bryan turned the corner and leapt into the kitchen just before one of the bullets hit the corner of the wall right behind his head.

"Fuck!" he shrieked as he snatched the doors open and bolted down the steps.

"Naw, don't leave now, nigga!" Raelyn jeered as she fired two more shots at him. The wind of one of the bullets whizzed past his right ear before the lead knocked a huge chunk out the trunk of the oak tree in her yard.

Bryan sprinted down the street like he was gunning for gold in the Olympics. He jumped into his car and hadn't put it completely in drive before he smashed on the gas to get away from Raelyn's house.

"Fuck!" he roared as he punched the steering wheel. "Who the fuck taught that bitch to shoot like that?"

~ Two Months Later ~

"NO, sir. I'm quite sure... I know, and I apologize. I know it's disheartening news, but I've dug deep into this over the past few months, and I'm quite confident in my report... Yes, sir. I understand. It was quite a shocking discovery. I'm just glad I caught it when I did... No, sir, thank you... Of course, of course. Anytime... Will do! Thank you... Bye."

Iyana placed her phone back on the receiver, rose from her desk, and approached the coffee maker perched on a shelf in her office. It had been a long nine months since she packed up and moved to Seattle, Washington, but as she gazed out the floor-to-ceiling windows of her corner office at her amazing view of Elliott Bay, the Space Needle in the near distance, she found affirmation in her decision to leave Memphis behind.

There had been no decision to make at all. When Iyana's supervisor pulled her into her office and presented the offer to her, Iyana was both flattered and shocked. For years, her job was thankless, and she felt unseen, unrecognized, and unappreciated. The offer of a promotion to Lead Case Investigator at the organization's headquarters and completely covered relocation enlightened her to exactly how valued she truly was.

Iyana's salary nearly tripled. After she worked at the headquarters for six months, she received her first and last performance evaluation, which resulted in another salary increase and a contract granting her a yearly pay raise and quarterly bonuses.

Though she no longer worked directly with the children, she still found her job incredibly fulfilling. In Memphis, she was a case-worker, but she also shed light on some of the malpractices and misdeeds some of her co-workers participated in. When news reached the higher-ups, they watched Iyana and found her to be the perfect candidate for a new position they never knew they needed.

The title of case investigator was usually given to case workers who visited homes to follow up on reports of abuse and neglect. Iyana's title as Lead Case Investigator was a facade for her investigation of other employees' behaviors in an effort to uncover any misappropriation of funds, falsified documents, and general breaking of the organization's policies. Having been successful at doing just that, Iyana discovered employees who were forging their supervisors' signatures on documents, claiming to have visited homes or met with families they made no contact with, and obtaining clientele under false or shady pretenses. One of her investigations also resulted in a group of employees at the Atlanta office being arrested after it was discovered they were stealing company property and writing stolen company checks out to themselves for cash.

Iyana communicated with several of the Vice Presidents for months before she disappeared on Bryan. Completely discontent in her relationship, she seized the promotion and relocation to escape her predicament. Simply breaking up with Bryan would be dangerous and completely useless, as he wasn't the type to go quietly. He'd more quickly assault and threaten her if she tried to make him leave, and she'd never be able to get rid of him and be free of his toxicity. If he knew about the promotion, he would've forbidden her from going and arranged a set of circumstances to prevent her from being able to leave.

Because of this, Iyana chose to play it smart. She informed Bria, Celeste, and her mother of her plans and made all the necessary arrangements to have her belongings packed and moved. She gave Celeste and Bria most of her furniture and a few clothing items and had everything else moved out in the middle of the night.

Bryan's actions, followed by his absence, played in Iyana's favor. She had the time she needed to peacefully pack, move, and move on with her life. She left without sneaking out, fighting her way out, and she was spared the inconvenience of listening to the sob story of a man whose lies were more believable than his truths.

As successful as Iyana was in her professional life, she was equally successful in her personal life. Though she missed Bria and Celeste terribly, and she hated to leave them behind, she quickly made friends with two of the first black women to greet her at her new job. The three of them went out after work for dinner, drinks, and occasionally karaoke twice a week. Celeste had already flown out for a weekend, and Bria promised to visit her as well within the next two months. She hadn't thought about a man or even entertained the thought of a relationship the entire time she was in Seattle, and she had no plans of changing that anytime soon.

Iyana was living. She was enjoying life. She was having fun. She was successful. She was prosperous. She was content.

"What are we doing tonight? Are we going to Rock Box again?" Iyana's friend and colleague, Telaina, suggested as she, Iyana, and their friend, Esmaé, approached the elevator together after work.

"Nah." Iyana shook her head as they waited for the elevator. "I'm not in the mood for karaoke tonight. Plus, I'm hungry as hell. Let's do Some Random Bar tonight. Their food is pretty good, and the drinks are on point."

"We haven't been there in a while. I'm down for that. I'm desperate for one of their watermelon mojitos," Esmaé agreed while nodding her head full of curly, sandy brown hair.

"Cool! Meet you guys there around seven?" Telaina queried as she adjusted the button of the plum business suit currently complimenting her chestnut complexion. Standing an inch taller than Iyana, Telaina was equally admired by both her friends for both her beauty and her consistent level-headedness.

"Hell naw! Let's go now! Happy Hour ends at six, and I'm starving!" Iyana exclaimed as they all stepped into the elevator.

"Damn! We can't even go home and take a shower first?" Telaina frowned as she flipped her long, curled auburn weave.

"If I go home, I'm going to bed. We haven't been anywhere but to work. It's not like we look or smell bad."

"Whatever. Let's just go. I'm hungry too, and I could go for some crab nachos," Esmaé confessed while licking her lips.

⁘

"Still no news?" Telaina questioned Iyana after they ordered their drinks.

"News? About what?" Iyana frowned in confusion while glancing back and forth between Esmaé's almond-shaped gray eyes and Telaina's upturned brown ones..

"A potential. A hopeful. A prospect," Telaina teased.

"Girl, no, ma'am! I told y'all that is not where my mind is right now. I'm focused on work, not on these little mannish-tail boys, like my grandmomma used to say."

"You work way too hard to not play hard, too." Esmaé shook her head and commented. The product of a Caucasian mother and Black father, Esmaé had perfectly freckled olive skin with a beauty mark just to the right of her lips. Standing two inches shorter than Iyana, she was thin framed, while Telaina sported an hourglass shape.

"All these fine-ass men out here, and you're telling me you haven't seen anything that has piqued your interest?" Telaina interrogated her in disbelief.

"What I'm telling you is I've had blinders on. I haven't seen anything that wasn't work-related, so there's nothing to be interested in," Iyana clarified.

Telaina and Esmaé glanced at each other and shook their heads.

"What?" Iyana questioned them.

"Look, sis." Telaina's long, slender fingers reached across the table and grabbed Iyana's hand as if she was about to console her. "I hate to be blunt with you, but you need some dick."

"I do *not* need no dick!" Iyana howled. "Dick does nothing but cause problems."

"Oh, sis, you just haven't had the *right* dick yet!" Esmaé bragged as she pursed her heart-shaped lips and batted her long eyelashes at Iyana as she corrected her. "Dick is a magnificent thing! Dick doesn't cause problems. It solves them."

"Got a headache?" Telaina queried. "Dick can cure that."

"Got a stomachache?" Esmaé chimed in. "Dick will knock that right on out."

"Got in-grown toenails?" Telaina countered as her full lips turned up into a smirk.

"Now wait now!" Iyana cackled as she stopped them. "How the hell can dick cure in-grown toenails?"

"Dick will make you give a fuck about your appearance, so you'll go to the nail shop and get that fixed," Telaina explained as she winked her mink lashes at Iyana's intrigued face.

"Oh my God!" Iyana burst into laughter.

"Attitude fucked up? Been cursing everybody out?" Esmaé continued. "Dick will definitely smooth that shit out."

"Hell, dick will make that *POOF!* Disappear!" Telaina cracked up.

"Y'all are so damn extra! How is either one of you sitting here fussing at me? Neither of you heffas have boyfriends!" Iyana pointed at them both.

"Oh, sweetheart, I don't have a boyfriend because I don't want to be in a relationship right now. I never said I didn't have somebody keeping the cobwebs from forming, though," Esmaé clarified.

"What you said!" Telaina high-fived her. "I'm like these niggas out here. I have commitment issues. I ain't got no man, but I got a nigga, though."

"Okay, so what's the difference?" Iyana wondered as the waiter placed their drinks in front of them.

"Pause this conversation," Telaina interrupted while holding up her finger. "Yes, sir. We're ready to order," she stated as she smiled sweetly at their blonde-haired, blue-eyed waiter.

"Okay, what can I get for you ladies?" he inquired with a smile as he removed a notepad from the pocket of his apron.

"Firstly," Telaina began, "you can go ahead a start working on our second rounds because we're going to need that like yesterday." She giggled as she scanned the thin White waiter up and down. "I'll have the ten-ounce hangar steak. My friend here will have the crab nachos with extra white cheddar, and her country ass," she said as she pointed her French manicured finger at Iyana, "will have the fried chicken dinner," Telaina ordered for them.

"How would you like your steak?"

"Medium well," she ordered as she batted her mink lashes at him.

"And the collard greens and potato salad are fine with the fried chicken?"

"They sure are!"

"Got it! I'll get this order in for you. Can I get you anything else?"

"A bag of dicks? Extra hard?" Telaina blurted. Esmaé and Iyana gasped at her remark.

"Laina!" Iyana fussed. "Oh my God!"

"I'm sorry, ma'am. We don't sell them by the bag here," the waiter joked back with her.

"How about a penis-colada then?" she continued.

"Ehhh, I don't think you'd want this particular bartender to make your penis-colada." He chuckled. Leaning closer, he pretended to whisper, "I hear his is a bit weak."

They all burst into laughter, and the waiter excused himself to take their order to the kitchen.

"Where were we?" Esmaé pursued.

"What's the difference between you having a man and a nigga?" Iyana repeated to Telaina.

"When you have a man, you're in a relationship. You do everything together. Post pictures on social media, possibly even live together. That's not what you do with your nigga," Telaina explained. "Your nigga fucks the shit out you when you need it or want it. If your car quits on the side of the road, your nigga will come fix it. If your light bulb blows, and it's too high for you to reach, your nigga will bring a ladder and change the bulbs out for you. He'll buy pizza or wings on Fridays, and you can Netflix and chill. He'll rub your back or your feet, and you can even spend the night, but you don't belong to each other. You don't trip on each other about fucking other people. You're there when you call each other, but then you go on about your business. That's your nigga."

"Basically, it's a friend with benefits?"

"Not exactly because it's mostly on the low. You aren't going out on dates with this guy or being seen with him. For the most part, nobody even knows you know each other, but he's always there in the background, waiting on your phone call," Esmaé clarified.

"Esmaé, you got a nigga, too?" Iyana was shocked.

"Girl, please! I've got a few niggas! They're all trying to play starting forward, but they should just be glad they're even on the team," she bragged.

"I mean, that's easy for you," Iyana admitted to Esmaé. "You're all bi-racial, gray-eyed, and shit. All you have to do is blink those long-ass lashes and flip that curly-ass, sandy brown hair and men come flocking to you like Canadian geese!" She shook her head and stated, "Look at me. I'm dark-skinned, all skin and bones, with nappy-ass hair. These men out here don't even glance my way."

"Girl, are you serious?" Telaina stopped her. "This is Seattle! Maybe down there in Memphis, where dark-skinned women are in abundance, the men don't pay you much attention, but up here, where it's about seventy percent white girl, dark-skinned Black women are a real commodity."

"She's right, Yana," Esmaé agreed as she sipped her drink. "I'm obviously mixed, and I have a whole group of niggas. Telaina's more of a medium complexion, and she has a steady nigga and a few that come and go. Girl, if you jump your ass out in that pond, you'll come back with a whole cooler of niggas because they're definitely going to bite."

"No doubt about it," Telaina confirmed.

"I don't know." Iyana sighed. "I've never been the type of person to mess with multiple people at the same time."

"Oh, I understand that," Esmaé assured her. "We're not saying you need four or five, but you need at least one!"

"Yeah, you need some dick, Yana. You're so tense and uptight. You need somebody to loosen you up, knock the kinks out your back, put a little pep in your step. You know?"

"Honestly, guys. I've been fine," she tried to sound convincing, but she wasn't fooling them.

"Yana, we've known you for how long now?" Telaina queried as she glanced from Iyana to Esmaé.

"About a year now?" Esmaé thought aloud.

"That's about right. You two were the first Black women I met at the company when I moved here."

"And we've been rocking ever since." Esmaé nodded.

"Right, so we've seen most sides of you. When you first moved here, you were bright and cheery. You've lost a bit of that since you've been here. It's been too long since someone slid your panties to the side, honey," Telaina acknowledged.

"I don't have time for all that. I've been so busy since the day I first stepped into the office. When do I have time to go somewhere and meet someone?"

"Sis, you just need some dick," Telaina stopped her. "The next time we go out for drinks, we'll go somewhere that has a dancefloor. You've got a whole donk back there! Shake that ass! It won't be long before you have your first candidate."

"You aren't going to hire the first applicant for the job, though. The first one to approach you is usually crazy," Esmaé informed her. "You'll talk to him for a little while to show the other guys you're approachable and available. Most men don't want a woman no one else is interested in, so while you think he's in your way, he'll actually draw all the other guys' attention to you."

"Exactly," Telaina confirmed. "You'll go to the restroom, decline his offer to escort you, and when you come out, there will be a guy waiting to introduce himself."

"Y'all have put entirely too much thought into this shit," Iyana commented and giggled.

"Oh, honey, it's not a thought." Esmaé frowned.

"No, ma'am. It's a routine," Telaina corrected her.

"A routine? Y'all do this all the time?"

"How do you think we accumulated our whole stable of niggas?" Telaina bragged.

"Oh my God!" Iyana cracked up at Telaina as the waiter placed their plates in front of them, and Iyana thanked him with a bright smile.

"It's no problem. A1?" he offered Telaina.

"Yes, please." She accepted the bottle of A1 Steak Sauce from his tray.

"You ladies enjoy. Let me know if you need anything," he insisted with a smile as he scurried away.

"Are you down?" Esmaé pressed Iyana as they ate.

"I don't know. It sounds like a recipe to concoct a crazy-ass stalker from a guy who doesn't know how to handle good pussy," she declined and shook her head.

"I haven't had that issue yet. You have to lay out the rules before any skins get slapped," Telaina schooled her.

"I mean, getting my oil changed does sound appealing right about now." Iyana sighed. "Let me think about it, guys. It's been a long time, and I've been doing fine by myself. The last thing I need is to jump back into the water and land straight on a snake," she grumbled.

"You're right," Telaina agreed, "especially after everything you've told us you've been through."

Y'all don't know the half of it, Iyana thought as she simply nodded and shoved a forkful of potato salad into her mouth as she was reminded she had refrained from telling Esmaé and Telaina about the repeated rapes she had endured with Bryan among other extreme pieces of details about their relationship. *Not even half.*

Chapter 24

IYANA STOOD NERVOUSLY behind her date, wringing her hands as he unlocked his apartment door. She examined him again from behind as if she hadn't been staring at him all night. He was a normal guy, not too muscular, not too tall, not exceptionally handsome, and yet, there was something about him that was so sexy to Iyana. She was immediately attracted to him when he approached her in the club several weeks before. Since then, they talked on the phone several times daily and became uncommonly intrigued by each other. Wrapping up their third date, Iyana found herself loving everything about him.

The clicking of the key in the lock jolted her back to reality as he turned to face her and welcome her inside while holding the door open for her. He tapped on a table lamp as she stepped into his modernly furnished apartment. A smile spread across her lips as he approached her after closing and locking the door.

"You have a gorgeous place," she complimented him.

His pearly white smile faded as he stared into her eyes. He intended to acknowledge her compliment, but found himself rendered speechless. Gently grabbing her face with his right hand, his thumb on her left cheek, other fingers on her right, his palm cupped her chin, he tilted her head upward and pulled her into his lips.

Time stood still. Silence echoed throughout the room. Iyana melted in a way that threatened to bring her to tears. His kiss was effortlessly passionate and filled with a burning desire solely for her. Though she was hesitant to kiss him back, Iyana was engulfed by a level of comfort she never had the pleasure of becoming acquainted with. There was something so familiar about him, something she missed without ever knowing it existed. Her heart moaned as his kiss filled her up like soul food, and his love stuck to her ribs.

He pulled her against himself with his left hand, the bulge in his pants growing as it pressed against her stomach. His right hand found its way to her throat and grasped it with a gentle roughness. Iyana gasped in a near panic at the feel of a hand around her throat, the traumas of her past life with Bryan rearing their ugly heads, but as she reminded herself, those days were long gone, and Bryan was nowhere near. He could never hurt her again, and this sweet hearted, incredible man before her had made it clear that he only wanted to love her. Iyana glanced up into his eyes and found reassurance there that she could trust him, and as if her body realized it as well, her muscles relaxed in his arms. Using his thumb to turn her head, he trailed kisses behind her ear, down her neck to her shoulder, across her collarbone, and back up the other side. Roughly tilting her head back, he ran his tongue up the soft tissue covering her throat before pressing his lips against hers once again, sucking her in even deeper.

He wrapped his arms around her and held her close, emitting a cloud of safety and security around them. She was his for the night, and perhaps forever, and at that moment, Iyana had no rebuttal for any request he could possibly make.

Their tongues tangoed as they lost themselves in the sweet rhapsody. He abruptly slid his hands beneath her and lifted her, wrapping her legs around his waist. Carrying her to his bedroom, he laid down with her on the bed, their lips never missing a beat. His fingertips caressed her cheek under the slivers of moonlight that rolled into his window like a gentle tide. She could barely see his face when she opened her eyes, and yet, it was as if she was viewing an old photograph she hadn't seen in years. His familiarity was comforting, relaxing, soothing.

Sitting up on an elbow, he kissed from her chin, down her neck, to between her breasts. He stared into her eyes as he slid the straps of her navy-blue dress over her shoulders. Iyana sat up and removed the entire dress, revealing a navy-blue lace thong and strapless bra underneath. He stared at her body, shimmering in the moonlight, enticing and eager to be enjoyed. As they kissed again, Iyana unbuttoned his shirt and slid it over his shoulders and arms. His shoes, his pants, and the t-shirt he wore under his button-down all tumbled to the floor as Iyana's fingertips explored the smooth skin on his arms, familiarizing themselves with the feel of his flesh.

His lips graced her navel, and she released sweet sighs into the warm air. Her inhibitions escaped her grip and scampered out the door. His hands cupped her breasts and slid beneath her to unfasten her bra. He placed kisses up and down her stomach that sent chills up her spine. Unable to control himself, he eagerly wrapped his lips around her left nipple and gently pulled back on it before caressing it with his tongue.

Iyana's fingers ran over the smoothness of his low-cut fade as he switched nipples. His neck twisted as he made sure to lick and suck it from every angle possible. When he came up for air, he slipped his fingers in the sides of Iyana's thong, slipped it off, and tossed it to the side. Spreading her legs tenderly, he stared at her juicy center with the ravenous hunger of a starved man with a steak placed before him. He ran his tongue over his lips and dove into her pussy face first.

Iyana gasped and released a low whine as he slowly licked it with adoration. As he quickened his motions, she gripped the sheets, nearly pulling them off the bed as she writhed in pleasure.

"Ahhh! Ahhh!" she squeaked. "Oh, shit!" Her back arched involuntarily as he flicked the tip of his tongue rapidly over her clit, sending her body into its first set of convulsions for the night.

"That's it, baby. Cum in my mouth. You taste so damn good," he encouraged her between licks.

Iyana sat up on her elbows and forced her eyes to focus in preparation in the darkness, wanting to take it all in before he slipped inside her. He stared into her eyes in the twilight, eager to see her reaction, as he rose to his feet, slid his boxer briefs down, and stepped out of them. One eyebrow raised, Iyana was pleased with the sight of the rock-hard eight inches that bounced out of his boxers. His chiseled abs and flexing biceps glistened in the moonlight as he approached her, his phallus leading the way and ready for action. *Those business suits sure can be deceiving,* she thought. *Here I was thinking he was just a normal guy, and he's built like a Mac truck under his Dolce & Gabbana blazer. Fuck!*

Swiping a condom from the top drawer of his nightstand, he strapped up before turning to Iyana with a smirk and a twinkle in his eye. He gently grabbed her face again and kissed her with a soft passion she had never experienced. Then he relaxed in the bed with his back against the headboard.

"I don't want to just make love to you tonight," he whispered after she had straddled him, his erection resting against her stomach. "I want you to make love to me, too. I want you to take control and go as fast or as slow as you want. Use me however you need. I'm here to do nothing less than please you. This is your dick. Cut up on your dick."

With a straight face and steady gaze, Iyana grabbed his rod, lifted herself on her knees, and slid down on his pole. He groaned in awe as she worked her muscles around him, surprised by how good she felt from the first stroke. Gripping the headboard as she moved, Iyana slid up and down, up and down, and he immediately regretted telling her to take control. She rode his dick like a stallion, and he couldn't take it. His hands moved from her hips to her breasts with a mind of their own. He squeezed lightly, running his thumbs over the dark chocolate tone of her areolas. Unable to resist, he leaned forward and wrapped his lips around her right nipple as his arms encircled her.

"Fuck, girl! Shit!" he frowned and groaned as he picked her up, laid her on her back on the bed, and dug deep inside her while Iyana moved against him, keeping time with his rhythm.

Iyana adored the love faces he made while making love to her. The care and attention he put into her experience with him impressed her. He was sure to listen for her deeper moans and aim for the same spot that caused them, determined to hit every crevice left untouched by those who had come before him.

It should be illegal for this shit to feel this good, he thought as he swam in Iyana's lake. Iyana experienced a high just as ecstatic as his. They hooked each other with their line, reeled each other in, and there was no throwing them back. Their moans turned to groans, their groans to shouts, their shouts to screams, and before they realized it, they had switched positions three times without missing a beat. Iyana's shoulders knocked pictures off the wall as he pumped into her deep and hard. She took all he gave her while he tried his hardest to fight the urge to shoot man milk deep inside her.

"Oh, dear God! Right there! I'm about to cum, baby!" she screamed. He carried her back to the bed, still on beat. Laying her on her back, he lifted her hips and held them as he pounded into her.

"Cum for me, baby. I love how you're taking this dick like a good girl. Now make a mess on daddy's dick."

"I can't take it!" she cried out.

"Yes, you can. You're doing such a good job, baby. Look in the mirror and watch."

Iyana glanced over at the dresser mirror, the image of his dick pumping in and out her womb turning her on even more. She felt as if she was watching an X-rated movie of herself, and she was captivated by it.

"Look at you. You look so fucking good. You're so pretty, so sexy."

"You're so deep, baby," she whined.

"That's how I'm supposed to be," he reminded her. "Come here. Don't run. You wanted this dick, right?" he taunted as he pulled her back.

"Oh, baby!"

"Is that it, baby? Right there?"

"Yes, daddy!"

"I'mma dig it out for you, baby. Let it out. You like it, baby?"

Iyana was speechless. He knocked half her words out of her voice box, and she wasn't even able to formulate the other half. She choked on air, cotton-mouthed from screaming, strangled by her own words trying to escape her throat.

"Talk to me. Tell daddy you like it. Like that? Huh? It feels good, don't it?"

Iyana could only whimper in response as he repeatedly hit her spot, his sex talk becoming as debilitating as his stroke.

"I already know you're about to cum on my dick. Go ahead and give it to daddy, baby. Throw that shit back and cum on this dick. Let me feel it," he whispered softly to her.

"Oh! Oh! Oh! Oh!" was all Iyana could manage to get out as he thrust.

"Mhmmm, mhmmm, mhmmm," he moaned with her, on the verge of exploding himself.

Tears were running into Iyana's ears as she prepared for what she knew would be the hardest orgasm she had ever experienced. She stared at him, still unable to speak, and completely in shock of how amazing he made her body feel the first time he touched it. *Everything he does feels so good, like he knows by body so well already. I could've sworn he studied a book on how to please me. We must've known each other in a past life,* she thought. *I must've been his husband. Maybe he was my wife.*

"Oh, my God!" he gasped as he hit a different spot. "I'm in your stomach."

Two strokes later, Iyana's floodgates opened, and she squirted juices all over his dick. Seeing her nectar dripping and running down onto his sheets sent him over the edge, and he shot the whole clip, his condom catching it all.

"Fuck, baby!" he groaned as he laid her down and collapsed on the bed next to her. Iyana struggled to catch her breath, her chest hurting, her head throbbing, her own heartbeat pulsing in her ears.

"Oh, Iyana," he moaned in a whisper as he reached over and engulfed her in his arms.

"Deion," she whispered as she dozed off in his arms.

~ One Month Later ~

BOISTEROUS LAUGHTER POURED from a table in the corner of Metropolitan Grill, where Iyana was seated on a Tuesday evening with her friends. Celeste and Bria accepted Iyana's open invitation and flew to Seattle together to visit. Telaina and Esmaé joined them for dinner with their boy toys in tow. Iyana also invited Deion, the man she met the first night she, Esmaé, and Telaina went on their *sack safari* in search of unattached intimacy for Iyana. Iyana and Deion discovered they had a great deal in common, and they genuinely enjoyed each other's company. They couldn't keep their hands off each other, which added to their connection, but because they mutually desired to turn their situationship into a relationship, they decided to slow their pace and focus on building their bond and getting to know each other better.

"I love him for you, Iyana," Celeste admitted as she, Iyana, and Bria stepped out the front door of the restaurant into the pleasant autumn night air. Celeste handed their ticket to the valet, and they waited together for him to pull their rental car around. "He's a great guy, and you two are so content together."

"I agree," Bria chimed in. "I've never seen you this perky. He's put a smile on your face."

"We'll see," Iyana sighed and blushed. "I don't want to get ahead of myself. I've only known him for three months."

"Yes, but he must truly be someone special if you introduced him to us. I believe he's a perfect fit for you. I know you feel it, too." Bria playfully elbowed Iyana.

"Yeah, he's a perfect fit in more ways than one," Iyana mumbled slyly.

"What was that?" Celeste inquired.

"Nothing," Iyana quickly responded, but Bria heard her.

"Ooooooooooh, girl!" she jeered. "If he's laying it down like that, you'd better wrap your legs around that nigga and hold on for the ride!"

"Stop it!" Iyana giggled. "After everything I've been through, I think I deserve a little happiness."

"You deserve a slew of it, sis," Celeste assured her.

"Yeah, you just be careful. Seattle is a long way for us to drive to take you to get your car back from a nigga," Bria teased.

"He's got his own car, so I don't have to worry about that," Iyana stated.

"Hell, the last one did too, sis!" Bria cracked.

"Naw, the last one had Oscar the Grouch's trash can for an automobile." Iyana cackled.

"That motherfucker was riding around in The Blur II from *The Little Rascals* and calling it a car," Celeste cracked as their car arrived.

"Look, sis, we're happy for you. You're doing great up here, and it looks like you've found a great guy," Bria gushed as she touched Iyana's arm. "Just take it slow, okay? You rushed into things with the asshole, and we all know how that turned out. Take your time this time."

"Girl, who are you supposed to be? Oprah? Iyanla?" Celeste snickered.

"You don't always have to be the one to make the mistake to learn from it," Bria hinted with a smirk.

"I hate to be the one to leave dinner early, sis. I'm so sorry," Celeste apologized. "That flight just has me drained."

"Oh, Leste, it's no problem. I definitely understand. The time zone change doesn't help much either. It may only be nine here, but it's eleven in Memphis. Your bodies need time to catch up. Get some rest. We've got plenty of time to catch up. I'm just glad to have y'all here," Iyana assured them.

"We love you, sis. See you in a couple days?" Celeste confirmed.

"Of course. I'm still taking Friday off, and we'll spend the whole weekend together before y'all go back to Memphis Sunday," she assured them. "What are y'all going to do tomorrow and Thursday, though?"

"There's a spa at our hotel and a couple of restaurants nearby we want to try," Bria informed her in a feigned British accent.

"Girl, I put y'all up in the Four Seasons! There's a bomb-ass restaurant inside the hotel!" Iyana chortled.

"I know, but it looked expensive as hell," Bria, the queen of balling on a budget, whined.

"Sis, charge it to the room. I'll take care of it."

"Excuse me?" Celeste questioned. "Say what now?"

"Go to the spa, go to the restaurant, order room service. Do whatever you want and charge it to the room. I'll cover it," Iyana repeated.

"Damn, Yana! You rolling like that? Okay then!" Bria exclaimed.

"I meant to make sure, but you guys found the debit cards I left for you, right?" she inquired, referring to the two prepaid Visa cards she loaded with three thousand dollars each and left with the front desk clerk for them.

"Yeah, they left them on the counter in the room for us." Celeste thanked her as she hugged Iyana and stepped into the driver's side of the Benz Iyana rented for them.

"Anything for my girls," she replied with a smile. "Call me if you need anything and have fun!"

"Will do!" Bria assured her as she hugged Iyana too and climbed into the passenger seat.

"Love y'all!"

"Love you, too!" they both chimed as they pulled off.

"I was coming to check on you," Deion advised as he stepped out the front door of the restaurant to see Celeste and Bria drive off and Iyana turn to come back inside. "I didn't want to run the risk of anyone snatching you up and running off with you," he joked.

"How sweet! Thank you!" Iyana beamed.

"Ready to head home? I think your friends are, ummm..."

"You don't even have to tell me." She giggled. "I already know." They cracked up as he held the door open for her, and they returned to their table where Telaina and Esmaé were both preoccupied flirting with their boy toys and giggling girlishly.

"So, Deion," Telaina addressed him in a sing-songy voice once they were seated again. "You and Yana sure are getting pretty close. You feeling my friend here?" she surveyed and nodded in Iyana's direction.

"I think it's pretty safe to say we're feeling each other," Deion confirmed as he sipped his drink with a nod. "She's a highly intelligent, strong woman. We have some of the most interesting conversations, and we enjoy each other's company."

"Deion, baby, is it okay if I order a dessert to take with me? That turtle brownie a la mode looks so delicious," Iyana requested.

"Of course, dear. Whatever you want. You don't even have to ask."

"Do you always say yes to her?" Esmaé pried. She was half curious and half genuinely impressed.

"Why would I tell her no? So someone else can tell her yes? I don't understand the question," Deion countered.

"Oh, no, sweetheart. You answered it," Telaina assured him. "Esmaé, let's leave the man alone. I think I've heard enough for tonight. He's clearly got his head on straight."

"I see." Esmaé smirked at him. "Love, I'm ready to go," she informed her date, whose arm was wrapped around her waist. "My kitty's purring."

"TMI! TMI!" Telaina jeered as they all split their sides.

"Ain't no shame," Esmaé retorted as she waved them off. "We're all grown. I'm sure we're all about to go home and do the same thing."

Iyana and Deion only glanced at each other and smiled knowingly. Esmaé's date waved down the waiter and requested their bill.

"Add a turtle brownie a la mode to go, and then I'll take our check as well," Deion informed the waiter.

"Yes, sir. Right away," the waiter agreed before rushing off.

"Long day at work?" Telaina pressed Deion after noticing him trying to suppress a yawn.

"Yeah. Even longer day tomorrow," he admitted.

"What exactly is it that you do? Iyana told us you work for Amazon. What do you do over there?" Telaina inquired.

"I am a Senior Executive of the Engineering Department. Basically," he proceeded to explain, "the company develops and purchases all types of equipment and machinery to make our operations more efficient on the logistical and fulfillment level. I supervise those developments and approve those purchases. I also submit requests for the purchasing and testing of new machinery to keep the company on the cutting edge of technology and keep production and delivery at the rapid rates our customers have always enjoyed."

"Wow!" Telaina was impressed. "That sounds like an important job. What's going on tomorrow? Why is it such a long day?" she continued her inquiry.

"Tomorrow I will present a set of sorting machinery to the vice presidents. This particular set of machinery sorts boxes in record time and will allow our logistic centers to prepare and ship orders three times as quickly. It will also cut down on the jamming of the lines by fifteen percent," he explained.

"That's great!"

"Yes, and tomorrow's presentation is twice as important because the VP of Engineering will be retiring next month, and this will put me ahead of the game for his position. I want this presentation to be on their minds right before he leaves. I also have another set of even more revolutionary technology I plan to present after he leaves, as they're considering who to promote into his vacant position," Deion explained.

"Smart man!" Esmaé's date cheered. "I like your way of thinking. Put something on their minds before they go to the drawing board, so you'll have a foot in the door. Then seal the deal with another ground-breaking piece of equipment. It's ingenious."

Deion thanked him and revealed, "Yeah, I've been strategizing for quite a while on this one. My work at the company speaks for itself, so I'm hoping this seals the deal for me."

"Babe, I'm so proud of you," Iyana gushed.

"Thank you, babe," he replied, and they moved in for a kiss.

"Hey! Hey! Un-uhn! Don't nobody want to see that! Not today! No!" Telaina complained as the waiter returned with the checks and Iyana's dessert. "Now I know it's time for me to go."

"Yeah, because you're about two drinks past tipsy." Iyana giggled.

"Aye, bruh," Esmaé appealed to Telaina's date. "Go ahead and pay the check so you can take her home. You got cash? Yeah, just put cash in there. You don't need no change. Take her to the house."

"Esmaé! Esmaé, seriously?" Iyana crowed. "You're drunk, too!"

"Drunk? Who the fuck is drunk? I mean, I might be a little fucked up, but shit, work hard, play hard, right?" Esmaé acknowledged with a hiccup.

"You got that right!" Telaina agreed, and they tried to slap each other five but missed and nearly slapped each other's dates.

"Oh, dear God! Y'all, please take them home," Iyana urged the two men.

"C'mon, babe. Let's go," Esmaé's date cooed while mock-coddling her.

"Don't be rushing me! Always so pushy! Don't be pushing me!" she grumbled as she rose from the table.

"I'm not pushing you, baby. I'm trying to help you up from the table."

"Naw, you was pushing me. How about we see if you can push that dick? Can you push it?" she babbled quietly.

"Push it real good." Telaina cackled and mocked the dance from Salt-N-Pepa's "Push It" video.

"Oh my God! Let's go! Let's go, y'all, 'cause naw!" Iyana ushered them out of the restaurant.

"Are you sure you're going to be okay?" Deion worried as he opened Iyana's car door after trailing her to her apartment building's parking garage to be sure she made it home safely.

"Yeah, I'll be fine," she assured him as she stepped out her car and grabbed her clutch, keys, and bag with her dessert. "Thank you and thank you for following me home."

"Oh, it was no problem. I wanted to, actually. It's my job to make sure you get here without any hitch."

She thanked him again with her head down as she childishly toyed with her clutch. "Look, I apologize for my friends. I know they can be kind of overbearing and nosey. I know this whole situation isn't easy on you, and they made it quite awkward," she chuckled nervously.

"Hey, hey, you don't have to apologize for anything," he assured her. "I'm a big boy. I usually take my grilling with a couple of mush-rooms and onions on the side," he joked. "I can handle it. You're right, though. It has been hard... literally," he hinted as he glanced down at his pants, "but you and I know what's going on, and believe me, you're more than worth it."

"Thank you for that," she murmured and blushed. "Do you... you want to..." she stuttered while motioning toward the elevator.

"Nope, nope. We agreed we would only have sex after every other date. We had sex two nights ago. If I go up there, there would be an instant replay of Sunday night," he warned her.

"I mean, I wouldn't have a problem with that," she insinuated with a raised brow and sly smirk.

"No, baby. We agreed, remember?"

Iyana nodded her head in disappointment. Deion stepped close to her and wrapped his arms around her. She laid her head on his chest, savoring the loving embrace until he gently lifted her chin and their lips greeted each other.

"Believe me, I want it just as bad as you do, baby. I can't wait to see you Friday so I can make love to you again," he whispered with his face in her hair.

"I think I want to stay in and spend some time together instead of going out."

"It's whatever you want to do, beautiful. It's your world."

"I just want you to make love to me all night."

"What you want is what you get," he agreed, and kissed her fore-head. "Now, get on up there so we can get started on getting through the next couple of days until we see each other again."

"Okay." Iyana smirked.

"Alright, babe. I'll see you later," he assured her as he got back into his car and rolled down the driver's window. "Good night, baby."

"Good night." She waved as he pulled off, and she turned to head to the elevator.

The eerie echoing silence that found its home in parking garages filled the air as the sound of Deion's motor driving off into the night faded into the distance, and the click-clacking of Iyana's heels against the cement reverberated off the walls of the garage. As tired as she was from a busy day at work and an eventful evening, Iyana was still on her guard, and her head was on a swivel. A sudden faint rustling alerted her she wasn't alone in the parking garage. She stopped in her tracks, holding her breath as if it would help her hear better, and examined her surroundings, glancing between cars and along the walls, but she saw nothing.

She was about to blame her paranoia for what she assumed was a hallucination when the headlights of a black sedan clicked on near the end of a far row of cars. Frozen in place, she watched the car slowly creep out the line of cars toward her. Her mind shifted to survival mode as she rushed toward the elevator door and frantically pressed the illuminated *Up* arrow. The creaking of the elevator rolling down the shaft filled the garage, and Iyana turned around to get a description of the car.

Black car, she repeated to herself silently. *Black car, two doors. It's a Chevy. Black Chevy, tinted windows, two doors. Black older model Chevy Impala, two door, tinted windows. Very dark tinted windows, chrome rims. Black older model Chevy Impala, two door, very dark tinted windows, chrome rimes, with pipes... expensive pipes, not the loud 'migo from the hood pipes.*

The car approached her and drove past slowly as she breathlessly hoped and prayed she wasn't about to be kidnapped or worse. The windows were too dark to see inside. As the driver's door was right in front of her, the ding of the elevator rang out, and Iyana stepped backward through its doors, the heel of her shoes finding the toe of someone else's foot and scaring her so badly the paper bag she carried with her dessert inside hit the floor.

"Oh, I'm so sorry," she apologized as she gazed over her shoulder to see her neighbor. He was six foot three, chocolate-skinned, and wearing a white t-shirt and grey sweatpants. He was towering over her. She had completely backed into him, stepped on the toe of his shoe, and pressed her butt against his groin, causing him to grab her by the waist.

"It's quite alright. Are you okay?" he inquired as he picked up her bag and handed to it her, quickly noticing she appeared frantic and afraid.

"Yeah, yeah, no, I... ummm... that car." She pointed. "It startled me. I don't know. I thought someone was—"

"It's okay. It's okay," he assured her. "They're gone now." He pointed out as the car's taillights sped out the garage.

"Yeah," she exhaled in relief.

"Do you want me to go up with you and make sure you get in safely?" he offered.

"No, no. I've held you up enough. I'm sure you have somewhere to get to," she declined with a nervous smile, embarrassed.

"Oh, it's alright. I was just going to my girlfriend's house. I'm sure she'll understand me arriving a few minutes later than expected to make sure my neighbor gets into her apartment safely. There's so much going on out here with domestic violence, sexual assaults, and sex trafficking, I wouldn't want anything to happen to you on my watch. Whether we know each other well or not, we have to watch out for our Black queens," he commented.

"That's so sweet of you. Can you just go up to the floor with me? I'm sure I'll be fine from there."

"Of course," he obliged. "C'mon." He ushered her into the elevator. "Let's get you home."

After pressing the button to take them to the twelfth floor, he stood on the opposite side of the elevator from Iyana at a comfortable distance. He gazed at her as she nervously fumbled with her purse and keys as the elevator climbed the floors.

"My name's Bryant, by the way," he introduced himself, attempting to lighten the mood.

"Brian?" she repeated with disgust on her face that made him want to quickly clarify.

"No, Bryant, with a 'T'," he corrected her, emphasizing the last letter in his name.

"Oh okay. Nice to officially meet you, Bryant, though I certainly wouldn't have wanted it to be under these circumstances. I'm Iyana." She offered her hand to shake, which he graciously accepted.

"It's great to finally meet you as well, Iyana, no matter the circumstances." He grinned while shaking her hand. "If you ever need anything, you just knock. If I'm home, I got you."

"Thank you," she gushed with a smile. The elevator dinged as it came to a stop and the doors opened. "Thank you so much for coming up with me," she reiterated as she stepped off. "You have a great night."

"Oh, I'm going to stand down here by the elevator and make sure you get inside," he informed her while stepping off behind her.

"You didn't have to. I know you had somewhere to be."

"Oh, I insist. You've got somewhere to be, too. Alive, and I'm going to make sure of it. Now, go on inside. You're not keeping me from anything important. Netflix and chill can wait until you're locked inside your apartment, believe me," he assured her.

"Thank you so much," she repeated sincerely, her gratitude clear on her face.

"It's no problem," he assured her as he watched her sashay down the hallway to the door across the hall from his own. There were only four condos on each floor of their building, two on each side of the elevator. "You good?" he shouted when she opened her door.

"I am. Thank you!" she shouted back.

"Alright. You have a good night."

"You, too. Thank you!" Iyana retorted and went into her apartment, closed and locked the door, and stood there with her back against the door, breathing hard, overcome with anxiety all over again.

No matter how she tried, she couldn't shake the feeling she had in the garage. She was the only one in the garage when that car crept through. It was too big of a coincidence, and she couldn't ignore the reality someone was possibly watching her.

Chapter 26

"OF COURSE. I'll be there shortly." Iyana was on the phone with Celeste that Friday morning. "I've got a couple stops to make, and then I'll be right on over," she stated as she stepped out of her car and closed the door. After hanging up, she took a deep breath of determination as she stood facing the building and proceeded inside.

"Good morning! Welcome to Pinto's!" a tall, blonde-haired young man greeted her.

He looks too young to be working here, she thought as she politely smiled back at him. Her eyes scanned the glass cases and shelving in the gun store. *He can't be a day past his college graduation.* Her eyes returned to him as she surveyed their inventory, and she quickly sized him up as a jock who was quite popular with the ladies because of his build and demeanor. *He looks like he plays rugby and is on the crew team.* She giggled as she peered over a case of Sig Sauers.

"Shopping for anything in particular?" an older, balding man with a dad belly inquired as he approached her.

Iyana sighed in relief at the offer of help from someone who appeared to have extensive knowledge of the store's inventory. "I have no idea what I'm searching for," she admitted. "All I know is I need something out this store." She chuckled nervously.

"You know more than you think you do," he assured her. "If you'd like, I'd be more than willing to help you pick out something as close to perfect for you as possible."

"Could you please?" she solicited help from the man who towered a foot over her.

"Of course." He chuckled. "I see you're looking at the Sig's. You see anything you like?"

"I don't know. They all look the same to me. They're just different colors or sizes. I have no clue what I'm looking at."

"Okay, so let me start with a couple of basic questions. Have you ever held a gun before?"

"Not at all."

"Okay. Are you interested in an automatic or a revolver?"

"A revolver? They still make those?"

"Oh yes! They do." He cracked up at her question. "And they're quite popular with the ladies."

"I think I'd like an automatic," she decided. "This pink one here is really pretty."

"Okay, let me stop you there. In the world of guns, pretty doesn't mean a damn thing. I've got plenty of pretty guns, but if you need a form of protection, you cannot judge any of these books by their covers. This pink one," he explained as he stepped behind the counter and unlocked the case with his ring of keys. He slid the door open and placed the pink gun on top of the glass. "It's pretty, alright. It's also worthless as a form of protection."

"What?" she questioned, shocked. "Why do you say that? It's a gun. It's a form of protection. All it has to do is—"

"Shoot. I know, and it doesn't," he informed her. Seeing her confused expression, he continued. "This is a Jimenez .22. Jimenez is known for making some pretty guns. Oh, they come in all colors and with all kinds of designs engraved on them. All that is to make up for the fact they aren't worth the metal they're made of." He chortled. "Jimenez's are a waste of money. If you pull this gun out to shoot somebody, you'd do better by throwing the gun at them and hopefully hitting them in the head with it."

"What do you suggest?" Iyana solicited his opinion as she giggled.

"We have a number of smaller caliber guns that will actually shoot," he suggested. "I'll let you hold a few of them and see if you like any of them."

She tried a Springfield .9 mm, a Taurus .45, a .22 Ruger, and a .380 Ruger, but when she picked up a Smith & Wesson M & P 9 Shield Ez, something about the way it felt in her hand assured her it was the one.

"That's a great gun," the man confirmed. "A Smith & Wesson is always reliable. This particular model has a slide that's tapered to make it easier to grip, which means you can chamber your first round effortlessly. If you find yourself in a situation and you have to whip that out, you won't find yourself struggling to rack the gun," he assured her.

"That's perfect. That's what I was worried about the most," she admitted, while turning the gun over in her hands. When she racked it, a smile spread across her face. She stared the man in his eyes and confirmed, "I'll take it."

After exploring the city all day Friday with Celeste and Bria, Iyana spent Saturday turning up with Celeste, Bria, Telaina, and Esmaé, and was exhausted. She enjoyed brunch with Celeste and Bria before they caught their flight back home on Sunday, and then spent the rest of the day lounging around her condo, catching up on housekeeping, and eating ice cream.

As she relaxed in the hammock on her balcony watching the sunset with a glass of wine perched in her hand, she thought back over her life. She truly was at home in her condo, with its amazing view of the downtown community and Elliott Bay. The state-of-the-art appliances, modern furniture and décor, and the consistent calm yet sophisticated ambiance all combined to create the absolute perfect environment for the woman she had become. She smiled at the thought of Deion and the memories of a few nights before.

"This is the life," she whispered to the sky. "This is *my* life," she stated with a smile as the sinking Sun's orange, fuchsia, and pink hues kissed the buildings in the distance. "This is my happy place. I'm finally happy."

Forty-five minutes later, after the Sun slipped below the shoreline for its nightly slumber, Iyana stepped inside to wind down for the night. As she placed her glass in the sink, there was a knock at her door.

"Who on earth could that be?" she wondered as she checked her cell phone for missed calls or texts while rushing to the door. Assuming it only could've been Deion, she threw the door open with a wide grin that quickly faded away when she realized there was no one there. Instead, a large bouquet of summer flowers in a vase had been left outside her door.

"Oh, wow!" She beamed as she picked it up. She glanced down the hallway, but there was no one there.

Closing the door behind herself, she took the arrangement inside and checked the card inside the bouquet.

I'm so sorry! Please forgive me!

Iyana frowned. Deion hadn't done anything wrong, and he didn't owe her an apology. Confused, she placed the vase on the kitchen counter, picked up her cell phone, and called Deion.

"Hi, you've reached Deion. I'm unavailable right now..." his voicemail played, and she disconnected.

Iyana was even more confused. Deion never missed her calls.

What on earth is going on? she thought as she plopped down on the edge of her bed, cell phone in one hand, card in the other.

She waited an hour for Deion to return her call, half watching TV, half trying to keep herself calm. She busied herself by taking a shower to allow time to pass, but when she got out of the shower, and her phone still hadn't rung, she called again.

"Hi, you've reached Deion. I'm unavail—" Iyana decided to leave a message.

"Hey, baby. It's me. I called a while ago, and you didn't answer, so I was just calling back. Ummm... call me back when you get this. Bye," she stammered through the recording.

Iyana watched TV for hours, waiting for Deion to call her back. She called three more times, and at one in the morning, she finally decided to go to bed.

As she lay there confused and worried, Iyana's mind replayed memories like old home videos. Dinner was great, and they made plans to see each other soon, but she was so preoccupied spending time with Bria and Celeste she didn't realize she hadn't heard from Deion since he pulled out of the parking garage that night. She frowned at the thought, disappointed in herself for not paying attention to him as she should. She didn't call to see how his presentation went, and he didn't call her with an update. The longer she pondered over the situation, the more evident it became something was terribly wrong. Iyana was desperate to know what was going on.

"Give me your phone," Iyana instructed Esmaé while she and Telaina lounged in her office four days later.

"We should call him," Telaina stated.

"Why are we calling him from my phone, though?" Esmaé frowned. "I don't want him calling me back looking for you."

"If he knows what's good for him, he won't answer your number, either," Telaina snarled. "Now, hand it over."

"Ugh! Here! Hopefully, he doesn't call back while my boo thang is over tonight." Esmaé giggled.

"Girl, whatever! Here, Yana. Dial his number," Telaina demanded, while handing Iyana Esmaé's phone.

Iyana dialed the number, but it didn't even ring. Instead, it went straight to voicemail. Feeling defeated at the failure of her last-ditch effort, Iyana returned Esmaé's phone and plopped down in her desk chair.

"Aw naw, bitch! No, the fuck you don't!" Telaina rushed over to Iyana's desk and snatched tissues out the Kleenex dispenser as Iyana's eyes filled with tears. "Not here, Yana. Not here," she whispered as she squatted next to her and held her hand. Esmaé stood in front of Iyana's desk to block the view of their passing colleagues by the glass office doors.

"You listen to me," Esmaé scolded. "Don't you let a single tear fall in this building. You can yell, scream, cry, and holler all night once you leave the parking lot. Hell, go home and blast "Unbreak My Heart," "Officially Missing You," "Bended Knee," and "How Do I Live" all goddamned day and night if you want, but while you're in this building, you're fierce, you're in charge, and you're unbreakable. Don't you let these hounds in here sniff out any weakness."

"I... I..." Iyana stammered as she dabbed her eyes with the tissues Telaina handed her.

"Hey! No, ma'am! Not here! Not at all!" Telaina adamantly shook her head. "We'll talk about this shit after work if it's going to get you this upset because there's no way we're going to let anyone see you like this. We're already at a disadvantage, sis. We're women in a corporate office full of men. We're Black in a white-washed world. We could be one thousand-piece puzzles, but in here, we must always give the appearance we have it all together. These wolves can smell fear like it's blood, and they prey on the weak. Fix your face, sis."

"Put your earbuds in and play "Fu*k Dat Ni**a" by Quality Control a couple times," Esmaé suggested. "Put on some Beyonce or some Latto or some Megan and say fuck this shit until we clock out because this shit here," she mentioned, making a swishing motion at Iyana's watery eyes, "this shit is a hell naw, sis."

Dabbing her eyes one last time, Iyana took several deep breaths with her head tilted back, fighting back the tears to pull herself together.

"You good?" Telaina inquired.

"Yeah. Yeah. I'm good," Iyana assured her.

"Alright. We're going to get back to work before they come looking for us. We can't give them a reason to say we're not working," Esmaé grumbled.

"Happy Hour after work, sis," Telaina promised over her shoulder as she and Esmaé headed to the door. "We got you!" Iyana thanked them with a weak but genuine smile. "We got you!" Telaina repeated.

Iyana returned home that night wasted. Telaina and Esmaé fully intended to get her fucked up. Iyana rode with Telaina to Rock Box, where she drank Hello Kitties all night, sang Adele's "Someone Like You" three times, No Doubt's "Don't Speak" twice, and then went down their Heartbreak Playlist until neither Esmaé nor Telaina could take it anymore.

"I'll come up with you and make sure you get in safely," Telaina offered as she pulled into the garage.

"No, no. I'll be fine. I got muh keys an' muh gun," Iyana shooed her off.

"Gun? When did you get a gun?" Telaina drilled her.

"Shit. I wasn't s'posed tuh tell yuh that," Iyana slurred and hiccupped.

"You know what? I'll let this shit slide this one time, but you're going to answer some questions when I pick your ass up for work in the morning," Telaina assured her.

"Yeah, yeah. Good night," Iyana murmured and pressed the elevator button. She used the mirrored wall to hold her up and tripped over her own feet while exiting the elevator on her floor.

"Watch your muthafuckin' step, bitch!" she spun around and cursed the elevator door in slurred speech. Fumbling with her keys as she stumbled down the hallway, she nearly kicked over the bouquet of sunflowers left in front of her door.

"Ohhhh! They're so pretty!" she cooed as she stuck her key in the door. "Hold on a minute." She held up a finger at the flowers. "Let me go pee first, and then I'll bring y'all inside."

Tripping through the house to the bathroom, Iyana was so drunk she missed the toilet, which resulted in her inadvertently peeing in the tub. After knocking a lamp over onto the couch while trying to turn it on, she brought the vase into the house and placed it on the kitchen counter next to the summer flowers.

"Another card, huh? Yuh can send flowers but can't answer muh muhfuckin' phone calls?" she slurred.

I could never apologize enough. I'm so sorry. Please accept my apology.

"I ain't accepting shit!" she swore at the empty kitchen. "If I accept this shit, I'll accept anything!"

After dropping the card on the counter, she set the alarm on her phone and fell asleep laying across the bed, fully dressed with tears streaking her cheeks.

Chapter 27

"HE DID WHAT?" both Esmaé and Telaina shouted the next morning.

"I don't even want to talk about it." Iyana waved them off as she raised her coffee mug to her lips again while trying to maintain focus on her computer screen in her office. Telaina and Esmaé weren't helping the hangover she had been battling all morning by grilling and yelling at her.

"Naw, heffa! I know like hell you ain't just say that man sent you another bouquet!" Telaina was heated.

"After you ain't seen or heard from him all week?" Esmaé, on the other hand, was disgusted.

"If I know you, I know you've been calling his phone at least a half a dozen times a damn day," Telaina scoffed while shaking her head.

"Naw, it's been going straight to voicemail. He's either blocked me or turned his phone off," Iyana informed them, the dismay evident in her expression. "I've only called once or twice a day the last two days."

"Iyana, don't you call that man's phone anymore. I don't know what the fuck he's up to, but this shit ain't cool," Telaina ranted.

"It ain't cool at all! He's on some slick-ass fuck shit, and you're entirely too good for this shit," Esmaé seconded Telaina's stance.

"Y'all! Y'all, please! Please stop yelling. My head is killing me. Just go back to your desks before they realize you're missing. I'll be alright. It's Friday. Let's make it through the day. We can talk about this later," Iyana suggested dismissively.

"You heard what I said, Yana," Telaina warned her as she followed Esmaé to the door. "Don't call his punk ass no more!"

"Ssshhh! Laina, you gone cause a scene with all this yelling!" Esmaé warned her.

"Whatever. Just come on out her office so she can get some work done."

"Don't start gossiping about me behind my back, either," Iyana warned. "You heffas go do some work."

"Girl, please!" Esmaé smirked at her. "You know everything we say about you at our desks we're going to say to your face at dinner tonight. The gossip is just practice." She cackled and closed Iyana's door before she could respond.

"Flowers," Iyana mumbled to herself. "Fucking sunflowers. Deion, what the fuck are you up to?"

"I have no idea, Bria. This isn't like him at all. I mean, I don't know him *that* well, but from what I *do* know, he's not the type to play these kinds of games."

"I don't know, sis. It sounds to me like you got ghosted," Bria's voice filled the cabin of Iyana's car. Iyana called Celeste the moment she got in the car after work, but when Celeste didn't answer, she called Bria instead.

"But why? I mean, if I did or said something wrong, if I was too much or not enough, if he wasn't happy, he should've verbalized that instead of disappearing. I would've at least liked to know what I did wrong. Maybe it was a behavior that could've been corrected."

"Yana, you gotta stop with that bullshit. You done lost your damned mind. What is this mess about not being enough? You're young, Black, successful, independent, beautiful, and smart. What more could a nigga want from you? If anything, sis, you're too much, but you're always more than enough," Bria assured her.

"Maybe that's it. Maybe I was too much, and I scared him off," Iyana reasoned.

"I don't think that's the answer, either. Think about it. He's not gone. He's just not there. There's obviously something going on you're unaware of that he doesn't want you involved in. He's sending you the flowers and the apology notes because he doesn't want to lose you. He just doesn't want you involved in whatever he has going on right now," Bria concluded. Iyana turned into her apartment building's parking garage after swiping her card at the gate.

"I'm at a loss here, Bria. I don't know what's going on. I go through a dozen emotions a day dealing with this shit. I'm emotionally drained," Iyana sighed as she pulled into her usual parking space.

"I know, sis, but this is a decision you have to make for yourself. I can't even begin to give you advice on this one. You know me. I'm quick to cut a nigga off, especially if he ain't acting right. This type of shit he's pulling would get a nigga erased and replaced fucking with me, but you ain't like that. You don't let go so easily, and you're always willing to give a nigga the benefit of the doubt. Plus, this guy... he's not like the hood niggas I be fucking with or any of the other niggas you've been with in the past. He's clean cut, got his shit together, and I could tell dude truly likes you. He was noticeably into you. Shit, that's an understatement! He was doting on you and shit, waiting on you hand and foot, with his ole T.I. you-can-have-whatever-you-like ass," she chuckled.

"That's what I'm saying. That's why none of this makes sense," Iyana whined as she leaned back in her seat and stared at the ceiling of her car. Silence surrounded her as they both became lost in their own thoughts about Iyana's situation. "I'm home now, Bria. I'm just going to pour myself a glass of wine and sit in the tub for four hours before I go to bed."

"I don't know about four hours, but have at it, honey. If you hear from him, let me know. I'll fill Celeste in on the situation when she calls me after work this evening," Bria promised, before they disconnected. Retrieving her gun from the armrest, Iyana got out, locked the doors, and headed toward the elevator.

As she whisked down the row of cars fidgeting with her keys, she was momentarily blinded by headlights. She stopped in her tracks, immediately recognizing the car as the same Chevy Impala that spooked her the night she stumbled into Bryant. Her mind raced as the engine started, the tires squealed, and the car took off in her direction. She gasped as she realized the driver had clear intentions of running her over. Sticking her hand straight into her purse, she whipped out her .9 and aimed it shakily at the windshield of the quickly approaching car. Seeing the gun, the driver turned off just as Iyana fired a single shot. The bullet skipped across the trunk and lodged itself into the concrete wall. The Impala darted down the next row of cars and shot out of the parking garage.

"What the fuck?" Iyana heaved as she frantically glanced around her while putting her gun back in her purse. "What the fuck?"

Iyana lost most of her hope for Deion's return. The bouquets of flowers became more of a nuisance than a flattering gesture, especially on days like the Sunday she returned home with an armful of groceries. She struggled to find her door key while maneuvering around the vase, desperately trying not to knock it over as she attempted to get inside and sit down the grocery bags. Already frustrated and wishing she had help with the bags, the vase made Iyana's situation even worse.

Iyana was up late the next Saturday night, watching old episodes of *The PJs*, eating ice cream, and flipping through ads for puppies for sale, believing a new fur baby would help her battle the loneliness she experienced. *I'm not ready for kids,* she repeatedly thought as she stared at her reflection in the bathroom mirror a few days before. *I'm not even ready to try the dating pool again. My first leap into the waters, I drowned.* An unexpected knock at her door snapped her out of her paw pal web probe.

"Ugh! Just leave the damned thing at the door! I'll get it," she growled toward the door. When she took her time getting up and answering the door, another set of knocks rang out. "What? Do I have to sign for this one or something?"

Her voice trailed off when she snatched the door open in frustration, and her heart tumbled out of her chest and landed at her feet. Her lungs constricted as if they collapsed and shriveled like raisins.

"I didn't bring any paperwork with me, but I'm sure I can scrape up an invoice or something for you real quick."

Iyana stood in the doorway with her mouth agape, staring. If she wasn't in a terror-stricken paralysis, she may have passed out or even screamed. Her immediate reflex was to close the door, but when she moved to do so, a shoe stopped it.

"Iyana, please! I'm not here to hurt you. I just... I just... I need to talk to you," Bryan pleaded as he dropped his head, the two-strand twists he now wore instead of the high top fade hanging into his face, completely understanding her fear, ashamed he was the reason she felt that way.

"I don't give a damn what you came here for! How did you find me?" she barked at him.

Fear boiled over into burning rage as Iyana believed all those months of living in peace were flushed down the drain. Bryan accomplished an impossible feat. He tracked her across the country, managed to afford the trip, and even pinpointed her apartment building. Now, there he was at her door as if he was an invited guest.

"It's a long story." He chuckled nervously. "And an even longer journey. Just... please. Can I come in?"

"Come in? I don't want you here! I don't want you anywhere near me!" she shrieked.

"Yana, I... listen to me. I know I'm the last person on earth you want to see. I know this, but I owe you an explanation, an apology, and so much more. Can I come in for a second? I promise not to take long."

"Look, I don't want an explanation, and I don't need your fake-ass apologies. All I want right now, and all I've wanted since two months after the day I met you was for you to leave me the fuck alone. That's it, and that's all. I don't know why you felt the need to come across the country to insert yourself back into my life, but just like you found your way out here, crawl your piece-of-shit ass back into the hole you escaped from in Memphis."

"I deserve that, but I didn't come here to fight or bother you or make things any worse than I already have. I want to heal the hurt I caused. Please... just... just a few minutes. I won't be long. I promise," he begged, desperation in his eyes.

"Just come on, Bryan," Iyana huffed in frustration. Realizing Bryan was not going to leave, she stepped back and allowed him into her house, into her safe space, something she promised herself she would never do again. *Hopefully, the quicker I get this over with and he gets whatever he has to say off his chest, the quicker he'll get the fuck out of here,* she thought as he breezed past her into her living room.

Immediately annoyed by Bryan's presence, when Iyana turned around from closing the door behind him, she noticed his eyes inspecting, exploring, and examining her condo, and she instantly felt naked, exposed, and violated.

"What is it you're so desperate to say, Bryan?" she hissed as she stormed into the kitchen and took a seat on a bar stool at the island. "Make it quick."

"I see you got the flowers I sent you," he mentioned in a casual attempt to lighten the mood as he glanced around nervously with his hands deep in his pockets.

"You?" Iyana shrieked, taken aback. "You sent these?"

"Well, yeah. I mean, who else is going to... ohhh!" he chuckled cockily. "My bad. You must've thought these were from some nigga you've been getting down with, huh? Is that what it is? You fucking with somebody?"

"Yeah, well, no. I don't know. It's complicated."

"Naw, it's not. Either y'all together or you ain't. Ain't shit complicated about that."

"I was seeing somebody. I guess I'm not anymore. I actually assumed all these flowers were from him..." her voice trailed off as she briefly lost herself in her thoughts. She quickly snapped back and glared at Bryan. "Look, it ain't none of your business, anyway. Why are you here?" she demanded again.

"You look good," he offered nervously, while leaning back on his heels. "I love what you've done with your hair, and your skin is—"

"Cut the nice-ass bullshit, Bryan. It's late, I'm tired, and my patience is thin. I don't have shit to say to you at all, and I'm not too keen on listening to shit you have to say, either, so I suggest you make this quick before you waste a two-thousand-mile trip because, believe me, I'm *very* eager to get you back on the first thing smoking to Memphis and the fuck away from me."

"That's... understandable." He nodded awkwardly. "I get why you feel that way, and I can't say I blame you. Look, Yana. Straight up, I came to apologize for everything I've ever done to you. I was dead wrong for taking advantage of you, stealing from you, abusing you... Iyana, I'm sorry. I'm so sorry. I- I'm ashamed of myself and my actions, and I- I can't believe I treated you the way I did," he stuttered.

"I can," Iyana interrupted. "I can absolutely believe it. I lived it. I lived through it," she growled through gritted teeth, "and I moved past it. I moved past you. You and all your bullshit, your gaslighting, your manipulation, your lying, your cheating… I moved past all that shit. You came here to apologize? The best thing you could've done, and what you *should've* done, was leave me the fuck alone!"

"Iyana, please, please don't be like this."

"Be like what? Are you going to pay me back all the money you stole from me? Are you going to take back all the fear and distrust you dumped on my doorstep when you repeatedly abused me? Are you going to give me back the dignity you embezzled from me when you raped me? *You raped me!* Are you going to refund all the time I wasted on you? *Are you?* I didn't think so. You don't have anything to say that I want to hear. An apology?" she scoffed. "You would've done better coming here with a check in your hand. At least I wouldn't feel like such a cheap fucking joke. You need to go. Get out, Bryan."

"But, Iyana, I wasn't—"

"I don't care! I swear I don't! I don't give a fuck! You need to leave," she repeated as she rose from the barstool and showed him the front door.

"I… ummm… I'm in town for a while," he informed her as he slowly approached the door. "I'd love to treat you to dinner so we can talk once you've had a chance to calm down," he offered. Pulling a card from his pocket and handing it to her, he continued, "Here's my number. Call me, and we'll set up a day and time."

When Iyana remained unbudged at the door with one hand on the knob and the other on her hip, Bryan laid the card next to the lamp on the side table by the door and sauntered out.

"Iyana, I—" he turned to speak, but she swiftly slammed the door in his face. Every single lock on the door clicked and clanked as he stood outside the door.

Fully expecting her to give him an extremely difficult time, Bryan came prepared for the cold welcome he received. After everything he did to her and put her through, Bryan was willing to put in the necessary work to prove he was a completely changed man. Releasing a heavy sigh as he pushed the elevator button, Bryan began formulating a plan to win back Iyana's heart.

Chapter 28

"IYANA, YOU SHOULD CALL THE COPS!" Celeste shrieked into the phone three days later, after Iyana informed her of her unexpected visitor.

"Call them for what?" Iyana challenged as she lay under a blanket on her living room sofa.

"To file a report!"

"A report for what? What am I reporting, Celeste? The nigga didn't do anything illegal. He didn't break into my apartment or anything," Iyana grumbled dismissively.

"The motherfucker drove across the country to find you! He's fucking stalking you, Yana!"

Celeste was both livid and terrified for her best friend. After being front and center for their shit show of a relationship, Celeste was proud of Iyana for moving away, moving past her trauma, and moving on with her life. She also knew the last thing Iyana needed was Bryan's return to her life at a moment when things with Deion were so uncertain.

Iyana waited three days before telling Celeste about the encounter, determined not to freak her out. The truth was, Iyana was equally as freaked out about the situation as she knew Celeste would've been if she hadn't downplayed it. Since moving to Seattle, she found the perfect little hiding spot where she was comfortable and could be herself. Bryan's discovery of her safe place left Iyana feeling naked and desperate for cover.

"He's not stalking me, Leste," Iyana disregarded her concern. "He came here to apologize."

"I don't believe that bullshit for one second, Iyana. That slimy motherfucker hunted you down because he wants something for you. He's a controlling, manipulative, conniving sociopath. He can't handle being broken up with. He has to be the one in control at all times. He ran your relationship with him like a dictatorship. You had no say-so in anything, so how dare you break up with him? How dare you pack up and move across the country without his permission?"

"Celeste—"

"No, Yana! I'm telling you! Mark my words! That motherfucker wants something! As hard as he worked to drill it into your head that you needed him, *he* was actually the one who needed *you*. You *never* needed him. Never. Need him for what? What did you need him for other than dick? Not a damn thing! You're being way too calm about this situation. If it were me, I would've put a bullet in his bitch ass and called the police to come scrape his ass up off my living room floor, and that's on periodt!"

"Celeste, I'm not getting back involved with this guy. I let him say what he had to say, and he left. All I wanted him to do was leave. Hopefully, I'll never hear from his ass again."

"Let's pray that's the case, Yana, because you know if I have to come all the way up there to see about you, I ain't coming to do no talking, bitch! I'm blowing me a nigga's ass smooth off," Celeste warned her.

"I know, Leste. I know. Look, let me call you back. Okay? I ordered food from the Thai restaurant a couple doors down, and it should be ready now."

"Okay, just... take your gun and call me if anything happens. One call, and I'm on the next thing with wings, bitch. Plane, helicopter, maxi pad, Canadian geese. Bitch, I'm coming."

"Canadian... Celeste, get yo' ass off my phone, mane!" Iyana howled. "I'll call you after work tomorrow."

Iyana threw on her burgundy pea coat over the plum peplum dress she wore to work. Zipping her boots up the back of her calf muscles, she slung her chain wallet purse over her shoulders, tucked her gun down inside, and headed to the elevator.

She decided to walk the two blocks to pick up her food. Spring in Seattle yielded a breath-taking natural beauty. The air was crisp and refreshing, perfect for Iyana, who wanted to clear her head. Stepping out the front door of her building, Iyana inhaled the fresh night air deeply. The low hum of downtown traffic was barely loud enough to be noticed, but still quiet enough to be calming. A young couple passed her on the opposite side of the street, chuckling, holding hands, and completely in love. Iyana sighed as she remembered the feeling of anticipating happily ever after. The butterflies, the smiles, the comfort, the happiness, the calmness she found in true love. She realized exactly how much she missed that companionship, and the authentic desire to be in the presence of someone she adored.

I loved him, didn't I? she pondered. *I really loved him. I was so happy with him. I can't imagine what happened, and I may never know. I just know I miss him. I've missed him longer than I've even known him.*

"Ahhh! Back again? This pad king for you again?" The restaurant owner giggled as Iyana's entrance was announced by the bell hanging from the door. The short, elderly woman shuffled to the row of bagged plates to retrieve Iyana's usual order, her smile pulling her wrinkled eyes tight.

"Yes, ma'am, Mrs. Chen. How are you?" Iyana grinned as she exchanged the twenty-dollar-bill in her right hand for the bag with her left.

"Oooh, I can complain. It do no good, anyway. You know?" She smiled. "You look trouble. You okay?"

"Mehh. I'll be okay. Just going through the motions."

"Motions? Wrong motion make baby," she warned. "You be careful who you go through motion with."

"That's true. That's true." Iyana giggled. "Thank you, Mrs. Chen. See you later."

Still allowing her mind to wander off, Iyana conquered half a block before a familiar voice called her name from across the street. She turned to see Bryan flagging her down as he jogged across the street to meet her.

"Iyana," he huffed when he caught up to her.

"What do you want, Bryan?" she scowled as she increased her pace, her attitude obvious. "What are you doing? Following me, stalking me now?"

"No, no. I was having a cup of coffee at the shop over there and saw you walk past," he clarified with a smile.

"Coffee? At a coffee shop?" she scoffed. "Nigga, you don't know shit about coffee shop etiquette."

"You're right. I don't, but I'm learning," he humbly agreed, causing Iyana to cut her eyes at him. *Learning? At one point, you couldn't tell this nigga shit. Now, all of a sudden, he acknowledges he doesn't know it all. Aw, okay then.*

"You- you didn't call," he mentioned when she didn't respond to his statement.

"Did you expect me to? I told you I have nothing to say to you. I meant that. I let you say what you had to say, and I listened while you talked, but nothing has changed. I still don't want anything to do with you."

"Yana, I just want a chance to fully explain. I've changed so much since you last saw me. I'm not the same person, I swear to you. I just want the opportunity to show you that," he pleaded as they reached the front door of Iyana's building. Hands stuffed deep in the pockets of his own pea coat, Bryan's face was painted with desperation.

"You're standing here talking about chances as if I haven't already given you too many. You've blown enough chances and wasted enough of my time. You don't deserve even one more, and I certainly don't owe you any," she reminded him.

"You're right. You're absolutely right," he agreed with an understanding nod. "I'm completely at your mercy. Just... please... can we have dinner or something one night? Sit down somewhere and talk? At least let me explain and try to make things right."

Iyana glanced down both ends of the street while considering his request. *Companionship, love, sex,* her mind repeated three times before she turned back to Bryan and answered, "No."

She turned and whisked into the building, leaving Bryan standing on the curb, attempting to speak but unable to formulate his words.

"Fuck love," she stated aloud as the elevator doors closed, and she ascended back to her safe place, happily alone and content with being unaccompanied.

Chapter 29

AS A PART of her new self-care ritual, Iyana was enjoying dinner alone two days later at a restaurant several blocks from her apartment. She sipped her cognac and Coke while waiting for the chef to finish preparing her meal of locally caught sturgeon with a mushroom and thyme reduction, rice pilaf, and lemon butter broccolini. The day had been long, the week even longer. Telaina and Esmaé were both preoccupied for the evening with their respective beaus, so Iyana resolved to spend her Friday night having dinner and a drink alone. Afterward, she would return home to bathe and crawl into bed for at least twelve hours before getting up for no reason other than to empty her bladder. Always the perfect date, even when only to herself, she silenced her phone and tucked it in her purse with the intention of speaking to no one other than her waiter the rest of the evening.

As she placed her glass back on the table, someone unexpectedly slipped into the seat across from her in her booth. Iyana stared at Bryan's wide smile with an unwavering scowl. No longer annoyed at his presence or angry about his persistence, Iyana was pissed that despite her refusal to initiate contact with him and her clear statements that she wanted nothing more to do with him, Bryan was nearly forcing her to deal with him.

"Get out my booth, Bryan," she hissed through gritted teeth.

"Damn, baby! I can't even get a hey, how are you doing?" he joked, still smiling despite her display of animosity.

"No, you can't. Do you know why? Because I don't care how you're doing. I don't care about anything that involves you. I want you to leave me alone and stop harassing me and trying to force yourself on me. I want you to get up from my table, and when you exit that door, I want you to leave town and never contact me again. That's it. I want you to disa-fucking-ppear!"

"What? Like you did?" he poked sarcastically.

"Exactly like I did," she encouraged him with an exaggerated nod and grin. "That's exactly what I want."

"If all you wanted was for me to leave, you could've had that wish fulfilled a week ago. All I'm asking is to sit down and have a talk with you. If you still want me to go afterward, I'll leave. I could've been gone days ago if you only called me and had dinner with me like I asked."

"When will you get it through your head? What will it take for you to understand? I don't want to have dinner with you, I don't want to be seen with you, and I don't have anything to say to you."

"Here you go, ma'am." The waiter returned and placed her plate in front of her. "Oh! I was unaware you would have someone joining you. Are you ready to order, sir?" he greeted Bryan as he removed a small tablet from his apron pocket.

"Actually, he was just—" Iyana began, but Bryan interrupted her.

"Of course. I'll have the filet mignon, fully loaded baked potato, and buttered asparagus," he ordered. The waiter hurriedly entered the order and left the table.

"How dare you?" Iyana was outraged. "You've got some nerve! I'm not paying for your food. You should either cancel that order or get ready to wash dishes because not a single penny of my money will ever be spent on you ever again."

"I'm going to eat, drink, and be merry, just like you," he informed her.

"Well, you need to do that at your own table. Preferably at a different restaurant, but on the other side of this one will do."

"I can't talk to you from over there."

"I don't want you to talk to me at all! Why can't you understand that? I've told you several times to leave me the fuck alone. I don't want anything to do with you. You're trying to force me to deal with you. You can't insert yourself back into my life. That door has closed. That ship has sailed. I've already explained this to you. It should've been obvious. I moved all the way up here from Memphis and told you nothing at all. Clearly, I tried to leave you and everything that came with you behind."

"And I deserved that," he agreed in a quiet tone she had never known him to use and with a patience she had never known him to have. "I'm not the same person I used to be, Iyana. I... I've been through hell since you've been gone, and it's opened my eyes to how badly mistreated you. I owe you so much more than an apology. You deserve to be treated right, wined and dined, loved and made love to. At the absolute least, I need to heal the damage I've done to you. I need to take it all back. I need a do-over. I want the chance to do right by you, to give you the love you deserve, to treat you with respect. I know I don't deserve anymore chances—"

"No, you absolutely don't. You've already used up all your chances, and the next man's, too."

"I'm aware of that. I've made it easy for the next man to come in and be a better man than I was. I set the bar ridiculously low. I've also been such a bad boyfriend. I'm sure you're going to give any nigga who tries to date you pure hell. He'll have to work for and earn every damn thing from you at this point."

Iyana fought her face's tendency to reveal her thoughts as she peered at Bryan and tried to figure out who he was. Her conscience tugged at her heartstrings a bit, causing her to wonder if she should at least hear him out. After all, he had driven over two thousand miles to find her. *He can't force me to get involved in anything I don't want to be involved in anymore,* she assured herself. *He can't make me tolerate him or deal with him. The least I can do is give him the punishment he's asking for by making him start completely over.*

"Yes, and why should you be any different?" she questioned him. "You say you've changed and you're a whole new person now. Well, you're going to have to work and earn everything, like the next man. I don't know you. I don't know anything about you, right? I'm going to treat you as such. You're a stranger to me," she stated as she glared at him. "I'm going to give you this one blind date, this one conversation. After that, please respect my space. If I choose not to ever speak to you again, please respect that."

"That's fair. I can respect that," he stated as he nodded. "Let's treat this like a meet and greet so you can get to know me. I'll tell you all about myself, especially the things you don't know, and you can decide whether you want to continue to see me after you've heard what I have to say."

"Bryan, I—"

"No. Nope," he cut her off. "We're already here now. You might as well get it over with. Don't worry about the check. I have more than enough money to cover your food and mine."

Iyana entered her condo, hung her keys on the hook by the door, locked all the locks, and clicked on the side table lamp when she arrived home from dinner.

"Home sweet home," she whispered as she kicked off her shoes, picked them up, and headed to her master bathroom.

She undressed while sitting on the side of the tub while running herself a hot bath. Bubbles formed as she mulled over everything Bryan revealed to her at dinner.

"I should have let him speak before now," she scolded herself aloud as she slipped into the tub. "I've been so mean to him when he went through so much to try to find me."

As she soaked in the steamy, bubbly water, she recalled Bryan's story. After going to Zaria's house to retrieve the last of his belongings, Bryan realized she threw away all his clothes and found himself fighting her off him. Iyana thought about Bryan's living arrangement with Serita, the woman she caught him in her bed with, and how Serita had allowed him to become a father figure to her children before she put him out the house to move in another man. She mulled over the business Bryan started and how well it must've been doing before Serita stole all his money and tased him when he tried to retrieve it. Her mind wondered about Raelyn's real intentions with Bryan when she moved in with him but insisted on not being in a relationship. It was amazing to Iyana that Bryan opened his home up to her, and she stole, pawned, and sold all his valuables.

Iyana sipped a glass of wine as all Bryan's stories replayed themselves in her head, her guilt growing as she pondered. *How could I have been so mean to him without hearing him out first? How could I have treated him as if he never meant anything to me?*

She thought, re-thought, and over-thought the entire situation. The extensive detail and description Bryan had gone into leading her to never once even consider his stories could have been the lies they were. Even Bryan's story about tracking her down was completely fictitious. In fact, Bryan committed some seriously foul deeds to find Iyana and to accumulate enough money to pursue her.

The truth was, when they were together, Bryan often dropped Iyana off at work and borrowed her car while his own car needed repairs. Amid doing so, Bryan became unusually acquainted with the same supervisor, who informed Iyana of her offer of promotion and relocation in the most inappropriate ways. Unable to find Iyana on his own, he received the news of Iyana's new whereabouts during pillow talk one night a few months after Iyana disappeared, not by endless hours of tireless research and searching, as he claimed.

Armed with that information, money he stole from both Serita and his uncle Marlowe's sock drawer, money he was paid for electronics and jewelry he pawned after breaking into Raelyn's house, and money he scammed various unsuspecting women out of or stole out their purses, Bryan sold his Maxima and bought another car. Then he casually cruised across the country to Seattle, where he paid for a room at a decent hotel. Using the phone book from the room's nightstand, he was able to find the address for Iyana's job. He watched the entrance of her building's parking garage from a window seat at a coffee shop, searching for Iyana driving one of the vehicles coming and going from the building.

Five days into his stakeout, Bryan spotted Iyana pulling into the parking garage in her brand-new Audi RS Q8 twenty minutes before the usual morning rush. He jotted down her car's tag number, make, and model, noted the car's midnight blue color, and returned to his room where he slept the rest of that Friday. He decided to explore the city to sightsee that Saturday and Sunday, and mid-day Monday, he took up post in his car, following Iyana to her apartment building when she finally exited the parking garage after work.

In the tub's hot water, she considered what Bryan went through, but she was unaware what she actually understood was a bunch of lies Bryan manufactured, a group of untruthful stories he concocted solely to get back in Iyana's good graces by soliciting her sympathy. He manipulated her as he always did, despite having intentions to treat her right.

Chapter 30

"I'M TELLING y'all he's a completely different person," Iyana tried to convince Telaina and Esmaé as their waitress brought their drinks to the table.

"Iyana, I wouldn't give two shits if he pulled a John Travolta and Nicholas Cage and swapped fucking faces! You should *not* be dealing with this dude at all! You need to call the police about him stalking you, not having dinner with him." Telaina nearly shouted at her, outraged Iyana had hidden the fact that she seen and spoken to Bryan from the two of them.

"Telaina, I'm telling you I'm fine," Iyana insisted.

"You are not fine! You've lost your damned mind! Do Bria and Celeste know about this?" Telaina pressed.

"I told Celeste about him showing up at my apartment, so I'm sure she's told Bria."

"But you haven't told them about the other night?" Esmaé grilled her as Iyana sipped her second Hey Ya instead of tossing it back like the shot it was. The three of them were enjoying Happy Hour at Rock Box after work the Wednesday evening, following Bryan's intrusion on Iyana's dinner.

"No," Iyana admitted.

"Because you know they'd fucking flip!" Telaina concluded.

"What was I supposed to do, Laina? I was in a public place, and you know I hate causing a scene."

"Get up and leave! Leave his ass with the bill! He can pay it since he insisted on sitting his ass at your table and interrupting your dinner. You definitely weren't supposed to sit there and listen to his sob stories. You aren't obligated to listen to a damn word he has to say. Fuck him! Piece-of-shit-ass nigga! Ugh! I fucking hate him!" Telaina growled while tossing back the last of her third Smokestack Lightening.

"Laina, please calm down," Iyana quietly urged her.

"Calm down? Man, Yana, this dude has taken you through hell and high water. You finally got rid of his ass, and now he's popping back up to do it all over again. I don't care what happened to him since you've been up here. He doesn't deserve anymore chances. It doesn't matter what Deion has going on. You don't back track for no nigga you were just running from!"

"I wasn't running from him," Iyana denied.

"The hell you weren't!" Esmaé jumped in. "You said yourself you were already searching for a way to break up with him, and moving here was your way out and your ticket away from him. Don't try to take that shit back, Yana. Stay true to those ill feelings and hold on to those bad memories. They'll keep you grounded and help you wise up. Remember how he made you feel and that you never want to feel like that again, and don't let him force you to deal with him or his presence because you're not obligated to."

"I'm being cautious, Esmaé. I won't let him treat me the way he did before. If I see any signs of things going down that road, I'll cut ties with him," Iyana assured them.

"There shouldn't be any ties to cut, Iyana," Telaina mumbled as she shook her head in disbelief. "I don't understand why you're even entertaining this motherfucker. If it were me, I wouldn't be cutting ties. I'd be cutting his damn throat!"

"Shit, I'd be cutting that nigga's dick off and shoving it down his throat," Esmaé agreed.

"Y'all..." Iyana sighed exasperatedly.

"Naw, Yana, I get it. I know we're getting on your nerves," Telaina cut her off, "but I promise you it's only because we love you, and we're concerned. We don't trust this nigga. I know he says he only has the best intentions, and I know there's history there, and you want to believe him. All I'm saying is he sounds like a snake oil salesman to me, and I ain't buying his bullshit."

"I can appreciate the concern you guys are expressing about my wellbeing," Iyana assured them as she dipped a chip in the yuzu salsa the trio shared. "I really want y'all to trust me to make the right decisions for myself."

"We do, Yana," Esmaé promised. "Ultimately, we can't make any decisions for you. You're grown. You're going to do what you want to do, anyway, and there ain't a damned thing we can do to stop you. What kind of friends would we be if we didn't speak up when we recognize something that promises to be detrimental to you, though? A real friend would tell you the truth, even when they know you won't want to hear what they're saying. I'll always tell you the truth, Yana, and so will Telaina."

"Yeah, bitch." Telaina nodded in agreement. "I ain't Willy Wonka. I ain't sugar-coating shit for your ass. Sometimes the harsh truth is exactly what you need to wake your ass up from whatever dream you're sleeping through."

"I'm not asleep right now, Laina. On the contrary, my eyes are wide open. Believe me, this nigga ain't picking up where we left off and moving on like nothing happened. He's going to have to prove himself every second of every day, and he'll have to earn everything. He's not even starting out with the benefit of the doubt. I still don't trust him, but I heard him out the other night, and I could see the difference and sense the change in him."

"Alright, Yana. Alright. What song are you singing first?" Esmaé changed the subject. "'Reunited' by Peaches and Herb?"

Bryan spent the next month wining and dining Iyana, relentlessly showing her the man he had become. When she was hesitant, he was patient. When she wasn't as trusting as he hoped she would be, he understood. He encouraged her to be open and honest about her feelings and her fears. He listened more than he spoke during their conversations. He tried to be everything she always needed, everything he never was for her.

"Same time, same place next Saturday?" he confirmed as he returned Iyana to her apartment building after dinner and a movie a month after their first dinner.

"Ummm... well, my lease is up on my apartment, so I'm moving this week," she explained.

"Oh, okay."

"I'll send you the address, so you'll know where to pick me up."

"You need help moving?" he offered.

"No, I've got it under control."

"You sure?"

"Yeah, yeah. I've got everything already lined up."

"Okay, well, send me the address when you get a chance, and let me know if there's any place in particular you want to go next weekend," Bryan reminded her as he kissed her hand. Iyana smiled and nodded before heading inside to the elevator.

Chapter 31

SHE STRUGGLED to catch her breath as she collapsed onto the pillows piled on the floor, doubled over in laughter, Bryan on her back, still frantically fingering her most ticklish places.

"Okay! Okay!" Her pearly whites gleamed in the empty room's bright lighting reflecting off the eggshell painted walls as she surrendered.

Bryan finally showed her some mercy and rolled over to lie next to her on the plush carpet, smiling just as widely as Iyana released a relieved sigh, but when he gazed into her face, Iyana wasn't there. She appeared to be spaced out, her mind transporting her to another place and time, one they both ran from long ago. It was evident in her expression. The pain of that era of their lives, pain caused mostly by himself, was prevalent in her eyes.

Her eyes. Those big, alluring round eyes that had always gazed at him with so much adoration and understanding, even when he wasn't deserving of their grace. He didn't deserve her, and he knew it. Neither did he deserve the second chance she gifted him, and that made him appreciate it even more. He knew he wouldn't lose her again. This him, the new him, couldn't lose her again, and so, he was determined he wouldn't.

Her smile became his trophy, his only goal, and his sole focus. He had just extracted from her a joyous round of laughter after a long night of cute smirks and warm glances, intertwined fingers and locked elbows. He was in a heaven he had never known with a woman he had almost always known, and he didn't want the night to end. Desiring to pull her back into the present and rid her of the thoughts of things that no longer existed, he thinned out the air, thickened by the absence of her consciousness by inserting a simple question into the silence.

"What's wrong, babe?"

The wide smile on his face couldn't have contradicted his question more if it tried. Iyana shook her head as if to both shake the memories out of her head and deny there was anything bothering her.

"I'm just..." she hesitated, not wanting to kill the evening's vibe with her hidden truth. Peering into Bryan's eyes as they awaited her answer, encouraging her to be honest, assuring her she could, Iyana took a deep breath and finished her confession. "I'm scared."

"Scared? Scared of what?" he frowned as he sat up on one elbow, palm pressed against the side of his own head. He moved closer to her and placed his free hand on her folded legs.

Iyana stared at her manicured fingers folded in her lap as she perched on the throne of pillows. When her eyes returned to meet his, there were pools in the wells that may as well have been as deep as the Pacific and as blue as the waves off the coast of Tahiti because they made Bryan's heart drop just the same.

"This. Us. What we've become. Who we used to be." She shrugged.

"What'd I tell you? Huh?" he quizzed her as he grabbed her hand and held it tight. "What did I tell you? I'm never going back to who I used to be. I ain't that nigga no more, Yana."

She gazed back up at him as tears streamed down her cheeks. His expression was reassuring, and his eyes were sincere. He himself was a breath of fresh air. She exhaled deeply and nodded at him in under-standing, assuring him she believed him. He gave her another ques-tioning glance, to which she responded with another nod of confirmation and a teary smile.

"Come here," he whispered as he pulled her to himself and wrapped his arms around her. "I love you, babe. I love you. Right now, that means more to me than it ever has. You mean more to me than you could ever know, Iyana." He rocked her gently as she cried softly into his chest, releasing one last cry. When she pulled away to wipe her face, he inquired, "Are you okay?" She simply nodded, and Bryan grabbed his shirt off the floor behind him to dab her eyes. Locking eyes with him as he gently dabbed the tears on her cheeks, Iyana searched for remnants of the man he once was. His gentleness and sensuality were new. His compassion and understanding were refreshing. Her fingers graced his hand, and she pressed her cheek into his palm, finding a level of comfort with him she never had. The silence between them was deafening and stated everything they didn't. Their lips greeted each other as old friends, and she welcomed the embrace of a man she never believed to be capable of that type of love.

***

"What has it been? Like two or three months? Everything still okay?" Telaina questioned Iyana as she tried to recall how long it had been since Bryan popped back into Iyana's life.

"Yeah, I mean I have no complaints at all," Iyana shrugged and smiled as she sipped her daiquiri with her feet propped up on her living room coffee table.

"I was sure he would've fucked up by now and gone back to his old self," Telaina gushed as she sipped her own daiquiri Esmaé had mixed for them.

"Yeah, but after he bought her all that stuff for her birthday, I could tell she was extra flattered. She's all smitten and shit now," Esmaé, who sat on Iyana's right on the sofa, leaned forward to glimpse past Iyana and smirk at Telaina.

"I'm just enjoying the ride." Iyana giggled. "He's got some debts to pay to society, so I'm just sitting back and collecting."

"You're a bill collector now?" Esmaé joked.

"Damn right! Pay me, motherfucker!" Iyana cackled again. "Shit, I spent enough time and money on his ass in Memphis. It feels good to get some of that back."

"Yeah, but are you getting some, too?" Telaina inquired with a raised brow.

"Girl, naw!" Iyana sighed as she picked up the remote and flipped through the channels on the TV mounted to her living room wall. "I'm stringing that out as far as I can. I have to be able to fully trust him first."

"Fully trust him? I don't even know what that is with this nigga. I mean, will you ever be able to truly trust him after everything he put you through?" Esmaé wondered.

"It's possible," Iyana answered, the uncertainty clear in her voice. "It's going to take a while, though."

"What are you doing about dick in the meantime?" Telaina inquired.

"Girl, please!" Esmaé howled. "We both know what she's doing about dick! Not a damn thing!"

"Man, Yana, you have to quit mistreating yourself like that. You and that nigga ain't together, and you don't owe him shit, including loyalty. You better handle that shit."

"Handle it the same way that nigga handled it when y'all were together," Esmaé scoffed.

"Would y'all stop?" Iyana chuckled at them. "Y'all know I'm not about to do that. Mind y'all own nosey-ass business and let me worry about my own dick-tuation."

Chapter 32

IYANA LAY in bed in her new condo, thinking late at night two weeks later as a gorgeous news anchor read off the various stories of the happenings in the Seattle area. She texted Bryan, who returned to Memphis two days before to visit his mother in the hospital and planned to be gone at least another week.

I just don't understand why you couldn't have just spoken up when you saw me instead of scaring me half to death, she referred to the previous incidents of him speeding through the parking garage at her last apartment building.

I wasn't ready to approach you yet, and I was sure you'd be afraid and startled by my presence. A parking garage is a creepy place to approach someone you haven't seen in a year, especially when you're quite sure they never wanted to see you again, he replied.

Yes, but almost running me over didn't help the situation.

Almost shooting me didn't help, either.

She was in the middle of typing a joking retort when her doorbell rang. Nearly forgetting she ordered a pizza, Iyana jumped up and rushed to the door.

"Sorry it took me so long. I had almost for—" Iyana apologized as she opened the door, but her voice trailed off as she stood there in shock and disbelief.

"Yana," Deion greeted her with a bouquet of lilies and a nervous smile. "Hey."

Silence filled the space between them as Deion awaited a response, unsure of how he would be received. With her mouth agape, Iyana examined his navy-blue tailored suit and Italian dress shoes as he wore his uncertainty on his face.

"Hey?" she frowned. "Hey? You've been missing for months! You disappeared without a trace, weren't answering your phone, weren't at your house. You ghost me and show up here months later and all you have to say is *hey*?" she ranted as she snatched the flowers he offered her. "I could slap your eyes out right now, Deion! I could, and I should choke you out! I could murder you right where you stand!"

"Iyana, I'm sorry! Please let me explain! I- I didn't ghost you. I—"

"You didn't ghost me? What do you call it then?"

"Iyana, I- can I please come in? Please?"

As furious as she was, Iyana was still powerless against Deion's charming smile. Memories of how quickly her feelings had developed for him flooded her mind, and she surrendered and allowed him to step inside. Taking a seat on her new sofa, Deion surveyed the unfamiliar living room. When Iyana faced him after locking the door, he lightly patted the spot on the sofa next to him for her to have a seat.

"It's like I've seen a ghost." Iyana sighed quietly as her senses returned, and she became overcome with a sense of relief.

"I very nearly was a ghost indeed." Deion chuckled.

"Where have you been, Deion? What happened?" she demanded with tears in her eyes.

"It's such a long story, but I'll make it as short as I can," he promised. Taking her hand in his own, he heaved a heavy sigh while trying to decide where to begin. "Yana, I didn't ghost you, baby. I'd never do that to you or us. I've been in the hospital in a coma," he revealed, causing Iyana to gasp.

"A coma? Since when? How long? What happened?" she bombarded him with questions.

"Calm down," he whispered, while caressing her hand. "Do you remember the night we last saw each other? When I trailed you home after dinner with your friends?"

"Of course," Iyana nodded. "How could I forget?"

"When I pulled out of the parking garage, I headed home. About two blocks down the street, I realized I was being followed. This car came out of nowhere and drove dangerously close to my bumper. I just assumed I was driving too slowly for their liking, so I sped up as I got onto I-5, but they kept tailgating me. Eventually, they acted like they were about to go around, but instead, they swerved into the side of my car and pushed me into the side of a tractor trailer. My car spun out, hit the concrete barrier, and flipped into oncoming traffic. I was already unconscious by that point, but I was hit by two more cars. They used the Jaws of Life to get me out the car, which was a crumpled sardine can. When they airlifted me to Harborview, I was barely alive. The doctors put me in a medically induced coma. I've had several surgeries to repair broken bones, hence the limp," he chuckled. "Luckily, I'm a quick healer. I'm not a hundred percent yet, but I was well enough to be released from the hospital. When I got out, I didn't have a phone, and I couldn't remember your number. My landlord filed eviction proceedings while I was in the hospital, so I had nowhere to go. I'm literally starting over. Luckily, someone notified my boss, and I still have my job. When I went by your apartment, you had moved. It took forever for me to track you down, Iyana, but I finally found you. I found you." He gave her a relieved and teary smile.

"Oh my God, Deion!" Iyana whispered with her hands over her mouth in disbelief.

"I know it's a bit much," he acknowledged as he stared at his own hands. "I can only imagine how badly you've cursed my name since I've been missing, but just know I'm so, so sorry, Iyana. I'd never disappear on you."

"Deion, I—"

"It's okay, baby. I know you're in shock."

"I am. This is... this is a lot. I'm so sorry I was mad at you," she apologized.

"There's no need for that. I expected no less. You didn't know. There was no way you could've known. For all you knew, I could've been another trifling nigga doing what trifling niggas do."

"But still..."

"No, no. I'm here now, and I plan to make up for all our lost time."

"I just can't believe—"

"I know, I know. Hell, I can't believe someone in a damned Impala had the nerve to run my damned G-Wagon off the road," he chuckled as Iyana's phone sounded with three text messages. She picked up the phone and then glared at Deion with a frown.

"A what?" she questioned.

"A black Chevy Impala with dark tinted windows," Deion clarified. "Old-ass piece of shit."

Iyana fell silent as she leered at her phone and recalled the dent in the front driver's side bumper of Bryan's car with the freshly missing paint. *He tried to kill him,* she thought. *This motherfucker saw me with Deion in the parking garage. He tried to run me over, and when he pulled out the garage, he tried to kill Deion. This is insane! All that shit he was talking about being a changed man. He's still the same lying, conniving, self-serving asshole he's always been.*

"Helloooo! Earth to Iyana! You in there?" Deion waved his hand in front of her face.

"Yeah, yeah." She snapped back to the present. "I'm just glad you're here now, alive, and still just as handsome." She grinned, her renewed adoration for him evident in her eyes.

"I'm here, baby, and I'm not going anywhere ever again."

"Yana, baby, I've been calling and texting you all week. What's wrong with your pho—" Bryan queried as he used the key to Iyana's apartment he made without her permission to open the door and walk right inside, but what he found stopped him in his tracks.

"Bryan Kimbrough?"

Bryan turned to run back out of the empty apartment but ran straight into the chests of two uniformed police officers standing behind him in the doorway.

"You're under arrest, Mr. Kimbrough," one of the three officers awaiting him inside the apartment stated.

"For what?" Bryan demanded as he backed away from them.

"Here in Seattle, you're being charged with stalking, attempted vehicular homicide, aggravated vehicular assault, fleeing the scene of an accident, and most recently, trespassing and burglary," the officer informed him as he waved at the door Bryan had just opened. "However, I'm sure the great folks of Tennessee will be pleased to have you extradited back to Memphis for the several cases of aggravated assault, aggravated rape, breaking and entering, burglary, theft, possession of narcotics, possession of stolen goods, domestic assault, and attempted murder you're facing there as well. You see, it seems you've been getting away with shit for a long time, Mr. Kimbrough, and your victims will finally be able to sleep at night knowing you're paying for what you've done to them. Some of these charges are over a year old, but there's only so long you can run from the scales of justice. It appears you've run to the wrong place, and your time has run out. You visited the wrong victim this time, and she refuses to be a victim anymore. Let's go!"

"Hell naw! Where's Yana?" Bryan demanded as he attempted to

fight the officer, who was trying to handcuff him. "Y'all got me fucked up! Where the fuck is Yana? Yana! Yanaaaa!" he yelled. "Is she back there in the bedroom? I know she's back there. You hear me?" he bellowed again. "I know you're back there, bitch! Come out here and face me!"

"Mr. Kimbrough... Mr. Kimbrough!" the officer who explained Bryan's charges shouted. "She's not here. I suggest you calm down and allow these gentlemen to cuff you, so we won't have to add a resisting arrest charge to the list."

"I don't give a fuck! Fuck you and your suggestions, bitch-ass nigga! Fucking pig!" Bryan spat. "I know she's back there. Yanaaaa! Yanaaaa! I'mma kill you, bitch! You hear me? I'mma shelf your ass, bitch! You hear me? Huh? I'mma shelf you like a fucking urn, bitch! Ashes to ashes!"

"Mr. Kimbrough! Unless you want me to add these threats you're making and your insistence on making these officers' jobs hard by refusing to go in cuffs to the grocery store receipt of charges you already have, I highly recommend you close your mouth, put your hands behind your back, and accompany us to the car quietly. That's only if you aren't too keen on having fifty thousand volts shoot through you like a skewer. If you're fine with being a kabob, keep on moving around and resisting arrest. We've got more prongs than an elementary school folder," the officer warned again and then stepped so close to Bryan's face he could smell the hot Cheetos on his breath. "Try me, nigga," he growled in a low whisper.

"You have the right to remain silent..." the officer behind Bryan recited as he cuffed him and escorted him out the apartment.

Epilogue

"ALL I WANT to do is lay here up under you. I don't even want to move." Iyana sighed as she rolled over and placed her head on Deion's chest three months later.

"You're crazy as hell!" Deion chuckled, startling Iyana. "You can lie here all day if you want to. You'll be laying here by yourself. I didn't come all the way out here to Moorea to lay in nobody's bed all day. I'm about to go find some jet skis and enjoy the sunshine on this gorgeous beach."

"I thought we came out here to spend time together." Iyana frowned.

"You're more than welcome to join me. Throw your swimsuit on."

"Really, Deion?" she cracked up.

"Woman, we've been rumbling and tumbling all night. You've drained me of all my energy. I've got to get in the sun to recharge my battery. I'm solar powered, baby," he joked. "Now, get up, and let's get dressed. Room service will bring our breakfast any minute now."

Deion slid out of the bed they shared the night before and drew the curtains on the sliding glass door that opened to the deck of their over-water bungalow. The Tahitian morning was stunning over the crystal blue waters, and Deion couldn't get past their breathtaking view of it all.

"As much as I treasure making love to you, I didn't come here only to have sex with you all week," Deion whispered as Iyana wrapped her arms around him from behind. "We could do that at home. I took this week off work and had you do the same to spend it with me because we needed this time together. We both needed to get away from work and the hustle and bustle of the city and rekindle what was almost stolen from us," he explained. "There's a nervousness and an uncertainty radiating from you that didn't exist between us before," he explained as he faced her and lifted her chin to stare into her eyes. "I don't like it. I understand it, but I detest it. This week is time for us to get back to our place. I want to spend an amazing time with your gorgeous face in a breathtaking place to rebuild what was already so naturally divine. We need this time. We need the fun in the sun to become comfortable with each other again. We need the long walks on the sandy beach and the midnight love making in the sand. We need a picnic by a waterfall and snorkeling with the dolphins. I just want a serene environment to spend quality time with you to get back what was stolen from us, what was stolen from me."

"I understand, baby. It takes time, but I'm here, and I'm willing to do the work. I could never be stolen from you."

"Oh, but you almost were. It seems like I found you just in time before he pulled the wool all the way over your eyes again and plucked you from my grasp. After everything he's put you through and done to you, I'd be devastated for you if you ever went back to him to endure that all over again."

"What did I tell you, baby? Huh?" Iyana questioned as she gently caressed his cheek while staring into his eyes. "I'm never, never, ever... I'm never going back."

Made in the USA
Las Vegas, NV
05 September 2022

54648964R00143